I0740891

HELLFIRE CLUB: LORNE

AN IMMORTAL WARRIORS NOVEL

SARA MACKENZIE

To my readers who wanted this book

Prologue

—◆—

Hellfire Club, Blackfriars Abbey,
Lincolnshire, England

THE CREATURE CROUCHED LOW ON the ground. Filthy. Disheveled. There were blood stains on the animal skins it wore for clothing and unspeakable things beneath its long nails. The Marquis of Lorne and his companions had spent six days and nights hunting the beast over his Lincolnshire estate and the surrounding villages, and at last they had captured it.

There was only one problem. They could not send it back to the underworld, where it belonged. The door was locked.

"Instead the Destroyer must be bound by magic. Held fast. That way he will do no harm." The Sorceress sounded angry. It wasn't often, Lorne was sure, that she failed in her task. She also sounded puzzled, because the door to Hell was never locked.

She stood now in the shadows but shone with a light that seemed to come from within. Her gown and her fur lined cloak were a dazzling white and the diamonds about her throat twinkled like stars. Her auburn hair burned with a strange fire and her eyes were such a brilliant azure that no one could meet them for longer than a heartbeat unless she wished it. And worse than the domination in her eyes was what lay behind them—surging oceans full of writhing snakelike creatures. If one looked too long, Lorne wondered, would you be drawn into her domain, the between-worlds?

He tried not to shudder at the prospect.

"Why is the door locked?" he asked. "Who has locked it?"

The air crackled. "That I do not know. Yet."

The Marquis imagined some lowly minion being the object of the Sorceress's fury and this time he did shudder. He reminded himself that he had done his part; he had captured the Destroyer and surely now the Sorceress would set him and his friends free. Pressing a handkerchief to his bloodied cheek, where the creature had lashed out at him with a stout branch once they had cornered it, he reminded himself that he wasn't the only one with an injury. Lord Sutcliffe had a fractured collarbone and Darlington was favoring his ribs.

"Can you do that?" he asked at last, with a quick glance in the Sorceress's direction. "Can you bind it by magic?"

"So many questions, Lorne." She came further into the room and his companions stumbled back involuntarily, and though the Marquis managed to remain in place it was not an easy thing. He felt his legs tremble like a newborn foal and his head begin to spin. The Sorceress's long red strands of hair moved as if blown by an invisible wind.

Her smile was terrible to behold.

"Do not think that I have forgotten *you* were responsible for bringing this creature into the mortal world. Yes, I will bind it by magic and send it to sleep. A long sleep. And you must guard it, to be sure no one disturbs its slumber. And if for some reason it does wake *you* must stop it. The Destroyer must not be allowed to cause more destruction."

"Me?"

"Yes, you!" Her voice rose. "You have brought this on yourself. This is your doing, you and your dangerous, childish games. The Hellfire Club," she scoffed. "A diversion for silly boys. Well now you must take your punishment."

Lorne didn't want to die, and although it wasn't death she was sending him to, it sounded very like it. A sleep that could last for eternity? He may as well be dead.

But deep in the shadows of his soul he found the courage to admit she was right. He had brought this creature's evil into the world and therefore he must do what was necessary to stop it. He may have wasted his life and all the privileges birth and wealth had brought him, but at least, he thought with a bitter smile, his end would serve some righteous purpose.

It was just a shame no one else would ever know.

Lorne looked down at the creature huddled on the floor and saw that it was watching him, cunning eyes reading him like a book. It raised a lip in a snarl, showing pointed yellow teeth. A prisoner it might be, but it was still extremely dangerous.

They'd thought themselves so clever, bringing forth a demon from the pit, immersing themselves in the dark arts. It had started with drunken orgies in the cellars of Blackfriars Abbey, while he had thumbed his nose at his ancestors, sating his boredom with ever increasing acts of insanity.

And this is how it had ended.

"Are you prepared, Marquis?"

That melodious yet terrible voice grated his senses and Lorne raised his head. He glanced at the others, seeing sympathy and horror in their faces, and the knowledge that they were next. He forced himself to meet her eyes until he thought he would drown in their power.

"I am."

She came closer. The whole world began to spin. Her hand hovered over him, causing his body to shake with her authority.

"A pity," he heard her murmur softly. "You could have been so much more …"

And then there was only blackness and emptiness.

And a long, endless sleep.

Chapter One

—◆—

Present Day
The graveyard at Blackfriars Abbey

THE LIGHT WAS ALMOST GONE.

Professor Maggie McNab straightened her aching shoulders, the trowel dangling from her fingers. Everyone else had left after Owen uncovered the stone tablet—gone to celebrate at the village pub. But she'd stayed on. The stone tablet was all well and good, but it was the ancient barrow she was truly interested in.

This dig was her project and this might be her first and last season here at Blackfriars. Her sponsor had been making doubtful noises about forking out more cash for next summer. Since her husband Simon had died, her profile had slipped below those of other prominent archeologists, some of them more like television stars than serious professionals.

Simon had always been good for a quote or a spot on the BBC evening news. He was one of those people who caught the eye and was remembered. Maggie's sponsor liked some bang for his buck, a bang she wasn't delivering. Besides, no matter what Maggie might think about her dig taking priority, her sponsor believed there were far more worthy sites competing for his money. Or at least more media-friendly ones.

She pushed back the dark curls escaping her rose-pink knitted hat and looked across the graveyard to the woods that were part of the Blackfriars estate. They seemed darker and more sinister than they had been a few minutes ago. She really should pack up and go home, but there was so much still to be done and only a few more weeks to do it in.

Her gaze came back to the barrow that formed one edge of the graveyard and was barely more than a long uneven lump, rising to waist height above the surrounding ground. Geophysics had shown there was something interesting underneath, and she'd started the excavation at its highest point, with a rectangular trench cut right across the middle. They'd gone deeper as the days went on and they searched for something, anything, to prove Simon's hypothesis that this was an ancient burial mound.

He'd always believed the barrow held something extraordinary. It was certainly ancient, and it was their baby—hers and Simon's—and she was determined to finish excavating it.

For his memory. For his legacy.

Maggie was aware her thoughts could easily turn maudlin. At moments like these, she might even shed a tear or two—Maggie wasn't one for disclosing her deeper emotions to the world but on occasion they managed to leak out. It had been a year since Simon died, and she continued to miss him, although it was also true that her grief wasn't as keen as it had been in the beginning. She was moving on; she had to, and the dig was a part of that journey. Once it was done, once she had found Simon's treasure, she could draw a line under that part of her life and look toward the future.

Only she wasn't at all sure what that might look like.

Simon had been a big part of her life and without him there was a void she still struggled to fill. Despite them being happily married, everyone kept reminding her how he'd been so much older than her, that he was more like a father figure to her. It was true that, sometimes, the age difference showed, but Simon had been Simon and very special. Without him… well, despite being a child prodigy, it was unlikely she would ever have reached the lofty heights of professorship at the age of twenty-nine. Instead, she might have lived and died on the Govan estate in Glasgow where she'd been raised. Because of Simon—and her sister Linny, too, she couldn't forget Linny—she had so much more to be grateful for.

Damn it! Now she was getting weepy. Maggie raised a hand to wipe away the moisture from her eyes—just as something moved in the trench at her feet.

Brow creased, she peered into the deepening shadows where she'd been carefully brushing away at the soil, but there was nothing to be seen. Earlier she'd thought she'd found something, but it was just a piece of stone, similar to any one might find in the locality, and of no significance. She'd been disappointed. The geophys results had shown such promise. Shouldn't they have discovered bones or artifacts by now? And yet there was absolutely nothing to suggest that a body had ever lain in the barrow.

Simon had been so certain this was going to be a major find, that someone of great importance had been put to rest here. An ancient Saxon king perhaps, one who had ruled this piece of England long before the abbey had been built and later been dissolved by King Henry VIII. Long before there was a graveyard here, or the 4th Marquis of Lorne had cast his dark shadow across the land.

The Marquis of Lorne had owned Blackfriars Abbey—his family, the Escotts, had been given it by the Tudors—but the Marquis's true claim to fame had been the founding of a Hellfire Club. One of those notorious gatherings of bored aristocrats that seemed to be rife in the late 18th and early 19th centuries.

Simon had done some delving into the history of the place and found the Marquis to be a very murky character. He'd been privileged, wealthy, and utterly selfish. According to rumor, he and his Hellfire Club had been responsible for the kidnapping and murder of several of the locals.

Maggie could recall the gleam in Simon's eyes as he told the tale in his precise way.

"By this time the number of people who were dying under mysterious circumstances had become excessive. Remember, Maggie, this was happening in an era where disease could swiftly carry one away. Whole families, if it was an epidemic. But this was deemed to be different. These people were dying in grisly ways, their bodies shrunken and—as one account had it—sucked dry. Others vanished completely, never to be seen again. Eyebrows were raised in higher circles and the local worthies began finger pointing. And they weren't the only ones. The villagers began to believe that the Hellfire Club was to blame and the situation was on the verge of tuning very nasty indeed."

Maggie had laughed. "You mean yokels with torches and pitchforks? So what happened to stop them from marching on the abbey and dragging the wicked Marquis from his bed?"

What had happened was the Marquis had died, or so it was assumed—there were differing reports of how and where he might be buried. With a stake through the heart was one possibility. Once he was out of the picture, the whole matter was promptly hushed up by those in charge and what was left of the Hellfire Club disbanded. This was a period in history when the upper echelons were very much afraid of revolution—they just needed to look across the channel to see what had happened in France. Any disharmony among the working classes was swiftly and ruthlessly stamped on. And it worked.

The sleepy village and its abbey went back to being sleepy and soon all was forgotten. More or less. Of course, the story carried on, lingering like a nasty taste in the mouth, but time blurred the line between truth and fiction. These days the 'wicked' Marquis was only brought out to titillate the tourists and frighten naughty children.

Maggie's reminiscences came to an abrupt halt. Something had *definitely* moved just beneath her feet. She could feel the tremor getting stronger.

Could it be a minor earthquake?

Again the earth shook and shifted near her well-worn, mud caked boots. She heard a rattle. And then a sigh.

The hairs on the back of Maggie's neck stood up as the oldest part of her brain screamed out in warning. *Danger! Run!* And yet the trained, rational part kept her right where she was.

The stirring came again, just beneath the surface. *A rat, perhaps …? Ugh.* This time she moved to step away, but as she did so a yellowing leg bone suddenly appeared from under the earth. Bobbing to the surface like a lifebuoy thrown from a sinking ship.

Followed by another one.

In quick succession came a pelvis and a rib cage and then a skull. In a heartbeat she had an old but complete skeleton lying before her, perfectly intact.

This wasn't possible. Things like this didn't happen. Instinctively, she reached out to touch, to feel, to prove to herself that this was real.

The bones began to fill out.

Horrified, Maggie snatched her hand back. She no longer wanted to touch but she couldn't help but stare in appalled fascination. It was as if time was running the wrong way, and much, much faster. The flesh and muscle and skin that had fallen away in death were reforming. Veins, sinew, and ropes of muscle began shaping its limbs. In a blink of her shocked eyes, flesh crept over the raw meat, giving it all the appearance of a living and breathing being.

But not human. There was something very wrong …

It gave a deep groan, and Maggie stumbled back, losing her balance, her head spinning. This couldn't be happening. It just couldn't. A skeleton had become a living body, and she was wide awake.

She began to edge away, still not taking her eyes from the … the thing. Her foot twisted on a tool someone had thrown carelessly aside and she fell back, landing hard on the ground. Pushing with her boots and clawing with her hands, she slithered away from the barrow. When she could no longer see it she got back to her feet, only to almost fall again as she tripped over the rolled up tarpaulin they had been using to cover their work at night.

Oh Lord, oh Lord …

She wasn't normally one to call on God, but with her heart banging against her ribcage, she did so now. Because it … he …*whatever* this thing was had risen up from the trench in a dark silhouette against the night's first stars. It—she decided now that it was definitely an *it*—wore animal skins instead of clothing, like something from a horror film. Once again her feet had frozen to the spot, and she stood staring, seeing and yet not able to comprehend.

The thing turned its face, sniffing the air, with an action that was less human and more like that of a wild animal.

Maggie must have made a sound because it abruptly swung toward her. Despite the growing darkness she could see it quite clearly, its white face framed by pale hair hanging in braids and, when it moved, she could hear the soft rattle of beads. And the way it moved … testing the air and standing slightly hunched forward, as if it was about to spring, hands clenched and its long nails … or were they, God, could they be claws?

Blind panic overwhelmed her. She turned to run, not realizing the tarpaulin was still at her feet. She fell in an ungainly sprawl and at the same time her boot knocked against a box of tools. On such a still night the ensuing noise was deafening.

It came at her with blinding speed. Before she could get to her feet, before she could do anything, it was right in front of her, stooping over her with its face pressed up against hers. There was a smell, rank and primeval.

Petrified, aware of the childish desire to close her eyes and pretend none of this was happening, Maggie forced herself to look up into its face. The scientist in her wanted, *needed*, to see. And what she saw was worse than she could ever have imagined.

That face wasn't human. There was something so fundamentally wrong about it that she, who had thought evil was what human beings did to each other, knew she'd never properly understood what the word meant until now.

The creature smiled and she saw it had sharp, yellow teeth. It was perhaps the least human thing about it.

Maggie screamed and once started she couldn't seem to stop. This thing meant to kill her. She knew it deep in her heart and soul. She was going to die.

And Maggie McNab wanted to live.

Chapter Two

———————

MAGGIE'S SCREAMS STILL RANG IN her ears, but she was already searching the ground for something—anything—to use as a weapon. Her hand closed on the shovel she'd had earlier. With a wild swing she struck out and hit the creature on the side of the head with a loud clang.

It stumbled back, but only briefly, before it turned to her again, eyes blazing. She realized that instead of saving herself she'd made matters worse; she'd made it angry. Mouth open, teeth glinting, it loped towards her.

This was her final moment. Her hands shook as she gripped the shovel, holding it in front of her as though it would save her from those teeth and claws. When in a rush of air another figure—with gleaming naked flesh and silver hair—appeared out of the night and flung himself at the creature.

With a deafening roar the two collided, and the air was rent with a sound like thunder, while the ground shook violently.

It was too much for Maggie. She turned and ran. But she'd only taken a couple of steps when a hand grabbed her shoulder. The nails penetrated her clothing and raked across her flesh. Rank, hot breath and yellow fangs snarled close to her face. She fought to be free, and once again it was the silver haired man who came to her aid, shoving her captor hard so that he fell away and at the same time released her.

Maggie staggered and might have fallen as well, but her savior caught her, pulling her close. He was naked alright, no denying it. She found herself gazing into a pair of pale eyes in a face so handsome she knew it couldn't be real.

"You must run," he said, his voice deep and aristocratic.

She couldn't move, couldn't stop staring at him, her thought processes barely functioning.

"*Run!*" he shouted, and spun her away, just as the creature leapt upon him. Once more, the two of them were locked in combat.

Shaking, stiffening her knees to hold herself upright, Maggie knew she wasn't going anywhere. She watched the fight, mesmerized. At first one seemed to be winning and then the other. She was hoping the man would win, her life depended upon it, but she could see the effort it was taking for him just to hold the creature at bay. It snapped and snarled in his face, and his arms were beginning to shake with the effort of keeping those clawed hands off him. The next moment he'd fallen back onto the ground and the creature was standing over him.

It had won, and as if to celebrate the victory, it flung up its head with a roar of triumph.

The shovel was still lying at Maggie's feet. She

couldn't stand there and watch the man die, not after he'd tried to save her, so she snatched it up again. Lifting it high in the air, she ran toward them, yelling at the top of her voice. She didn't know what she was saying but it was probably swearing—the sort of bad language Linny disapproved of in her little sister.

She fully expected the creature to turn on her and take her down, but to her surprise it took one look at her and loped off, with a snarl, into the night. Emboldened by this, Maggie followed it for a few strides and yelled a bit more but it wasn't coming back. She peered towards the dark woods, just to be sure it wasn't lurking. When she felt confident it was really gone she turned back to the fallen man.

Suddenly her body was one big ache. Scrapes and bumps that she hadn't noticed in all the drama were now shouting out for her attention. She limped toward the man, who throughout all of this hadn't moved, and dropped to her knees beside him.

He was lying on his side, his back to her, and she couldn't help but check out his broad shoulders and the column of his spine, down to the muscular curve of his buttocks and his powerful legs. It was difficult to ignore the fact that he was completely naked but she did her best.

Tentatively Maggie reached out a hand to touch his shoulder, wondering if he might vanish before her eyes in a puff of smoke. Instead, her finger tips encountered warm skin. He was real and he was alive.

"Eh … hello?"

He raised his head, and his silver hair fell forward

to cover his face. It was long enough to reach his shoulders, and he pushed it away so that he could see her. Handsome wasn't a strong enough word for him, but she tried to ignore that too.

"Did he hurt you?" he asked, and she realized again how distinctive his voice was—deep and aristocratic and very English.

"Only some wee bruises," Maggie said, her own voice not cultured at all and very Scottish. "Are you? Hurt, I mean."

He went to sit up, but something was wrong because his breath hitched and he sank back, muttering.

"We need to get away," she said, trying not to look at the concave of his stomach and what lay below. She glanced away and then right back again because—well, he was a very attractive man and there was certainly plenty of him. "Do you have some clothes you can put on?"

He met her eyes before looking down at his naked self. Hadn't he known? That was the impression she was getting, that he hadn't been aware of his own unclothed state. He said with a droll sort of quality, "You have me at a disadvantage, madam."

Maggie blinked. "Well that's one way of putting it. You haven't answered my question though. About your clothes. Where are they?"

She was starting to feel flustered. Maggie was a modern woman, but she had never been entirely comfortable with the type of man who oozed sexual attraction. The sort of man other women panted after. In fact, she tended to steer well clear of the breed. She told herself it was a self-preservation thing, but truthfully she just couldn't believe any man like that would be interested in a woman like her. They were worlds apart.

And there'd been an incident once, long ago at school, but that was before Simon and best left forgotten.

He pushed his hair out of his eyes again and frowned at her as if she was irritating him, or he had a headache, or both. "I have no clothing about me, as you can see." Then, in a lower tone, talking to himself he added, "There is no time for this. No time …"

He had managed to get up onto his knees, so that the two of them were now level, but again the movement caused him pain. He put a hand to his side with a groan and hung his head, breathing shallowly as if his ribs hurt.

Maggie looked over her shoulder at the dark woods. They couldn't stay here much longer. Whatever that thing was, it might come back, and they needed to get to safety. "I think we should go," she said, giving the trees one more searching look before she turned back to him.

He was so close they nearly bumped noses. Just like before, she was staring into his eyes. It was the oddest thing, but she felt as if she couldn't look away. Didn't want to. Those icy blue irises drew her closer and closer.

That was when it occurred to her that this might be another monster, just one that was better looking. Who was he? Where had he come from? Why was he naked?

She opened her mouth to ask, but as if he'd read her mind, he said, rather breathlessly, "There is no time for polite conversation. It'll be out there, somewhere. Watching us. Will you help me to stand?"

So polite!

He didn't wait for her answer, however, and was already struggling to his feet. Maggie put her arms around his waist, his body warm and hard muscled, taking his weight, trying not to hurt him. It took some effort, but eventually he was upright, leaning against her, gasping, his silver hair tickling her cheek. There was nothing rank about him, either. She thought the scent that clung to him was a combination of herbs. Parsley, sage, rosemary and thyme …

Between them the cold air puffed white with each breath. Up close there was no sense of him lacking humanity, as had definitely been the case with the creature.

This was very much a man.

His legs were shaking with the effort of staying upright. He took a step and nearly toppled over; she had to steady him. If she hadn't seen him in action, she would have thought he'd just awoken from a coma, or been bedridden for many weeks. Luckily, she was strong from all her years working on archeological sites around the world—she'd always preferred the physical aspects of her job over the endless paperwork.

Had he come out of the ground too? That thought might have sent her screaming into the night, but there wasn't time for such contemplation. Just keeping him upright and looking out for the creature was keeping her busy enough.

They took several halting steps before he seemed to get the hang of it but he was obviously working hard. She could see the gleam of sweat on his skin despite the chill in the air.

"Do you want to rest a moment?" she asked him. He seemed to be putting more weight on her now and she was struggling to keep them both from falling. "You can wait here and I'll bring the Land Rover over. Look, rest against this gravestone here."

He shot her an irritated look. "We keep going," he said. "Where is this land rover?" He said it as if he'd never heard the words before.

She wanted to point to the fence where she'd parked this morning but that would have meant taking away her hand, and they both needed her to hang on. "Not far," she said instead, gritting her teeth. She told herself to look on the bright side. She hadn't encountered many naked men recently and certainly no specimens as perfect as this one. She should be making the most of it.

And he wasn't old, despite the silver hair. He was probably her age or a bit older, maybe in his early thirties. He was about a head above her height and she was tall for a woman. *Perfect, really, in every way,* Maggie thought, and smiled to herself.

He'd turned his head and was looking at her; she wondered if she'd spoken it aloud. "Are you all right?"

"We need to find shelter before the creature returns," he replied, his voice getting weaker. Maybe he was talking to himself. She considered whether she should take him to the hospital but it was thirty miles away, and the cottage was so much closer. She could always ring for an ambulance from there. He was right; they needed to get to shelter before that monster returned to finish what it had started.

She shuddered. "Do you know what that thing was? I've seen wild animals at the zoo, and I've dug plenty up, but none of them looked like *that.*"

He stopped, and she was glad of it. Her arms were aching and her back wasn't much better. "Did you hear me?" she asked, steadying him when he swayed to the side.

He gave her another of those looks, arrogance in every line. Despite her annoyance, she found herself once again admiring the perfection of his face. Straight nose, firm lips, strong jaw, and dark brows slashing over those pale eyes. Now the expression in his eyes grew bleak.

"It is a demon. I know it only as the Destroyer." He spoke in the tone of someone who had seen it in action before.

"But how—"

"No time," he said. "I need to rest. I need to regain my strength. I need to sleep and eat. If it comes … I cannot fight it, not as I am. You will not survive without me, so you must get me somewhere safe."

"So you know it, then? This demon?"

"What part of 'no time' did you not understand, woman?" he growled, and for a moment seemed to waver, as if he was uncertain whether his feet could take another step. His head fell forward onto her shoulder and his hair shielded his face.

They took a moment, both of them struggling now. His warm breath made her aware he was very much alive. Real. Not a dream, although she was inclined to think this whole situation was part of a nightmare, and at any moment she would wake and find herself in her bed.

"We'll go to my cottage." Maggie spoke in her practical voice, giving him a pat on the back—well it should have been his back but her arms had slipped down and it was actually his buttock. She could hear herself blathering on, talking nonsense. "It has thick walls and it's cozy. I like to think of it as a bit of a sanctuary. If we bolt the door we can keep that creature out for a while, and you can rest and eat, until you get strong again. And, by the way, do you usually fight demons naked?"

He lifted his head at last and she had the feeling he was laughing at her, although his face was perfectly composed. "That would be most generous of you," he said. "And no, this is not my usual state of dress."

They started walking again, slowly but steadily, and Maggie was glad to see that the Land Rover was getting closer. It was old and battered but reliable. Owen, her assistant on the dig, had taken the utility truck after loading it with most of the tools. It was Friday, and despite the isolation they weren't keen on leaving things here over the weekend. He'd taken it back to the village pub where the rest of her team were staying and was probably already celebrating their find.

The stone tablet they'd unearthed earlier today had been about the size of a paperback book, carved with runic writing. They'd found it wrapped in an oiled cloth near the barrow. She and Owen had carefully packed the tablet into a crate with protective wrapping and left it in the back of the Land Rover. By rights they should have told Blackfriars Abbey's owner, Mr. Stewart, but they'd been keen to take a look at it first. He was a strange sort of chap and they'd been worried he might lock the tablet up and refuse them permission to examine it.

Maggie knew she hadn't been entirely honest with Mr. Stewart. He believed they were excavating the graveyard in an attempt to uncover the truth in the stories surrounding the infamous 4th Marquis of Lorne.

Blackfriars Abbey and its grounds have been undisturbed for two hundred years, and would probably have remained undisturbed if Simon hadn't come along and found it 25 years ago. He had been on a cycling holiday and it was quite by accident, but he'd always said that as soon as he saw the barrow he'd know it was special. By the time he'd pedaled away he was already one hundred percent certain that one day he would be back to dig.

Simon had no real interest in investigating the story of the Marquis, that early 19th century devil worshipper, but he'd been willing to play along with Mr. Stewart. It was the only way he could get permission to do the dig. When he'd discovered that the current owner of the abbey was obsessed with his wicked predecessor to an almost unhealthy degree, Simon hadn't had any qualms about using that obsession for his own ends.

Simon had set everything up—found the money and the team. He was so positive there was something here at Blackfriars worth finding, and Maggie had teased him about it, telling him he was as bad as Mr. Stewart. But just as they were ready to start work he'd fallen ill, and he'd never had the chance to fulfill his dream.

Now, a year later, Maggie was doing the dig for him, as her tribute to his memory.

And what am I doing thinking of that now, she asked herself grimly as she stumbled with her wounded rescuer toward the vehicle. The night air was getting colder and every few moments he gave a shiver that shook them both. The ground was uneven, which didn't help, and their progress was punctuated by him muttering the sort of words Linny would not have approved of.

Her nose began to itch and she didn't have a free hand to scratch it. Without thinking, she tilted to the side and rubbed it against his shoulder. He stiffened, as if he wasn't used to such familiarity.

"Sorry. Itchy nose."

He smiled and then he began to laugh. The sound was rough and shaky and she wasn't sure he was entirely sane.

"I'm glad you think this is funny," she said, her face hot with emotion. "Personally, I don't find much to be amused about."

He choked and eventually stopped. When he looked at her again with his remarkable eyes all laughter had gone.

"I don't think this is funny either," he said. His gaze slid past her to the Land Rover, and his body seemed to go rigid, the shock evident on his face and in the flare of his nostrils. He was like a thoroughbred stallion about to be forced into an inferior horse trailer.

"What is this?" He pulled out of her arms and promptly staggered back at a dangerous angle.

She grabbed and steadied him, only just preventing him from falling over. What was his problem? The Land Rover might be old but it had been her faithful companion on many digs. "If you want to get away from here you'll just have to lower your standards and get in," she said irritably. "Come on, your Highness. You said we needed to go. Well let's go."

Again he stared at the Land Rover and back at her but she wasn't having this. Maggie walked him to the vehicle and propped him up against the bonnet so that she could open the passenger side door.

He required her help to climb inside; his strength seemed to be rapidly deserting him. At one point she found her hand high up on his firm thigh. When she saw she was within an inch of those well-endowed private parts she pulled it quickly away.

They were both breathing hard, and she hoped he hadn't noticed, but when he swiveled his pale eyes toward her she saw that the laughter wasn't very far away.

"Unlike the Destroyer, I don't bite. Not unless I'm asked." His cool stare slid over her face and rested on her lips.

Those lips tingled. Was he hitting on her? It seemed so wildly unlikely that she was inclined to think she'd misinterpreted his words. Instead, she gave him a none-too-gentle final push into the car and reached over the back and found the dusty blanket she sometimes used to wrap around the bits and pieces they found at their digs. She tucked it around him, relieved that he was finally covered.

He was holding his ribs, his eyes closed and his

head thrown back against the worn seat. Was he seriously injured? She wondered again if she should take him straight to the nearest hospital. But what was she going to say when they asked her who he was and what had happened to him?

She hesitated, watching him, while she considered the matter.

The rest of the team were lodged at the hotel, but Maggie had taken a lease on a nearby cottage for three months. It was conveniently close to the dig and yet she didn't need to join in with the others, not if she didn't want to. She didn't have to pretend that everything was the same as it used to be.

She made up her mind. "We'll go to the cottage, it's closer." *If I need to I can call an ambulance from there.*

And anyway, the most important thing right now was getting away from the graveyard as quickly as possible.

Maggie climbed in on the driver's side, slamming the door and starting the engine.

The man jumped, staring about him wild eyed.

"Not far," she said. "Hang on."

He turned and gaped at her as if she was crazy. "What should I hang on to?" he asked, but seemed to lose interest and closed his eyes again, snuggling down under the blanket with a groan.

Maggie's practical mind wanted to pepper him with questions, but it was obvious that the man at her side wasn't going to answer them.

The old Land Rover shook as it took the turn in the narrow track that wound through the dense woods, headlights picking out individual trees.

Ahead, the way diverged, one route heading for the abbey, the other toward the cottage. Maggie followed the road to the cottage, knowing there was a ford over a stream ahead of them. After that it was plain sailing.

The ford was really just a dip in the road with a shallow gleam of water running through it. Maybe in the winter it flooded but right now it was just a trickle. Maggie drove down into it, hitting the bottom with a splash, and it was only as the Land Rover began the climb again, with the headlights tilting up, that she saw it.

The creature. The *demon*.

It was standing in the middle of the road. Right in front of them. She knew they weren't that far from the dig but somehow she had expected it to run the other way.

Now, with the headlights on, she could see it in more detail, though that wasn't a good thing. Its furry clothing hung stiff about it and there were leggings tied with leather strips, and a ragged cloak. It was as if these things were more than just clothes, they were part of it. Braided yellow hair framed the narrow, animal-like face and her eyes were drawn to the pointed teeth protruding from between its lips. It stared at her and instead of proper eyes, with white surrounding the irises, she saw only blackness.

Terror caused her brain to work overtime, everything becoming crystal clear, and she could see there was more than animal cunning in the way it looked at them. There was an intelligence. A horrible intelligence.

The moment didn't last all that long. It just felt

like it did.

She revved the faithful old Land Rover harder than she should have. The motor roared, then spluttered and died. The vehicle began to roll backwards and she slammed on the brakes, staring up at the creature. Afraid to take her eyes off it.

Any moment now it would spring onto the bonnet and crash through the windscreen, and that would be the end.

Chapter Three

L ORNE WAS DOZING. HIS SITUATION was so far beyond his experience he found it easier just to accept it as it came to him. This was the future. The Sorceress had warned him he may wake into a strange and exotic world, but that he couldn't allow any of it to distract him from his task.

He wondered what game she had been playing, bringing him into this place like some newborn, stripped bare and naked. Was it another of her tests? Well, apart from the amusement he'd derived from the Scotswoman pretending to avert her eyes, he couldn't allow that to distract him either.

He'd been asleep for a long time. And as he slept, he had relived his life, over and over again, raking through every detail, delving into each word and gesture. Every wrongdoing. He felt as if he had been taken apart, piece by piece, memory by memory, and put back together again. And in time the gap between who he had been and who he now was had widened. In short, he was a different man in the same body.

Not that the Sorceress believed him.

The last time she had come to him, striding into his sleep as if she owned him, she had said he still had to prove himself to her. "So easy to slip back into your old ways, Marquis," she'd mocked, her fierce blue gaze drawing on his blood like moon tide. "Convince me, and then perhaps you may have a chance to live again. When the Destroyer is dealt with."

When the Destroyer is dealt with.

Perhaps the Scot had done him a favor, waking the demon and bringing Lorne back with it. This might be his chance to finally complete the task of sending the demon back to Hell, so that he could resume his life.

Unfortunately, his sleep had left him physically weak and his abrupt awakening, followed by the violent fight with the creature, had depleted most of his remaining energy. The demon was at its most vulnerable when in its true form, and he should have been able to secure it. An opportunity gone begging. He told himself there would be another chance and when it came he must be ready. This was why the Sorceress had buried him beside the demon.

In case some ignorant Scot brought it back to life.

He heard his voice, the Lorne he had once been, deep in his brain. He understood why he had thought as he did, why he had once loathed the Scots. Now the woman's image flashed into his mind, and even on such a short acquaintance it was unexpectedly detailed. Her odd hat, the color of rose petals, tugged down over that wild dark hair, her eyes luminous as pools of lamp oil. She was tall for a woman, long legged in tight trousers that admittedly had given him a pleasurable view, and soft where she'd been pressed against him earlier.

She was a woman, he reminded himself, and it had been a long time since he'd bedded one. In the days before the Destroyer he'd not been particularly fussy. As long as a woman had the correct anatomical attributes he would bed her. But a Scot?

Even now her accent, so similar to that of his grandmother, brought back memories that struck him like cudgels, making him feel bruised and battered … although to be fair he supposed the bruises had more to do with his fight with the creature.

The machine she'd called a land rover had stopped. In the silence he heard the woman make a breathy sound, as if she wanted to scream but couldn't quite manage it.

The pain in his ribs was excruciating and, although all he wanted to do was sit very still and pretend he was somewhere else, Lorne forced his eyes open. There, through the window of the strange machine that drove without horses, stood his enemy.

The Destroyer stared back at him with its bottomless black eyes, cloaked in its animal hides, and the hair hanging in braids. He hated its eyes even more than the glistening teeth that hung lower than its lips.

Lorne's head spun, but he forced himself to focus, to stay alert. The Destroyer was back and if need be he must fight it again. Fight to the death.

He knew with a bleak certainty that if the creature decided to attack now then he was done for. Weakened or not, it still held the advantage over him. The machine would offer them some protection but the Destroyer wasn't going to let that stop him. He would crack the windows like the shell of a nut, to get to the flesh inside. Even a Scot did not deserve what the Destroyer would do once he had hold of her.

"Have you any weapons?" Lorne asked, not taking his eyes off the creature.

"Weapons?"

"What was that you were swinging around your head back in the graveyard?"

Her face cleared. "The shovel? I left it there. I couldn't carry it and you." Then she seemed to have a miraculous thought. "Hang on."

"What should I hang on to?" he asked impatiently.

She ignored him and turned and leaned over her seat, rummaging around in the back of the machine. Lorne tried not to be distracted by those tight trousers molding the shape of her bottom. When she appeared again she held a long metal bar. "Tire lever," she muttered out of the corner of her mouth, then held it up so that the creature could see it. "And I know how to use it too!" she shouted.

Lorne winced.

"Do you think it heard me?" she whispered, hands white knuckled as she clutched her weapon.

"I rather think it did."

"I won't die without a fight," she added for good measure, shaking the metal bar threateningly so that it knocked against the metal rectangle fastened above the window.

"Can't you start your rover carriage?"

She didn't answer so he assumed not.

Lorne didn't really believe her posturing would frighten off the Destroyer, but after a moment it began to back away from them. Slowly. Watching them all the time. Before it turned and vanished into the woods. No doubt it too wanted to rest and regain its strength.

His shoulders sagged with relief, and then he caught his breath as the movement caused pain to stab his chest where his ribs were either broken or bruised. He needed to be fit and well; an injury might mean he would fail in his quest.

Lorne swore softly.

"Watch your mouth."

Startled, Lorne turned his head. The woman still stared at the place where the demon had stood, her dark eyes wide and frightened, her tangled hair a frame for her face. There were beads of perspiration above her full upper lip and her skin shone pale in the greenish light that came from the machine.

There was beauty in her face, and strength, but there was also suffering to be seen. He recognized suffering; it was something he understood only too well. For all his privilege he had never been a happy man.

But this was not the time for pity. He reminded himself that she should suffer after what she had let loose on the world. Her meddling may well mark the end of mankind. And yet … it was true that if he could capture the demon again, if he could please the Sorceress, then it might mean the beginning of an entirely new life for him.

"Where has it gone?" the woman wondered aloud, her accent like fingernails on slate, reminding him of his hated grandmother, the Dowager, and the way she had treated his poor mother.

"To kill. To feed," he answered harshly, his head still half in the past. "That is what he does."

She turned to look at him, and that was when he noticed that the metal rectangle she'd knocked sideways was a mirror, and he could see his reflection in it.

His hair was white! His face had not changed, but his hair … He was too surprised to do more than stare. Then she spoke and broke the spell.

"What is it?" she whispered. "Dear God, that … that thing. What is it?"

"A demon from the underworld."

"But there's no such thing as the underworld," she said forcefully.

"Do you doubt your senses?"

"Of course I do! I mean, I have to. Otherwise …" her voice trailed off, as if unable to finish the thought.

"The Destroyer is as you saw it. Evil and unnatural, but all too real."

She wanted to dispute his words, he could see her struggle, but instead she said, "And now it is free?"

"*You* set it free," he said. "You dug it up. It was you, wasn't it?"

"Yes, I—"

"Then it's your doing that the demon is free."

But if he expected her to show remorse or to grovel and apologize he was very mistaken. Instead she took immediate offence.

"*My* doing? I'm an archeologist. I was digging a site. And last time I checked there was no sign that said '*Warning: ancient demon buried here.*' What was it doing there? What were *you* doing there?"

It suddenly seemed to occur to her that his being in the ground hadn't been natural, either. Expecting a barrage of questions, Lorne decided he would prefer to wait and answer them later, when he had more vigor.

"Can you set this machine moving, madam?" he asked rudely, cutting her off. "In case you've forgotten we need to get to safety. We can deal with your excuses later, after—" He stopped. He'd noticed the anger sparkling in her dark eyes.

Oh God, a fight! A verbal scrap. Once upon a time, Lorne would have loved nothing more than to annihilate someone in a war of words, and he could probably have reduced this woman to tears in minutes. His tongue, according to some, was a vicious weapon that he could wield as well as he did his rapier, often with the same deadly results. Lorne had once found pleasure in hurting others with his words, but as he slept, and reviewed his life, he understood that while he might have been enjoying himself, his victims had suffered. Now his actions shamed him.

"I don't need to make excuses," she retorted. The anger seemed to drain out of her and she leaned closer, giving him a look of concern. "Are you in much pain? Maybe we should go to the hospital so they can check you over." He noticed she stole a glance down at his body, now decently covered by the paisley blanket.

Just for a moment he had the mad temptation to fling it off, to see what she'd do, but he knew he was being childish. His exhaustion had made him lightheaded. So lightheaded he even wondered what her lips might taste like, if he ran his tongue lightly across their plump surface.

He shook his head, causing the darkness to spin. "No," he managed to say through his now over-powering exhaustion. "No time for dalliance."

"Dalliance?" Her eyes narrowed suspiciously. "Who's dallying?"

He dismissed this with a wave of his hand. "I have to find the demon. But first, I need to regain my strength. It has been a long time since I walked this earth."

He could tell by her silent look that she was debating whether or not to ask him, but in the end she couldn't seem to help herself. "Just how long has it been since you, eh, 'walked this earth?'"

He stared back and had the oddest sensation, that he might fall forward into those dark eyes and drown. This was a pleasant change from the Sorceress, whose blue stare was utterly terrifying.

She was awaiting his answer.

"What year is this?" he asked.

She told him.

He couldn't disguise his amazement. "Really? So long ..." No wonder this world seemed so very strange to him. Suddenly he realized that every mortal he had ever known, and even their children and grandchildren were dead and ashes, and the sense of his own solitude swept over him like a great wave.

"Hey." She rested her hand on his shoulder. "Are you all right? Look, it doesn't matter. Tell me later. I think I'd prefer not to know, actually. Not yet."

Her kindness took him by surprise—he'd had little of that emotion in his life. Reaching up, he took her hand in his and held it a moment, examining the flesh of her palm and her fingers. She didn't resist, watching him curiously as he inspected the calluses and scrapes and the other signs of hard work. She had a washer woman's hands, he thought with amusement, but decided it would be ungenerous to say so aloud.

"It has been more than two hundred years," he said, and looking up caught the look of shock in her eyes. Was she going to scream? He hoped not. He didn't know if his head could stand it.

"*Two hundred years?*" she echoed. "That can't be …"

"I come from the year of our Lord eighteen hundred and eight," he added, rather enjoying her expression as she struggled between disbelief and amazement. "I have been in the earth for over two hundred years and now you have brought me back to life."

She shook her head. "I saw that—that *creature* reform in the barrow and I still can't believe it."

"The first thing you must learn is that you cannot win the fight if you do not believe."

She didn't answer. She didn't seem to know what to say, but he thought he saw the beginnings of a grudging acceptance in her.

Lorne closed his eyes. After a time he heard the machine falter then roar once again. With excessive caution she eased it up out of the ford and back onto the road. Lorne's thoughts began to drift.

He was thinking of rose petals. It was because of that blasted hat she was wearing. Strangely, the faded pink color reminded him of the crypt below the abbey and the long nights he and his friends had spent there, indulging in the pleasures of the flesh. A bowl of scented water—filled with rose petals—resting at his elbow, a naked woman sprawled across his lap, pleasure growing from her busy mouth.

Darlington, with his scarred face, would grin at him as he tossed his own woman over his shoulder and limped off into the shadows with her—Darlington preferred to do his pleasuring in private—and Sutcliffe drunk as the lord he was, would roar with laughter as he was whipped by a woman dressed as a very lude abbess.

They'd been foolish boys indulging themselves with what, in hindsight, seemed to be relatively innocent pursuits. Certainly they were when compared to what happened after. After they'd decided to call up demons from the underworld.

He wondered what had happened to his friends. Had the Sorceress allowed them to remain in their own time? Perhaps, somehow, he would see them again. He hoped so. Lorne desperately needed them by his side, to help him recapture the Destroyer. The Sorceress had set him a monumental task. Could he do it entirely on his own?

"More than two hundred years." He heard the Scotswoman at his side mutter the words under her breath again. "I'm sitting beside a man who's over two hundred years old."

But of course, Lorne realized, he wasn't alone. She was with him. The 4th Marquis and his Scottish troublemaker. He felt his mouth twitch with the irony of it, and he suspected this was another of the Sorceress's maneuverings, another test to enable him to prove himself.

The witch probably believed that he would be furious to be placed in such a position, and the man he had been would have been very angry indeed, but Lorne was that man no longer. He was done with those futile and wasted years.

But it was too late to go back and change them. All he could do now was make whatever amends were in his power—to recapture the Destroyer and this time to send it to Hell where it belonged.

And if he failed? Well, no one would ever know what he had tried to do. How he had stepped up to the invisible marker that distinguished the heroes from the villains.

He would know though, and that would have to be enough.

Chapter Four

MAGGIE DROVE VERY CAREFULLY ALONG the track through the woods. She was still trying to come to terms with what the man had said, but her mind must have been frozen with shock because she couldn't seem to grasp any of it. Rather than try to make sense of the two hundred year old naked man beside her or the demon somewhere out there, her thoughts kept drifting.

If only Simon were here. Simon, alive and warm and comforting at her side. Now that Simon had gone she sometimes felt as if she was becoming a different person, and she wasn't quite sure who that person was.

She shot the stranger a sideways glance.

Was he really a man? Or was he another demon?

He seemed to be asleep, or at least his eyes were closed. His handsome face now looked drawn and haggard, and his skin was greenish in the light of the dashboard. Her heart gave a thump as she wondered if he was dead, but then she saw the steady rise and fall of his chest, where the blanket had slipped off one shoulder.

Good. Not dead then.

Her gaze swept over the curve of his pectorals and the darker circle of his nipple, travelling along the line of dark hairs that disappeared beneath the blanket. Did that mean his hair had been dark before it became silver? His hand lay in his lap and she found herself admiring the long capable fingers and their trimmed nails.

Her own fingers twitched, remembering the way he had touched her. His were not the hands of a manual worker by any means—*or an archeologist,* she thought with a wry smile. The calluses on his palm were probably from holding the reins of a horse rather than standing out in the blazing heat or pelting rain and swinging a pick and shovel.

She'd been asking herself what he was but now she began to ask another question altogether: *Who* was he? And she wasn't at all sure she wanted to know.

The twisting road had almost taken them through the swath of forest. Blackfriars Abbey had one of the largest forests in private hands in the country. Maggie thought it a shame the public couldn't drop in to enjoy it. Mr. Stewart was an odd, reclusive fellow and he liked his privacy too much to allow any strangers onto his land.

Maggie had heard that very few people in the village had actually sighted him—the woman who came to clean for him also brought his groceries and other supplies so he rarely ventured out. The only reason he had allowed the dig to go ahead was because Maggie had reiterated Simon's story about discovering more about the 4th Marquis of Lorne, as well as a plea to grant her dead husband's final wish.

Mr. Stewart had written back swiftly to give her his permission and suggested she stay in the cottage on his estate. 'It has been lived in by some of the foresters,' he wrote, 'but I am assured it is in good condition.'

All of their interactions apart from one had been by letter, and it was only when he made that single telephone call that she realized he was American. As for the abbey, she'd seen the outside of it when she drove up one day soon after the dig had started, hoping to see him and thank him. He hadn't answered the door. Instead, Maggie had spent a moment standing and staring up at the historic building, noting how shabby and in need of repairs it was.

Her thoughts refocused as she saw the clearing ahead, and the cottage reared up before them, a dark shape against the stars. She'd been told by the estate agent who'd handed over the key that it had once been the gamekeeper's cottage, a la Lady Chatterley's Lover, but Maggie had yet to find any signs of passionate encounters within its walls.

The last occupant had left it neat and clean, although he'd neglected to pack all of his belongings, but the furnishings were rather scruffy and it could have done with some paint. At least there was running water and a roof over her head, absolute luxuries compared to some of the digs she had been involved in.

Maggie drew up outside and turned off the engine. In the silence that followed she wondered if her sense of relief was premature. Perhaps the demon had followed them and was now ready to pounce on them from the shadows.

It wasn't a nice thought and she shivered, and then jumped when her companion spoke.

"He's gone."

"For good?" she whispered, and cleared her throat. "I mean, has he left for good?"

"Of course not."

Maggie stared at him a moment more in the darkness, waiting, but when nothing else was forthcoming she opened her door and jumped out into the chill air.

"Wait here," she told him. "I'll come back and help you."

It wasn't that she didn't believe him, but she preferred to check for herself before they made their way into the cottage.

This place might be isolated but it did have modern conveniences. She unlocked the door and walked in, switching on lights as she went. The incandescent bulbs weren't of the highest quality, but the glow was comforting. The downstairs consisted of a sitting room, kitchen, bathroom, and laundry. Upstairs were two bedrooms and a study. She was hesitating, looking up the narrow staircase, when a voice spoke behind her.

"What is up there?"

She jumped and turned to her rescuer. "I thought you were going to wait?"

"I never intended to wait," he replied, and if he looked a little pale he was putting up a good front. He nodded over her shoulder at the stairs. "Does anyone else live here?"

"No. You don't think he's up there, do you?" she added, unable to keep the anxiety from her voice.

"I don't." He turned away as if that was the end of the matter, leaving her to trail after him. He got as far as the kitchen, walking very carefully, then stopped and leaned heavily on the back of a chair. Maggie noticed the sheen of sweat on his skin and the tightness about his mouth, as if he was holding in his pain. She waited, wondering what he was planning to do next, but it seemed he'd reached the end of this second wind. Cautiously, he lowered himself onto the plastic seat with a soft groan.

Two hundred years.

How could that be possible?

How was *any* of this possible?

Beneath the blanket, whose hem barely reached past his thighs, was a lithe, healthy, masculine body. She glanced at his legs with their sparse covering of dark hair, and his bare feet with their fine coating of earth.

Two hundred years old.

Why didn't that make any difference to how she was feeling—awkward and interested and strongly attracted? There hadn't been a man in her life since Simon, not in that way. Owen and her colleagues and her team here at Blackfriars … well, they were different. She didn't feel uncomfortable in their company, she didn't feel as if her equilibrium was under threat, because on some fundamental level of her being, that was what was happening to her right now.

"I'm not going to vanish." He spoke in that rich, posh voice and she felt her face flush as she became aware how long she'd been staring. He opened one eye to look at her and then he opened the other. He smiled. "At least," he qualified, "I don't *think* I am. The Sorceress has plans for me."

Sorceress? "You're blathering," she said brusquely, not wanting to know. There was only so much her poor brain could handle at a time. "Now, I have some first aid training. Do you mind if I take a look at you?"

"Do your worst, madam."

"Okay." Maggie eyed him a bit uncertainly but she wasn't a novice. She'd gotten her first aid certificate when they first started their own digs—Simon said one of them had to be able to put their eager volunteers back together—and she'd dealt with her share of broken bones, and plenty of cuts and bruises. She knew what she was doing, more or less; it was just that her patients weren't usually two hundred year old naked men.

Best to pretend this was nothing out of the ordinary, she told herself, and began to draw down the blanket to his waist. But instead of staying put it began to slip further. She made a grab, intending to save his modesty, at the same time as he did. For an awkward moment they fumbled together, and he gave that rough laugh, followed by a groan as he jolted his ribs.

Maggie stepped back, knowing she was making a fool of herself. "I'm sorry."

"There's no need for you to tend to me, madam," he said, still slightly breathless. Under the kitchen light he looked paler than before and the hand holding onto his covering was shaking slightly. *Some men don't know when to stop being heroes,* she thought irritably.

Maggie's attention focused on his chest. On the lower left hand side she could see what was the beginning of a large bruise. "Of course there is a need for me to tend you," she retorted. "You saved my life. And my name is Maggie."

He looked surprised and strangely vulnerable, but it only lasted a moment before his expression turned impassive, making it very difficult to read what he was thinking.

Time to take charge, Maggie told herself.

"I'll try not to hurt you," she said, already bending over and placing her hand against his ribs to examine him. Once or twice he caught his breath and held himself stiff, but he didn't cry out or protest. The last time she had met a man this stoic was when Simon was on his death bed.

Maggie closed her eyes and concentrated, moving her hands gently but firmly along each rib, testing the injured area. When she was finished, she took a step back, hands on her hips and met his eyes. His pallor was tinged with green now, as if he might be sick, but his gaze was unwavering.

"I can't feel any bones sticking out, so no serious breaks," she said. "Your ribs are either cracked or bruised. I won't strap them, but you should rest until they heal. Two weeks at least."

That laugh again. He winced and shifted on the chair, trying to get comfortable. "Resting for that long is not an option, Maggie. I have to capture the Destroyer."

"Then you need to see a doctor," she replied tartly. "A, eh, physician," she clarified, wondering whether that was a word more relevant to his time period.

His dark brows slashed down in a frown, and his voice was haughty. "I know what a doctor is and I do not require one."

"As you wish." She forgave him, knowing he had to be in considerable pain. A doctor would give him some nice tranquillizers, but if he preferred to suffer that was up to him. She had more important matters on her mind, which reminded her …

"Why do you call that thing the Destroyer?"

"That is its name," he said impatiently. He glanced at her, and as if he realized she needed more, added, "That's the only name I know it by." He put his hand on the table and tried to stand, but the strength for it was beyond him. Maggie knew she could wait and make him ask but such games seemed pointless right now. She slipped an arm about him, propping him up as he found his feet.

"You're not going to fight it again right now?" she asked.

"No, Maggie, I'm not going to fight it now." He'd spotted the sofa set under the windows in the lounge and began to make his way toward it. His voice sounded husky. "Now I need to rest, just as he is no doubt doing."

The sofa was old, with a wooden frame and foam cushions, and it had a dip in the middle. There were some odd stains on the bright blue cover, but he lay down on it as if it was a feather bed, tugging the blanket over himself as best he could. His long legs hung over one end and his head rested on a pillow that had seen better days.

"There's a bed in the spare room," Maggie offered, watching him, but it was already too late. Her guest was asleep.

Chapter Five

"YOU MUST MEND WHAT YOU have broken."

The Sorceress had been awful in her fury, her blue eyes hard and sharp as blades, her hair moving about her with that invisible wind. She was a creature like no other and Lorne, not one to be afraid of much, had been so in awe of her he could barely think.

How stupid they had been to interfere with the structure of the corporeal and spiritual worlds! They'd been like children, poking at a dangerous animal, believing everything was there for their gratification alone.

"You could have been so much more …"

The Sorceress's last words returned to him, spoken as he'd fallen back into that long dark sleep.

He turned over on the sofa, groaning at his ribs, and felt the Scotswoman covering him with something thicker and more substantial than his blanket. She carefully tucked it around him, her voice a distant murmur, but he couldn't wake. Her kindness to him was not unexpected, as she'd said he had saved her life, but it had been a long time since anyone had cared whether or not he was comfortable.

Whose idea had it been to bring the demon up from the underworld? Sutcliffe's? Darlington's? No, it had been his and his alone, although his two friends had been quick to fall in with the plan. The nights and days of debauchery in the crypt, so exciting when they'd begun, had grown stale. They needed something more, something to titillate their senses further, something to fill the void inside them, and what could be better than summoning a dark soul from the bowels of Hell?

Stupid, stupid, *stupid*!

Because the demon, when it came, was beyond their expectations, beyond their limited imaginations, and beyond their control. It hadn't wanted to play their silly games. All the demon had wanted to do was kill. To destroy.

"But that isn't all, Marquis."

The Sorceress was there, in his dream, her face pressed close to his, her power paralyzing him beyond speech. He couldn't even blink. "Since you've been sleeping I have discovered that The Destroyer is not alone."

"Not alone?"

"You will see. Concentrate on finding the demon and capturing him. Bring him to me."

"Yes," he said hoarsely. "I will."

"The woman," she added, with a little smile. "She will help you."

"She's a Scot," he said drolly, "in case you hadn't noticed."

But she had noticed, of course she had. This was all part of her plan to remake him into a better

Lorne. He might feel resentful at her lack of trust, aware as he was that he was doing his best, but he'd learned long ago that it was useless to argue.

"Aye, so she is." She assumed the accent perfectly, mocking him. "You hated your grandmother, didn't you, Lorne? But to catch the demon you will have to learn to get on with Maggie McNab."

"Was that why you took away my clothes? So that I can get on with her?" he asked her dryly.

"It may have been. Do you think it is working?" The Sorceress stepped away and some of the oppression lifted from him. Her voice deepened, became a command.

"*Make* it your business to get on with her, Lorne. It will take the two of you to complete this task."

"And if I don't?" he said, just to hear her response.

"If you fail and the demon is not captured, then you must take his place in the underworld. Well?"

She was waiting for his promise of obedience. They'd been down this road before in the two hundred years since they had met. He really wished she trusted him, believed him when he said he had changed, but he understood why she did not.

"I will do as you say, madam. I will find the demon and bring him to you."

She smiled, but it was difficult to watch when he could see the monsters behind her eyes. "One day, my fine Marquis, I will trust and believe you. But not yet. No, not just yet."

She'd read his mind, Lorne thought with disgust. And now she was fading. In a moment she had gone and the darkness descended upon him once more, and he slept.

Chapter Six

MAGGIE FOUND HERSELF WATCHING THIS man from the past, unblinking. For some odd reason she couldn't keep her eyes off him. Or maybe it wasn't so odd, under the circumstances. Perhaps he would wake up and begin to explain himself?

He didn't. He lay still. Pale and still. Like a dead man.

Well he was a dead man, wasn't he? Technically. A dead man two hundred years old, if he was to be believed. If her own eyes were to be believed. Those same eyes that had seen a demon rise out of the ground just hours before.

With a sigh, Maggie finally unzipped her jacket and shrugged herself out of it. She was wearing a close fitting, turquoise colored, long sleeved shirt that had seen better days, and was now liberally splattered with mud from the barrow. She tugged her woolen hat off her unruly dark curls, running her hands through them. Making her way over to the combustion heater, she began to stack it with wooden logs and some kindling paper, then lit it. The paper caught, igniting the wood, and everything began to burn nicely.

That was better.

She turned away and her eye was caught by a parcel left on the coffee table. She'd collected the mail from the village this morning and had planned to save this particular treat until she was settled in front of the fire with a glass of red in her hand. Now, with a mixture of anticipation and regret, she picked it up and ripped off the paper.

Maggie thought she'd prepared herself, but even so a wave of sadness washed over her. Inside was a book. The cover was the one Simon had chosen—an old sepia photograph of a rocky island in a grey sea—but she was more interested in what was on the back.

Turning the book over she found Simon's photograph. His smiling face brought a lump to her throat. She stroked his image with her fingertips, as if he could feel her. Of course he couldn't, but she hoped that somewhere, somehow, he knew that his life's work was finally in print.

Secrets of Moyle. That was the title of the book, and it told the story of the island of Moyle, concentrating on what life had been like there in the 19th century, when it was still a thriving community. Among the inhabitants were Simon's ancestors, the Frazers, and the island had always drawn him. He'd spent many of his early years as an archeologist working there, discovering its past, learning how the people survived on that small lonely rock in the Atlantic, far off the Scottish west coast. *Secrets of Moyle* had been one of his proudest accomplishments.

And he had never seen it in its published state.

Tears filled Maggie's eyes but she forced them back. There had been enough crying. Simon was gone and she should be celebrating his life rather than mourning his death.

"Underworld… down in the dark… no, no…"

The muttered words caused her attention to jump to the sleeping form on the sofa. He'd thrown out one of his arms and seemed to be trying to sit up. Almost immediately he fell back, still asleep. He was having a dream and it didn't appear to be a pleasant one.

He turned his head toward her on the cushion and she noticed the stubble on his lean cheeks. Dark stubble. Dark like his eyebrows and the hair on his chest. Had the stubble been there before? Somehow that one detail, the idea that the hair had grown since they met, made him seem more real and alive than any other. She was tempted to move closer so that she could examine him better, but decided that wasn't a good idea.

Not until you know exactly what you're dealing with.

Maggie's brow creased. No, that wasn't right either. She wasn't touching him under any circumstances, not in *that* way. She wasn't the sort of woman who fondled strange men, even if they were spectacularly handsome. In fact, spectacularly handsome men were usually her worse nightmare. She was the sort of girl who preferred to spend time with the shy eccentrics, huddled in a corner and listening to their stories about life's misfortunes.

This man was more Linny's type. Or was that unfair? Linny normally went for men who were handsome—and rotten to the core. She didn't think this man was a bastard, but she might be naïve about that. You'd expect someone as gorgeous as him to be spoiled rotten, the sort who expected all womankind to fall to their knees in admiration. And yet she didn't think that was the case. When she'd told him she wanted to help because he'd saved her life, he had looked at her as if she'd given him the keys to the kingdom of heaven.

Spoiled men who expected such things didn't look like that.

She would have to question him when he woke up. She didn't even know his name. Once she had the full story, or as much of it as she could get, then she could decide what to do. Call the police? Possibly. Although she doubted they would believe her. Maggie could see the headlines now: *Archeologist claims to have found 200 year old living man in cemetery after demon attack.*

No, best if she took this slowly, and tried to work out exactly what was happening in a rational and logical way.

An image of the Destroyer replayed in her head and she knew that the rational and logical had already left the building.

She scrutinized the sleeping man. Maybe she should check to see if he was too warm now that she'd covered him with the quilt from the spare bed? Check his pulse and bathe his brow?

Or maybe she should just keep her hands off him, for her sake and his.

Linny would tell her she needed to get laid. Maggie and her sister shared a strong bond, something that some even described as a psychic bond. If there was trouble brewing for one then the other knew.

Lately, Linny seemed to be always on the phone. Her sister liked to remind her that even before Simon had died there'd been barely any exciting action of that sort, not for quite some time.

"Go out and find a man and bring him home with you for the night," Linny suggested once after they'd shared a bottle of wine. "You don't have to be engaged to him to enjoy yourself."

"I'm not like that," Maggie had insisted. "I don't do casual sex. I never have."

"Your loss, sis."

"You know there's only ever been Simon, and now he's gone … I'm perfectly fine on my own."

"I can buy you a vibrator?"

Maggie gave her a look.

"What? It's a reasonable alternative."

"Not for me."

Linny had wrapped her up in a hug, and they'd both shed some tears, and Maggie had hoped that would be the end of it.

Simon Frazer had been all of fifteen years older than her and she'd admired him tremendously, even before he'd began to take an interest in the young lass from Glasgow with the prickly personality and the unfortunate habit of blushing whenever she was complimented on her work. He took the time to listen to her, to understand her, and to encourage her—all the things she'd had in starvation rations when she was at home in Govan, the rougher side of Glasgow.

Her mother had been a junkie, her father in and out of prison all his life, and if it hadn't been for her sister Linny she would probably have ended up one or other herself. But Linny had taken her in hand, smacked her down when she needed it, and hugged her when she needed that, too.

With Linny's help, Maggie had fulfilled her potential and gone on to university to become an archeologist. A professor, no less. But beneath the smoothed down edges, there was still the old Maggie. Tough, mouthy, and so vulnerable inside. Even now, she didn't believe she deserved her success; failure was more expected where she came from.

Simon had adored her despite everything that made them different, and in turn she adored him. Their work had brought them together, and kept them together through the years. They were a team, and it was his friendship that Maggie missed more than anything. Evenings discussing their latest finds, looking up at a dig and seeing his fair head across the trench, knowing he was there if she needed him. They had planned to make the barrow at Blackfriars Abbey the pinnacle of their achievements.

"What if we find a warrior with his sword, Maggie, or even a prince with his royal regalia and hunting dog? That would make a career. You'd be able to write a book on it, maybe even star in a documentary. You'd never have to kneel in the freezing rain with a trowel again."

"Well then it would be worth it," she'd agreed with a laugh, even though she quite liked digging with her trowel, rain or no rain. The thought of fame wasn't important to her, not without Simon to share it. In fact, after this dig, she had been thinking of taking a long sabbatical.

That was until, instead of a warrior or a prince, she had unearthed a demon from hell and his silver haired adversary.

There was a noise outside.

Maggie's eyes flew to the door. It gave directly onto the sitting room. There was a back door too, in the laundry, but she'd made sure it was locked and bolted. This one only had a lock, no bolts, and she'd always thought it would be easy enough to break in if someone really wanted to.

She waited, but then everything was silent again. Perhaps it had been a fox on the scrounge and she was being hypersensitive. Maggie relaxed and took a calming breath.

Then the sound came again. Sharper. Louder. As if claws were scratching on the wooden surface.

Something is trying to get in.

Maggie's attention went to the man on the sofa, thinking he might have heard it too, but he was still asleep. Maggie didn't even consider waking him up—he was injured and he had already saved her once. This time it was her turn.

She took the few steps needed to reach a wooden cupboard in the corner of the room and turned the key to unlock it. Simon's shotgun was inside, and she lifted it out, with some shells from the box on the shelf below, and loaded it.

She knew how to use the weapon. Simon had shown her when they were on Moyle for that final visit. He'd told her he wanted her to learn to shoot. "In case your father comes looking for you," he'd said with black humor, but she'd known it was because he'd wanted to comfort himself with the knowledge that she could take care of herself when he was gone.

Simon had always brought the shotgun with

them when they were on site, just in case someone took exception to their presence. Or the thieves who saw an opportunity to do some digging of their own. He'd never fired it at anyone, and the one time he'd had to get it out, just the look of it had been enough to scare away the problem.

Maggie walked carefully back to the door and stood before it. She took aim. She was glad to find her arms were steady and her hands weren't shaking. She wasn't afraid, or perhaps she'd gone beyond fear now. All she felt was a calm determination to protect herself and the sleeping man.

Outside, the scratching came again and then the door knob rattled. Violently. She watched it twist back and forth as someone gripped it from the other side. That was no fox. She could no longer pretend that there wasn't someone out there. Trying to get in.

"Go away!" Maggie shouted. "I mean it. Go away or I'll shoot. I have a gun!"

"Let me in!" a deep voice growled.

Her heart jumped. Did the Destroyer *speak*? She swallowed, tightened her grip on the shotgun, and found her voice again.

"I'm warning you—"

"Let me in or I'll smash the bloody door in!"

The next moment something big and heavy threw itself against the wooden door, shaking it on its hinges and rattling the windowpanes. The door was too flimsy to withstand another assault—she could see the wood splintering—and when it fell whatever was out there would be in here. She had no option. Maggie aimed and pulled the trigger.

Just as a forceful hand thrust the barrel up into

the air.

The shot went through the ceiling of the spare room above the door, smashing through plaster and wood which then rained down upon them. The air was filled with dust and the pungent smell of gunpowder.

"What do you think you're *doing*?"

But he said nothing and walked to the door. She watched in wide-eyed horror—or perhaps more rage than horror—as he unlocked it and flung it wide.

We're going to die, Maggie thought, hysteria bubbling up inside her. *That thing is going to tear us to pieces.*

Chapter Seven

A SHAPE BOUNDED IN. SHAGGY, GREY, pale eyed.

A wolf!

Maggie stumbled backwards before she realized it wasn't a wild wolf at all, but some sort of domesticated wolf—even a husky.

The animal leapt at her man from the past and he pushed it away, though gently, before giving its thick grey coat an affectionate ruffle.

"Down Loki, down."

Loki, however, didn't take much notice. The dog had spotted Maggie and was about to leap on her when a huge man with short dark hair came through the open door and grabbed its collar—something she'd only just noticed—and pulled it back.

"Loki," the giant growled. "Leave Lorne alone. You'll turn him into a eunuch with those claws."

So she finally had a name for her rescuer. Lorne.

Maggie watched the two men clasp hands and exchange a jumble of excited words—"I thought I was—""We feared you were—""Loki found your scent—"

With eyes as dark as his hair, the visitor looked Lorne over. "Where are your clothes, my friend?" His attention then shifted to Maggie, as though she might have had something to do with it, and he chuckled.

Entering the room behind the giant was another man, his hair not quite as dark, his face as sharp as a hawk. He had a decided limp, and a scar ran down his cheek, as though someone had sliced it open with a blade. There were more handshakes and exclamations of relief before the third man turned to her. "Darlington, at your service, madam," he announced, in a voice as aristocratic as Lorne's. Then, to Maggie's bemusement, he actually bowed.

It felt as if she was trapped in a Jane Austen novel. Any moment now she would be curtseying and sending the maid off for tea and crumpets.

Maggie put a hand over her mouth, not sure if she was going to start laughing or screaming. She'd prepared herself to die, not take part in a costume drama. She turned away and saw that someone was staring back at her from the mirror on the wall. Dark curling hair, brown eyes wide beneath strong brows, skin flour white, and lips that had lost their rosy-color. For a moment she didn't recognize herself. She could have been a ghost.

Another reflection came up behind her, so suddenly she gave a squeak. She swung her arm and would have struck Lorne, except that he wrapped his arms about her and pulled her back against his body, holding her fast.

"It's all right," he said. "Maggie, it's all right."

He was far stronger than he'd been before when she helped him up from the kitchen chair. She could feel his body pressed behind her, the heat of him, his wide chest and flat stomach and… oh God, he was becoming aroused.

Maggie's disbelieving eyes flew to his in the mirror and for a moment they stared at each other. She saw confusion in his face followed by a sort of derision, but it was for himself rather than her, as if his physical reaction was a lack of self-control he wasn't happy about.

As for herself, as soon as he touched her every one of her senses fired up only to melt back down. She was a woman on heat and her biggest fear now was that he should find out the truth.

Lorne cleared his throat but his eyes remained fixed on her. "Don't be afraid," he said, in the voice of a man striving to be reassuring when he had a serious hard on. "You're safe. You have my word we will not harm you."

Perhaps he was as far out of his comfort zone as she was, but Maggie wasn't thinking of him. She opened her mouth, and closed it again. She'd been standing in the circle of his arms, spine like steel, unbending, her hands clenched into fists at her sides. Mainly because she was afraid that if she relaxed she might do something foolish, like turn and kiss him. The very thought of it was embarrassing and humiliating, and she couldn't let him know she wasn't the virtuous damsel she was about to portray.

"Safe?" she repeated, her voice rising. "If I have your word then let me go, you … you *fiend!*"

His eyes widened and he gave that harsh bark of laughter, the sound of someone who wasn't much used to laughing, but enjoyed every minute of it.

Furious, she began to pull herself free, slapping at his arms as he lifted them away. "How dare you?" she gasped, completely out of her depth. "What gives you the right to touch me?"

"Maggie, I meant no harm," he said, holding out his arms in surrender. "My cock … it has been so long since I held a woman. Forgive me …"

"Your *cock*!" she hissed. "I'd ask you to keep it in your pants, but you'd have to be wearing some first. I'll have you know I am a respectable woman." She knew she sounded like something from a 1950s movie with strong moral overtones but she couldn't seem to stop herself.

Lorne's eyes flamed. God, had she gone too far? She didn't really know him, after all. For a moment she was catapulted into the past and her first months at university, before Simon came along, when she had learned that a friendly smile was not always to be trusted. Just as she had on that awful, memorable night, Maggie prepared herself for his retaliation.

But the big man had arrived, towering over them, his hands on his hips and his face expressing his impatience with such childish behavior. "That's enough, Lorne," he rumbled. He shot Maggie a frown. "The lass doesn't like your way of showing affection."

Lorne frowned at his friend. "I *have* let her go, Sutcliffe. However, I am in rather a delicate condition."

Maggie had already noted his 'delicate condition'. She shouldn't have looked. She wasn't at all sure why her eyes had disobeyed her brain, only that her gaze had been drawn downward.

Sutcliffe sighed in weary exasperation, as if Lorne had behaved in just the way he'd expected. He looked around and spotted the blanket on the sofa, and picked it up. "Here," he said, throwing it at him. "Now sit down, Lorne, and behave yourself. There isn't time for this. We need to talk."

Lorne looked as if he'd like to argue, but after a glance at Maggie, he began to carefully wrap the paisley wool around his hips, like a kilt, and then went to the sofa, where he sat down gingerly.

Maggie wished he'd be quiet so she could forget it had ever happened, but he didn't seem to know how. "My pardon," he said quietly, watching her face. "I appear to have as little control over my base urges as a savage animal."

Maggie shot him a look, made all the more bad-tempered because of her own confused feelings and 'base urges'. "If that's an apology then it's too feeble to deserve a reply."

Lorne smoothed the wool over his lap. "At the moment, feeble is not a word that applies to me, Maggie."

She caught a flash of warmth in his eyes and her heart ratcheted up a notch. Jesus, when would it end! He was like a virus she couldn't shake off and she'd only known him a couple of hours. The trouble was, Maggie was very much afraid that there was a part of her she barely recognized that didn't want to shake him off.

Her eyes skittered about, looking anywhere but at him, and landed on Simon's book, resting on the coffee table in front of him. Straight away she wanted to grab hold of it and remove it from his contaminating presence. And at the same time, for the sake of her own sanity, she didn't want to be anywhere near him.

Her body was hot and tingly, as if she'd just been in a warm bath. She felt … sensual, that was the word. Needy in a way she did not remember ever feeling before. When she should be repulsed she was actually turned on, and she felt as if Lorne had touched something far deeper than her skin. She felt as if he'd delved inside her and now he was there, like the virus she had just likened him to, spreading through her blood, and there was no getting him out.

You're being idiotic, she told herself angrily. *It's the adrenaline. You thought you were going to die and now you feel the need to have sex. It's natural, normal, so stop beating yourself up over it. Anyway, he's not your type. Simon was your type. Not this upper-class Englishman who thinks he's God's gift to women.*

"It looks like I wasn't the only one being punished," Lorne said in a voice that sounded quite emotional for a 'fiend.' "What happened to you both?"

"The Sorceress put me in your family mausoleum," Darlington complained as he limped to the stove to warm himself. "Had a devil of a job getting out once I woke up. I was sharing a coffin with one of your upstanding ancestors and he had his bony arms wrapped around me. I think *she* did that, to be honest."

"And I was in a graveyard. I think it was a pet's grave. I suppose that was for Loki." The dog had flopped at Sutcliffe's feet, panting, looking from each of them as if he knew exactly what they were saying.

"I had hoped you'd be allowed to remain … back there. I thought I might be enough for her."

The two visitors exchanged a glance and Maggie thought they seemed surprised. "We were all in it together," Sutcliffe said gruffly. "Only fair the punishment be shared out."

"So, why are we awake?" Darlington reached down to massage his leg as if it hurt him. "Why has the Sorceress brought us back now?"

There was a pause before Lorne said in a voice heavy with meaning: "It is free."

The two men stared at him. Darlington muttered a curse. "How?"

Lorne raised his dark brows at Maggie. "I think you should ask Maggie here that question."

"Professor McNab," she snapped before she could stop herself.

She'd backed away as far from them as she could, until she was standing near the open door. Outside the air was cold and the cloudy night sky gave little light. She was tempted to run away from the craziness of this situation, but where could she run to? And regardless, the demon was out there and as much as she wanted to escape Austen Land, she didn't want to become its next meal.

She straightened her back, telling herself she wasn't about to be intimidated by these Sassenachs, even if they should have been dead for over two hundred years.

"I'm an archeologist."

"A what?" asked Darlington.

"I think she means an antiquarian," said Sutcliffe. "*Archaeologia* means ancient history."

Maggie looked from one to the other but decided

not to go there. "I am conducting a dig at Black-friars Abbey. How was I to know that *thing* was there? Someone should have put a sign up to warn people." But honestly, would that have mattered? The mummy's curse wouldn't have kept Howard Carter away from King Tut's tomb.

Sutcliffe gave a surprised chuckle while Darlington seemed to be studying his boots. They were waiting for Lorne's response, she realized. He led and they followed.

But at the moment Lorne wasn't responding. He was listening.

"I need to know what's going on," she blurted out, his voice rising as her emotions spilled free. "For the love of God, I need you to explain to me *what the hell is going on!*"

Lorne had always found that women were ruled by their hearts rather than their heads. His grandmother, even at her cruelest, had been irrational in that cruelty.

Of course, irrational behavior was not the sole domain of women. Just now, when he'd held Maggie, he'd lost all of his fabled self-control.

But was it really so irrational?

It had been a long time since any woman had been in his arms, so naturally he would become aroused by the touch and scent of one, whoever she might be. Scottish or not. What other explanation could there be?

Sutcliffe thought he had interrupted Lorne *amusing* himself with Maggie—he had seen it in the big man's expression. He saw Lorne as the man he had once been and how could he know Lorne had changed?

Nevertheless it was frustrating. Lorne wanted to say, *No, this is me now. I wouldn't do that, not any more. I'm trying so hard to be better.* But how could he make his friends understand? They'd probably think he was playing another of his silly games.

Lorne considered himself a solitary man. Sutcliffe and Darlington were his closest friends and he would lay down his life for them if necessary. Even so, there was always a distance between himself and the rest of the world, and the most secret part of his soul was beyond a border few people were ever allowed to cross.

"Well?" Maggie was glaring at him. "Who are you?" Despite her bravery when she'd stood at the door with her shotgun, he knew she was frightened. Although she was demanding an explanation, would she be able to cope once she had it? Lorne prepared himself for female hysteria.

A glance from Sutcliffe to Darlington showed him they weren't about to step forward—as usual it was up to him. A shame, because exhaustion was fluttering at the edges of his vision like black wings, and although his cock had finally relaxed, he felt as if that little performance had drained him of all his energy. Maggie, if she but knew it, was perfectly safe from being ravished by him.

He cleared his throat and got unsteadily to his feet, one hand clasping the blanket in place about his waist. For a moment he thought he would collapse, but he steadied and gave her a gentlemanlike, if slightly wobbly, bow from the waist. His companions promptly followed suit.

"Allow us to introduce ourselves," Lorne said.

"The Hellfire Club, at your service," Sutcliffe added.

"We are the roaring bad boys," Darlington finished with more than a hint of pride.

There had only ever been one Hellfire Club at Blackfriars Abbey.

"And your names?" she asked in an uncertain voice.

Lorne smiled. He was enjoying this. "Charles Escott, the Marquis of Lorne, my lady," he said. "The 4th Marquis," he added, so that there could be no mistake. "Those of my acquaintance know me as Lorne."

"The wicked Marquis." It was a whisper, as if she hadn't meant to say it aloud. Suddenly she looked rather pale.

"Lord Aiden Sutcliffe," the giant rumbled, "and you've met Loki."

"Nicholas Darlington," the man with the scarred face said. "I had a title once, but I was stripped of it. Rightly so." He gave a quick glance to the others, as if he thought they might find his acceptance curious.

She took a breath, as if she needed to gather her strength for this next question. "So you've been dead. Sleeping. Whatever. For two hundred years?"

Everything in her was rebelling against those words. She was a rationalist, and he could see her mind struggling. He couldn't blame her.

"Correct."

"The Destroyer...? What is it?"

"The Destroyer came into the world because of

me. It is my fault." He watched her face, expecting her to fall onto his admission that this was his fault with glee, but she simply stared at him. "I called him up from the underworld and let him loose into the world. Not one of my cleverer ideas, I agree, but I assure you, my heart was filled with mischief, not murder. It has been my job to guard him to eternity and beyond, if necessary, which is the reason the Sorceress placed me in the ground beside him."

Maggie seemed to be trying to come to grips with what he'd said in a logical way. Perhaps it would be all right after all.

"The Sorceress?" Maggie spoke the name cautiously. "Who is she?"

"She rules the between-worlds. It's a gateway and she is a gate-keeper. The Sorceress decides who passes through the between-worlds from the underworld to the mortal world. Or vice versa."

"Underworld, mortal world ... I'm familiar with these places, but they're not real. If they were I would know." Maggie shook her head in bemusement, her dark eyes rather wild, her curls flying about her head. "What does she look like, this Sorceress?"

Lorne gave her a humorless smile. "You will know her when you see her."

She looked like she wanted to argue the facts with him, and Lorne was relieved when Darlington interrupted, speaking to him rather than Maggie. "We know the Destroyer will be weak at first, as we all are." His friend limped closer, and his scarred face was gloomy. "He'll need to find a place to hide, and from there he'll go out to hunt. To eat.

He needs to feed."

He rubbed his stomach through his rumpled white linen shirt. "We all do."

———◆———

Maggie was still reeling from their revelations. Eat? She knew she should ask for details, get an understanding of just what that creature was likely to find tasty, but the words couldn't get past the narrowing of her throat.

The big man joined the conversation, a note of urgency in his voice. "The more he eats the stronger he'll become. We have to find him before that happens."

Maggie interrupted. "And if we don't?"

They exchanged another of their glances, and as if by some unspoken rule, it was Lorne who answered her.

"Then this village, and soon this country, is in dire trouble."

They were insane, they had to be, but if that was the case then so was she. She had seen the truth with her own eyes and now she had no choice but to deal with it. Was she really standing before the Hellfire Club, that band of trouble makers that had disappeared in 1808?

They were the 'roaring bad boys,' there was truth in that. She remembered Owen saying—one of the few things she did remember—that they made the antics of Byron and Shelley pale into insignificance.

The three men were watching her, probably expecting her to faint or come over all girlish, so for the sake of her pride Maggie decided to disappoint them.

"I'll make some sandwiches," she said, and disappeared into the kitchen.

Chapter Eight

SUTCLIFFE GAVE AN APPRECIATIVE CHUCKLE and Darlington raised an eyebrow. They were impressed by Maggie's sangfroid and Lorne had to admit she was impressive. But he'd caught their knowing glances in his direction.

They assumed he was starting one of his seductions.

It had been a joke between the three of them and they'd even wagered on the outcome several times. Not that the outcome was ever in any doubt. Lorne was a notorious rake and women seemed to fall into his hands, and his bed, with predictable regularity.

Women saw his handsome looks and thought they knew him. They didn't, and he made sure they never did. They were just a procession of faces and bodies that meant little to him, and he was ashamed to say he didn't much care what happened after he'd slaked his desires.

His behavior shamed him now and he burned with a desire to be a better man.

The thought that his friends still believed he was capable of such egocentric hedonism angered and upset him, but they didn't know the changes that had been wrought on him over the past two hundred years. The demons of a different sort that he'd been forced to face. He would have to show them, and more importantly, he would show Maggie, that he was no wicked Marquis, not any longer.

And why does what she thinks matter?

He reflectively eased his bruised ribs. Loki seemed to sense his inner turmoil and came to rest his big head against Lorne's knee, allowing his ears to be gently tugged. The dog pressed closer and he let his thoughts drift. Once again, they drifted in Maggie's direction.

She was a woman who preferred her head to rule over her heart.

She'd been warm in his arms, soft in the right places, though she was a bit on the skinny side. He'd always preferred his women well-covered—*fat*, according to Darlington's standards—but that seemed of little concern to him now. The faint scent of her still clung to him, and he was startled to find that despite his exhaustion he was becoming aroused again.

The Sorceress wanted them to work together to recapture the Destroyer, but it wasn't going to be easy. He would need all his powers of persuasion to convince Maggie to help, because they needed her. This was her world, not theirs, with its strange machines and devices. She was vital if they were to succeed.

The alternative was too horrible to imagine, and Lorne wasn't going to let that happen. Apart from the havoc the Destroyer would wreak if it was not reigned in, there was his own fate and that of his friends to consider.

If they failed, the Sorceress would not be gentle. She had threatened to send him to the underworld in the demon's place, and he was certain she meant it.

Lorne may have play-acted with damnation in the Hellfire Club, cavorting about and chanting, but it wasn't a place in which he was particularly interested in taking up residence. In the games he and his friends had played, their version of the fiery pit had been something to mock. Afterwards they could go up the stairs to the abbey and eat a hearty meal and sleep in a soft bed. The real underworld would be very different. There would be no reprieve, not even for a moment, just unrelenting torment.

He shivered and drew the quilt closer about him—he'd finally abandoned the blanket. If, he decided, he was going to die anyway then he was going to do his best to make good his mistakes. Not all of them, for how could he, but certainly the worst of them.

"Well, I hope there are plenty of sandwiches to be had. I feel like I haven't eaten for two hundred years." Sutcliffe's prosaic announcement interrupted his thoughts.

Lorne smiled and then laughed.

Sutcliffe frowned. "Are you all right, Lorne? You seem …" But he shrugged, as if he couldn't decide *what* Lorne seemed.

"Never better for a man who has been buried for two centuries."

Sutcliffe waved a hand at him. "What has happened to your hair?"

Lorne shifted in his seat, trying to get comfortable, but every movement seemed to jolt his ribs. Even when he kept still there was a nagging ache that wouldn't go away. "I'm not sure. Makes me look rather distinguished, don't you think?"

Darlington snorted, limping over to a shabby armchair and sitting down at an awkward angle, his lame leg stuck out in front of him. Unlike Lorne, whose discomfort was temporary, Darlington's pain was constant. Not that he ever asked for their sympathy—his stoicism was legendary.

"Why did the Sorceress leave you bare as a badger?" he asked. "At least I had my clothes on when I awoke."

Lorne knew why—the Sorceress had told him it was to break the ice between him and Maggie—but he didn't want to share. His friends would make sport of him. "I have the feeling she has more lessons to teach us."

A shudder ran through Sutcliffe's massive frame. "Well, I for one will not gainsay her." Darlington grunted in agreement.

No, thought Lorne, *there weren't many mortal men brave enough to gainsay the Sorceress.*

In the kitchen, Maggie had recovered from her meltdown and was occupying herself by slapping slices of buttered bread together with tomato and ham. As she worked, she nibbled on a crust with honey, and tried to come to terms with the fact that the naked man who had saved her life was in fact the 4th Marquis of Lorne. She'd had an inkling before but had kept herself in denial.

No chance of that now.

His legend was still very potent in this part of England—although nowadays he was more of a bogeyman to frighten children into obeying their parents. Simon had dismissed the man as a bored, spoilt aristocrat, whose legend far outstripped the reality, but Simon had never come face to face with him.

Was it just her, Maggie wondered, or was there something very compelling about the man? Charismatic, that was the word. He probably had women queuing up at his Hellfire Club, begging to join. And there was the other thing she'd felt … the desire. It was like an insidious tide, with her sitting on a beach thinking she was safe, only to find it suddenly up to her ankles, and her knees, and then completely over her head.

Maggie had never been a believer in love at first sight, but this wasn't love. This was *lust* at first sight. She remembered some of the girls she'd known years ago, with their bedroom walls covered in posters of boy bands and movie stars. Maggie had never been interested in either, but she supposed if she had to have a crush on someone it would be some heroic historical character.

And she certainly couldn't say that the Marquis of Lorne wasn't valiant and brave, not after what he'd done tonight, at considerable risk to his own life.

She paused outside the lounge and took a deep breath. What's the worst that could happen? Best not go there. She had to set her mind to be as open as possible and just let matters unfold, and at the same time try to keep a grip on her normally tightly wound self.

Carrying a plate piled high with sandwiches, she strode into the room as though she didn't have a care in the world, and placed them on the table. A moment later she had to take a step back, as the members of the Hellfire Club fell upon the offering ravenously. She had something for Loki, too—a dish full of tinned stew. The big dog moaned and licked his lips at the sight of it, and soon gulped it down.

Maggie did not consider herself much of a hostess but she guessed her guests were going to prove appreciative of her efforts.

In no time they'd finished the lot. Darlington and Lorne sat back, looking replete and sleepy, but the larger Sutcliffe was still searching for crumbs on the plate. When he spoke he sounded grumpy, as if he was still hungry, which she supposed he was.

"I miss my bed."

Darlington yawned. "It was very claustrophobic in your Mausoleum, Lorne. Not that I have anything to go home to. Nothing and no one." Maggie wondered why he had been cast adrift but this was hardly the time to ask.

"The sooner we catch the demon the sooner we go home." Sutcliffe wasn't listening to his friend. "Shouldn't we be out there now, looking?"

"We have to do it properly this time," Lorne spoke a warning.

"And what happens when we catch it?" Darlington asked. "Does the Sorceress put us back on guard duty and send us to sleep again?"

"The door to the underworld is open. She can

send it back where it came from."

They fell respectfully silent.

"Well what happens when we do go home?" Sutcliffe looked down at Loki's bowl, but that was empty too. "Can we return at the moment we departed?"

"May be awkward," Lorne murmured.

Sutcliffe and Darlington shared a glance. "What do you mean?"

"Well, the Destroyer had been busy up until that point. No doubt, someone will have to be blamed for the dead villagers."

"You mean us?" Sutcliffe said. "But we caught the creature. We saved lives!"

"Yes," Lorne agreed, "But we also summoned it." He straightened up with a wince and pushed his hair out of his eyes. "However, that was entirely my fault and I will shoulder the responsibility."

Another uneasy glance between the other two. Darlington raised his eyebrows at Sutcliffe, who gave a shrug. "Are you *sure* you're feeling all right?" Sutcliffe said at last. "You don't sound quite…" He shrugged again.

Lorne's brows came down in a scowl. "Don't sound quite *what*, Sutcliffe?"

"Nothing, nothing," the other man said hastily. "I'm sure it will take us some time to return to normal."

Lorne sighed and closed his eyes. "Normal," he muttered. His friends watched him in silence, waiting for him to finish the thought, but he had fallen asleep.

The conversation had been fascinating. It was like taking a peek back in time, and Maggie was enthralled. So the murders that history had laid at their feet had actually been perpetrated by the Destroyer. Lorne had summoned it, but was clearly trying to make amends. Did that sound like the wicked marquis of legend? A curl of heat started low down in her belly but she ignored it, told herself it was indigestion, and folded her arms.

"Do you think after this is over you will go back to eighteen hundred and eight?" she asked Sutcliffe, who seemed the most approachable right now. "I mean, eh, isn't Lorne right? Isn't it a bit dangerous to go back?"

Pitchforks and bonfires, that's what would be waiting for them. Assuming the local magistrate didn't hang them first.

"The Sorceress didn't actually tell us what she was going to do with us," Darlington admitted, shifting in his chair. He held his hands out to the warmth of the fire again, and Maggie saw that he wore a rather impressive signet ring on his little finger. "I simply assumed we'd go back." Sutcliffe stared off into space. "Could we get used to living in the future, do you think? It must have its compensations."

"Like no one wanting to hunt us down and kill us," his friend answered dryly.

A tingle ran down Maggie's spine. She gave the sleeping Lorne a cautious glance, and found that the thought of the Marquis ending his life so brutally filled her with dismay. Surely this Sorceress they held in such awe had some trick she could use to save them?

And yet, if they did stay, *where* would they stay? What would they do? It wasn't as if 'aristocrat' was a sought after profession. Her mind began to go down all sorts of strange paths—if they returned, would it change the past, and the present? Would she still exist? Would their presence now affect the future in unintended ways? What if their actions caused ripples that eventually turned into tidal waves? She was relieved when Loki interrupted them with a growl.

Sutcliffe had tried to set the door back in place, resting it up against the frame, but it wasn't secure. His earlier determination to force his way inside had damaged the frame, and there were gaps where the cold air seeped in. Now the animal was staring in a way that made the hairs stand up on Maggie's neck.

Sutcliffe got to his feet. "We need to fix that. Do you have tools?"

Lord Aiden Sutcliffe's eyes were as black as his hair, and his nose had been broken at some point. He was a great bear of a man, but strangely Maggie found herself liking him.

"There are some in a box in the laundry. Straight down the passage and in the bottom of the cup-board."

Sutcliffe lumbered off and for a moment there was silence.

"Lorne says he met you in the graveyard." Nicholas Darlington had lowered his voice, glancing at the sleeping Marquis. "And that you woke him up. I imagine he wasn't terribly happy. He's never at his best first thing."

Was he fishing for information or making polite conversation? Maggie didn't think Darlington was the chatty type. "He saved my life," she said. "And he was hurt, so you're right; he probably wasn't at his best."

Darlington leaned forward, dropping his voice further. "Lorne gets bored very quickly. He's always looking for new diversions. That's why he started the Hellfire Club. At first he was excited by the prospect, but it waned. As with everything, he grew bored. It's the same with women."

Was he trying to warn her off his friend? And if so, why?

"Darlington."

Darlington started guiltily at the sound of Lorne's voice, and then he relaxed again, turning with a smile. "You're awake," he said.

Lorne was looking back at him through half closed eyes. Darlington seemed to read something in them that Maggie couldn't. He stood up, awkwardly because of his leg, and said to no one in particular, "I'll go and help Sutcliffe."

Maggie really didn't want to be left alone in the room with Lorne. Had Darlington been warning her not to become infatuated with the Marquis? Did he think she already was? The thought was too embarrassing, made worse because Lorne had overheard.

"How are your ribs?" she asked quickly, to forestall anything he might be about to say.

"They hurt," he replied.

She'd been expecting him to brush the question off, pretend everything was fine. Honesty was a good change of pace. She much preferred it.

She turned away from his intense blue stare, and noticed Simon's book was still on the table. Lorne reached for it.

"No," Maggie said, and bit her lip.

His hand hovered above the cover. "No?"

What could she say? *Please don't touch my dead husband's book, it makes me feel guilty, it makes me feel as if I am being disloyal.*

He'd ask why, wouldn't he? And she'd have to make up some silly excuse because how could she tell him the truth? That they'd barely met and she was already thinking about him in terms of the bedroom.

Darlington had been good to warn her, though she didn't really need anyone to tell her she was being a fool. And she had no intention of following through on her fantasy.

When she didn't speak again, Lorne's hand closed on the hardback cover and picked it up.

"Moyle?" he read, with a quizzical lift of his eyebrows. "*Secrets of Moyle.* Written by Professor Simon Frazer." He turned the book over and examined the photo on the back. He seemed mesmerized by the likeness, and Maggie remembered that photographs were still unknown in the world he came from. Strange that he should have no problems with demons and sorceresses and the underworld, and yet struggle with a black and white snap.

"Do you know him?" he asked her, finally lifting his eyes, and holding out the book to her.

She hesitated, not wanting to get close to him or accidently touch him. She knew what had happened before. He read the concerns in her face and a smile glimmered in his eyes like distant lightning.

Jesus, don't do that!

"Eh, he's my husband. Or was. He died a year ago."

Lorne looked down again at Simon's smiling face, and she thought he was going to say something about being sorry and offering her his sympathy. What he did say was, "A year."

Maggie opened her mouth, meaning to ask him what he meant, but closed it again. She had a feeling that if she did ask she would wish she hadn't.

"Darlington was quite right, you know," he said, breaking the silence. "The man he was describing was me."

"Really, Marquis, it's none of my business."

Lorne leaned forward, his hand still resting on the image of Simon's face. "Maggie, you have to understand—"

She'd never been comfortable with gorgeous, charismatic men, and Lorne was the king of allure. In the brief time since they'd met—albeit under harrowing circumstances—he'd set her completely off balance. Her ridiculous attraction for him was a complication she didn't need, so she was more than happy when Sutcliffe shuffled back into the room.

His arms were filled with tools he thought might help him to fix the door, while Darlington, limping behind him, carried only a hammer.

They ignored Lorne and Maggie, propped the door open and set about unscrewing the damaged hinges.

Maggie could see the shape of the Land Rover parked outside. The runic tablet that Owen had found in the graveyard was still packed in its box in the back, and she knew that such a precious object should be inside here with her. Getting it would also give her something to do.

She got up and moved toward the doorway, picking up the shotgun Lorne had left resting against the wall.

Instantly the men, and even the dog, turned to stare at her. She could have heard a pin drop. Lorne tried to get to his feet, holding his quilt around him.

"Where are you going?"

"Eh, I need to fetch something from the Land Rover," Maggie said, wondering why it was such an issue. Then, seeing the incomprehension on Sutcliffe's face, explained, "The horseless carriage. Outside."

He and Darlington exchanged a glance. "I will assist you." Sutcliffe clicked his fingers at Loki, but before either of them could move, Lorne was on his feet.

"*I'll* go with her," he announced, ignoring their snorts of laughter as his covering slipped dangerously low again.

Sutcliffe turned to Maggie. "Don't you have anything he can put on?" he asked her with a grin. "I'm sick of looking at his bare arse."

"There were some clothes that belonged to the last tenant." She was smiling as well, despite herself. "He seemed to have left in a bit of a hurry."

"Then for the sake of everyone can you get them for him?" Darlington asked. "Your blushing is heating up the room and we already have a fire."

Maggie scowled as she climbed the stairs. She was beginning to think that the members of the notorious Hellfire Club were closer to silly boys than big bad wolves.

The bedroom felt like a sanctuary. For a moment she felt tempted to lock herself in and hide under the bed covers. But she decided against it. Not because it was cowardly, but because the men downstairs would probably come looking for her and demand she make them more sandwiches.

The thought caused a wry smile. Was she frightened of them? No. Well … not much anyway. They were a bit like some of the men of her dig team, professional and childish in equal measure. Except for Lorne. What had he been trying to tell her a moment ago, before they were interrupted? Maggie had the feeling that he was going to reiterate Darlington's warning about getting involved with him.

Was it *that* obvious she was infatuated with him?

She told herself firmly that she'd just have to try harder to convince him that she didn't give a damn.

Maggie gave the old wardrobe door a wrench to open it—it tended to stick. Inside, the last tenant's garments hung from a railing. Her own clothing was still in her suitcase—jeans and t-shirts, mostly, as well as underwear and socks. She had nothing that needed hanging up, anyway.

She fingered a black long sleeved shirt, and checked out a jacket, also black. They looked like they might fit. There were some trousers as well, and a pair of shoes placed at the bottom of the wardrobe. More black.

Clearly the previous tenant had a thing about black, but Maggie decided that black was the perfect color for the Marquis of Lorne. She took out the garments, piling them in her arms.

The open wardrobe door had hidden her view of the room, and she hadn't heard anyone come in. She didn't even know the Marquis was there until she turned and ran up against his warm, hard body.

With a muffled squawk she tried to back up, but it was too late. Taken by surprise, he'd reached to steady her, his hands gripping her arms, and she was trapped.

Chapter Nine

LORNE HAD COME UP TO the bedchamber because he was weary of his so-called friends making jokes at his expense. Had he ever found them amusing? Maggie had said there was clothing up here and he was sick of being naked for no good reason. He was also tired and desperately needed sleep.

But it was more than that. For some reason the thought of Maggie with her wild curls and brown eyes gave him a sense of ease. As he climbed the stairs, his legs shook with exhaustion, and he remembered her gentle hands on his aching ribs, and her kindness. He feared she might think he was the man Darlington had described. The man he once was. Listening to his friend try to warn her had filled him with dismay, and made him angry.

He wanted his friends, wanted Maggie, to know that man wasn't him, not any longer. He had changed. How could he make them see that?

After he reached the top he paused by the banister, waiting for his head to stop spinning, then followed the sounds he heard to Maggie's bed chamber. He found her rummaging through a tall dresser and muttering to herself. Curious, he'd walked right up behind her, not expecting her to turn around so quickly.

Now here she was in his arms once again, and he wasn't sure who was holding up whom. Not that he was complaining. In the old days, he would have quite happily remained here, and perhaps they would even have climbed into the comfortable looking bed together. But, he reminded himself, he wasn't that man anymore.

She pulled away and dropped the clothing she'd been holding. He noted that once again her dark eyes were angry and her face flushed pink.

"Maggie—"

"How the hell did you creep up on me like that?" Her loud voice hurt his head. "And who said you could come into my bedroom?"

Her reaction seemed rather extreme. Although, if she still thought of him as the wicked Marquis, always prepared for seduction, it made sense. He wanted to explain, but by now he had become very, very tired. As if from a distance, he noticed that his body had reacted to her again, which was remarkable in the circumstances. Perhaps he could tell her that? No, probably not. Maggie, he thought, would not be pleased to hear that every time she was near his cock stood to attention. It wasn't exactly a considerate thing to say.

But right now he needed to sleep, then he needed to eat again, and after that he needed to finish the task the Sorceress had set for him.

Lorne's legs gave way and he sat down heavily on the bed.

"Hey!" she burst out. "This isn't your room, Mister."

"Maggie," he murmured, "your voice is far too loud. Hush now."

"H-how dare you ..." She began a stammering tirade that seemed to be fueled by fear more than moral outrage. Lorne thought he should question her about it, but he didn't have the strength.

Ignoring her, he lay down and proceeded to pull the covers over himself. Eyes closed, he could smell her scent on the sheets—something sweet and fruity, like pomegranates. Meanwhile, Maggie still carried on about privacy and personal space, but he didn't answer and soon she fell silent. He felt her move closer, followed by the soft sound of her breath as she peered into his face.

Lorne opened one eye. She jumped like a scalded cat.

"Go away. Please," he said. "I need to sleep. And I can dress myself. I don't require your assistance."

"My help!" she blustered. "I'm not your valet, thank you very much! And this is *my* room!"

"Well, unless you want to watch I suggest you go away," he told her irritably, and gave a jaw breaking yawn.

"Watch? In your dreams, pal!"

Her accent was more pronounced. He'd noticed that happened when she was angry or upset. And it wasn't the same as his grandmother's, who had come from Edinburgh, and never tired of telling him how *civilized* and *enlightened* it was there compared to Blackfriars Abbey. As a child he'd often wished she'd go back there, but he'd never said it aloud. He'd known better.

Maggie was still huffing and stomping about, but

this time he kept his eyes closed. Finally he heard the door click shut, before her steps faded.

Lorne stretched out with a pleasurable sigh and slipped away into pomegranate scented darkness.

<hr>

When he woke it was still dark, apart from the soft glow of the lamp on the dressing table. It wasn't a naked flame, but another of the strange bulbs that he'd seen downstairs, that Maggie had turned on by clicking a switch on the wall.

He blinked up at the dingy ceiling and pretended he was back home at the abbey, that he was in his bed, and soon it would be early morning. The sun just beginning to rise and the lawns white-tipped with frost. In a moment, he would get up and throw on some clothes and go down to the stables. Then he would go for a ride, galloping through the woods and up to the hilltop where one of his ancestors had built a Grecian folly. Once there, he could stand and look out over the abbey and all the lands about it, as far as the eye could see.

His kingdom.

He knew now just how privileged he had been, and how little he'd valued it, any of it. The Sorceress had been right, he could have done so much with his life, and instead he had brought on his own downfall, as well as those of others. The one thing he could do, *must* do, to atone for his thoughtlessness was to recapture the Destroyer and return it to the underworld.

Lorne stirred, still restless. Pretend as he might he wasn't in his own bed. His bed was an ornate four poster with a canopy of green silk embroidered in gold thread, and this room would fit in his bed chamber five times over. He was quite certain that his valet was not waiting for him to pull the bell, and his servants were not busy cooking him a sumptuous breakfast.

With a groan he sat up. His ribs still ached but his head was no longer spinning and his thoughts were a little clearer. Physically, he was starting to feel more like his old self, although he knew the essence of that man was gone forever.

The clothing Maggie had found for him was lying in a heap at the bottom of the bed. He inspected each garment. Better than he'd anticipated, and they looked as if they would fit him. Slowly he began to dress, taking some time to discover the intricacies of the fastenings, but when it came to the shoes he could not find any stockings. Casting his attention about he saw more clothes in a trunk under the window, and went over to inspect his find.

Lorne discovered that these were Maggie's clothes. He picked up a pair of her tight-fitting trousers and then some scanty objects that could only be underclothes. He had a mental image of her wearing them that kept him fully occupied for a few delicious moments before he reluctantly laid them aside. Finally he found stockings, woolen ones, and though they were small and the pattern of pink roses somewhat dubious for a man with his reputation, they were stretchy enough that he decided they would do.

Then he noticed a framed portrait of a man on the window sill.

He picked it up, turning it to the lamp light, and saw the same face he'd seen on the back of the Moyle book—Simon Frazer, Maggie's dead husband. His hair was going grey, and he had strong but not unattractive features, and kindly eyes. Maggie would be drawn to kindness. He understood why Maggie had been a little overwrought. The book was precious to her, as was the man, and she had lost him to the reaper.

And probably that explained the suffering he'd noticed in her face. She missed him, and she was a young woman, and a year was a long time in the life of a young woman without a man. He was beginning to think that was part of the problem with her temper.

Lorne pulled on the stockings and laced up the shoes. He straightened his garments with a few tugs and turned to the looking glass. The clothes fit, and this was certainly an improvement over going about bare-arsed, as Sutcliffe had so kindly referred to it.

He gave his image a mocking smile. There was something to be said for silver hair above a face so young. Then his smile vanished and he leaned even closer, peering at himself intently.

There were two dark streaks running through his hair, one at each temple. Was this a recent development? The brief reflection he'd seen earlier had made him think he was completely white, so maybe his natural color was returning? Was that a good sign? It must be. He was regaining his strength and vigor and with it the color of his hair. Soon he would be capable of dealing with the Destroyer.

And after that ... that was anyone's guess.

Downstairs he found the others sitting around the glass-fronted fire box. Loki stretched out before it while Maggie sat on the rug beside him and stroked his thick fur. Darlington dozed in his chair with his mouth slightly ajar, and Sutcliffe was eating what looked like a concoction of apple with crumble on top. There were cups on the table and a pot for tea.

"Cozy," he said.

Maggie jumped. He felt a flicker of irritation. Why couldn't she look up and smile at him? Why couldn't she get used to him, as he must to her? Then he reminded himself that he didn't deserve a woman like this to smile at him or admire him or love him, or even tolerate him. Not without earning her attention and affection.

Sutcliffe swallowed his mouthful of pudding. "Had your beauty sleep?" he asked cheerily. "You're looking less like a ghost at any rate."

Lorne came to stand beside him. "What do you think?" He held out his arms to show off his borrowed clothing. "Not exactly Jermyn Street. My tailor would consider the stitching less than satisfactory."

Maggie wasn't looking at him, instead she stared into the fire. "I think they suit you," she said quietly. "You look like Lestat, the vampire."

"Vampire?"

"An undead creature from folklore that drinks the blood of the living."

"Thank you, I do know what a vampire is."

She reached for the tea pot and poured him a cup. He shook his head as she gestured at the milk and sugar, and noticed how she set the cup down rather than handing it to him. She didn't want to touch him.

Darlington gave a gentle snore and Sutcliffe took a sandwich. Maggie went back to stroking Loki's fur, her face flushed from the fire. There were shadows under her eyes and Lorne was just about to tell her to go to bed when he caught sight of something on the table beside the teapot. It looked like a stone rectangle with writings carved into its face.

His gaze sharpened. This was something he recognized, and the runic lettering upon it— something he had never wanted to see again. His heart sped up and suddenly he was both icy cold and furious. His finger shook as he pointed.

"What is *that* doing here?"

———◆———

When he'd come into the room in his black suit, Maggie had wondered if he could possibly get any more good looking. She felt herself slowly melting in his presence, fighting her feelings, everything at odds. What was going on? How could she want to throw herself into his arms and at the same time long to slap his face?

And now he was staring at her with those icy blue eyes, demanding answers, and she was tired of him.

"Don't take that tone here, pal," she said, as heated as he was cold. "This is my home and you are a guest in it. You saved my life, but if you don't show some manners you can bloody well leave."

His eyes narrowed but some of the ice had gone. She waited for him to let fly at her and was surprised when he didn't.

"You don't understand," he said at last. "That belongs to me. I used it when I summoned the Destroyer from the underworld. Don't you realize how dangerous it is?"

Her eyes widened and Sutcliffe swallowed audibly.

"*That* is the spell stone?" he said in awe, coming closer to examine the runic writing. "I don't think I ever saw it. You kept it to yourself."

Lorne ignored him, his eyes still on Maggie. She stood up, wiping her palms on her thighs as if they were suddenly damp. Her voice had that husky note that went straight to his groin.

"I dug it up. Or I should say, Owen did. It's old."

"It's not old, it's ancient. And to unearth it was perilous in the extreme."

"It didn't exactly have a warning sticker on it. *'Caution: may cause demonic summoning.'*"

Lorne picked it up and held it in his hand—it more or less fit in his palm. "I will destroy it."

"No!" He could see the anguish in her face. "You can't destroy it. This is part of history; it's precious and important. It could completely change how we understand ancient religion in this region of the world. It belongs in a museum, where people can see it. Where it can be studied."

"And where some other idiot can use it to call up a demon from the underworld?" he retorted angrily. "No, we cannot take the risk, Maggie. It *must* be destroyed."

She chewed her lip, looking torn, but this time she didn't try to stop him.

"Wait!" Darlington was on his feet before Lorne

could smash the stone against the fireplace. "What if destroying it makes matters worse? What if the demon becomes trapped here permanently? I don't think you should do that, Lorne. Not yet. Wait until we can speak to the Sorceress."

Sutcliffe rumbled his agreement.

Lorne hesitated. He wanted to crush it to dust. He wanted this blight to his life gone forever. But what if Darlington was right? Yes, he must wait. He handed the tablet back to Maggie. She took it with a sigh of relief, holding it as if it was made of fine china.

"In the morning we return it to the graveyard and rebury it," he said frostily.

His friends exchanged a look. "Will it be safe there?" Sutcliffe asked.

"It was safe for two hundred years."

This time no one argued.

Chapter Ten

DAWN CAME CREEPING THROUGH THE window, and Maggie forced her tired body upright, then flopped back against the pillows. She'd been so weary that by the time Lorne decided to order her upstairs she hadn't the will to call him out on it. Not even Darlington and Sutcliffe's knowing smiles could rile her enough to change her mind.

She'd given him a stony glare, but that had only caused his lips to twitch with amusement, and then she'd shuffled tamely off to bed.

The bedding had retained his scent. Throughout the night, she'd tossed and turned with her brain going over and over what was happening. She'd only fallen into a doze a short while before and now it was time to get up. She could hear stirring downstairs and the sound of Loki's woof.

Her unwelcome guests would be waiting to be fed.

Well, they could wait. Maggie needed a shower and a few moments to gather her thoughts. Who knew what had happened while she'd slept? And there was the matter of the tablet, and the task of reburying it in the graveyard, to return it to safe keeping.

Lorne had been furious when he saw it and she'd reacted before she properly understood the danger. She was guilty of certain assumptions regarding the Marquis because of the stories she'd heard about him, yet he constantly surprised her by acting out of character. Maggie wasn't ready to consider him the good guy, not quite yet, but she didn't think he was the villain either. Not entirely, anyway.

You're forgetting, he set the Destroyer free.

No, she wasn't forgetting. How could she when it was obvious he had never forgotten? He was a man trying to make amends and she should give him the benefit of the doubt.

Of course, that didn't address the other issue she was having with him, but Maggie told herself that was her problem. She was a clever woman, but she certainly didn't think of herself as a femme fatale. There was that incident back in her early days at university, and that had shown her exactly where she stood when it came to men who found her desirable. She doubted Lorne would have looked at her twice if she'd turned up in 1808. The fact that she was the only woman available right now was probably why he and the others were paying her so much attention.

Maybe the Hellfire Clubbers had always been competitive. Like a pack of hounds, and she just happened to be the only bone available.

***

Ah, that was better.

The warm water streamed over her back and she proceeded to wash her hair with her new pomegranate and apple shampoo. The foam stung a little on her shoulder, and she twisted her head, trying to see what was wrong. Then she remembered. The Destroyer had grabbed her, his sharp claws had pierced her clothing before Lorne had flung himself between them. The scratches weren't deep but she could see four shallow parallel lines.

Maggie shuddered. Those claws hadn't looked very clean, so she gave the spot an extra scrub with her soap. When she'd finished rinsing her hair, she found some antiseptic and managed to put a glob of it on the red marks. *Of course they would be in the most difficult place*, she thought, but the stinging had stopped by the time she'd finished and she told herself that would do the trick.

She dressed in some faded jeans and one of her favorite sweaters—cream with a blue Western Isles pattern—something Simon had bought for her when they went to Moyle that last time. Pulling her damp dark curls back into a pony tail, she sat down on the bed to tug on her socks and her knee-high boots with the zip-up sides.

When she'd finished dressing, Maggie glanced up at the window. It might be morning but the sun had failed to come out yet and the woods around the cottage looked dark and drab.

Where was the Destroyer now?

Was he out there somewhere, hiding, watching the cottage? Or had he run off to find shelter and food, to wait for his strength to return as the men of the Hellfire Club were doing? She didn't understand *why* the demon would hang about

Blackfriars Abbey when he could make his escape. It didn't make sense, but perhaps she wasn't getting the point. She'd have to ask one of the men.

Not Lorne, though. Definitely not him. But she could ask Lord Sutcliffe; he seemed approachable. Darlington was rather intimidating, but perhaps his habitual scowl was because of his leg. Maggie wished now she'd boned up a bit more on the history of the members of the Hellfire Club. Owen had shown her his book, he'd even read some bits aloud during their meal breaks at the graveyard, but she hadn't always been listening.

As she came downstairs, Maggie became aware of the smell of bacon and eggs cooking. Loki trotted up to her, tail wagging, and she paused to pat his big head before she followed the smell of cooked food into the kitchen.

She didn't know what she expected to see, but it certainly wasn't what confronted her.

Lorne stood before the wood fired stove in his black trousers with his shirt sleeves rolled up and a huge pan of food sizzling on the hot plate. She knew what he looked like without his clothes on, she reminded herself before she could stop the thought. He flipped the bacon and, now aware of her presence, turned and gave her a hint of a smile. He looked her over from her ponytail to her boots.

"We gave up waiting for you, Maggie. Do you always sleep until midday?"

"It is not midday," she retorted, knowing she had to be pink from his intense examination of her.

The only woman syndrome, she reminded herself. And if it wasn't a legitimate syndrome then it should be.

Refusing to let him put her off, she came closer, hovering over the pan and hoping to find him doing something wrong, just so that she could point it out to him. Apart from egg shells and unwashed dishes scattered all over the sink, he seemed to have managed very well. Perhaps if the stove had been electric or gas, it might have been a different matter, but a man from the past, even a Marquis, would have some experience with a wood fire.

She opened the pantry cupboard and found another tin of stew for Loki. Lorne was still watching her with close attention, but she did her best to ignore him, rinsing the bowl from last night and pouring the stew into it. The dog began to gulp his meal as he had the night before.

Maggie was tempted to leave Lorne to it. That was what he'd expect of her and it was probably the best idea for herself as well, but she was stubborn and contrary enough to do just the opposite.

"No sign of your friend, then?" she said, leaning back against the bench next to the stove.

He frowned as he moved an egg a little closer to the edge of the pan. "My friend?"

She crossed her arms. "The demon."

"It was you who released the Destroyer into the world," he reminded her.

"And from what I gather it was you who brought it here in the first place."

"Touché," he said, and moved the egg again.

"Do you really believe it's still around here?" she asked. "I was thinking that, logically, it'd want to get as far away from the abbey as possible."

"True, but the abbey is its home. The creature is familiar with the abbey and the woods. Like the three of us, it is a foreigner in a strange land, and until its strength returns it'll want to stay close to what it knows."

"That makes sense," she said.

"We have to capture it before it's ready to widen its hunting ground."

"How will you do that? Capture it, I mean."

He looked at her, hesitant for a moment, as if he thought to spare her feelings. "We'll follow its trail," he said eventually. "It's not called the Destroyer for nothing. We will know where it's been."

"You mean look for the bodies?" she said, remembering Simon reading out descriptions of those bodies from the reports of the time.

"Yes."

"When you said the Destroyer needs to feed ... what exactly does it do? Was it intending to eat me after I woke it up?"

He considered his answer. "Like any cornered beast, the demon will fight to survive. Had I not stopped it, then I'm sure you'd be dead now. But you are imagining death in a purely physical way. The Destroyer prefers not to destroy from the outside. It takes life from the inside. I don't entirely understand how, but I've seen the consequences. Picture a dry husk, Maggie, the life sucked out of it, and that is how this creature gains its strength. It collects mortal lives so that it can remain immortal. It destroys in order to live. I pray that we can find it before it harms anyone, but I am not hopeful of it ..."

He paused, as if waiting for another question, and when she said nothing, turned back to the pan.

Maggie chewed her lip. What they were discussing was truly horrific. So much so that, although she knew she should interrogate him further, she really didn't want to. Not right now.

Lorne, satisfied with his cooking, removed the pan from the heat and set it to one side.

"Plates are in that cupboard," she said, gesturing to the brightly painted door above her head. That was a mistake. She knew it as soon as he looked at the door, and then shifted his focus down to her. Maggie tried to move out of his way, but it was too late.

He stepped in and reached above her, so that her body was more or less a prisoner of his. His face came so close she could see the dark stubble of his beard and the dark pupils of his pale blue eyes. Her eyes fixed on his throat as he took the plates down and set them onto the bench at her side. He didn't seem to be in any hurry to move away. If anything he was even closer than before.

She could feel his breath on her lips and knew that it would take only a very small movement on her part for their mouths to meet …

Heat worked its way up her body, spreading like contagion, and her breasts tightened, nipples growing hard. Maggie should have been shocked and embarrassed by her feelings, but she was working too hard at containing this madness. She stared at the hollow of his throat, frozen in place.

"Are you hungry, Maggie?" he asked in a soft, deep voice that made her toes curl and her heart slow to a sensuous beat.

Oh God, was she hungry? She was starving! And it was all wrong, so very wrong …

"I won't harm you." The timbre of his voice

rolled across her senses, and it took a moment for her to take in what he'd said. "I would never harm you."

"You want me to trust you?" she whispered. She didn't think she was ready to trust the wicked Marquis.

He tucked a loose strand of hair behind her ear and she nearly swooned. Swooning was not something Maggie had ever done. It wasn't even something she understood, but right now it was the only word that went halfway to what she was experiencing.

"I know you can't. Why should you?" he said, and his smile became strained, as if it was taking an effort to maintain his poise. "I wanted to say … Maggie, I'm not the man I was. Two hundred years is an extraordinary length of time to think about the things I've done."

Two hundred years of thinking? It didn't sound very comfortable to Maggie. In fact, it sounded pretty awful, especially if you were Lorne and had so much to mull over. Maybe that was what they called Purgatory?

"The Sorceress told me that she wants us to work together," he went on. "And we need someone like you to help us catch the demon. Maggie, you're of this time and we are not. You have an advantage that neither we nor the demon possess."

She saw exactly what he was working up to. Working together would require them to be close. Did he know how out of control she was? Was he trying to explain to her, in case she was hoping for romance and sex, that this was to be nothing more than a professional relationship?

Memories flooded her thoughts. Her days as a naïve university student, so much younger than her classmates. Awful, embarrassing memories.

She tried to push Lorne away.

"Maggie." He held her hands and despite herself she let him, still staring at his throat. "Look at me."

She didn't want to but her disobedient gaze slid up to his face. For a moment she wondered what he wanted her to see, before, like a shock wave through her senses, she realized. Lorne's cheeks were flushed, his eyes heavy, and he was struggling as hard as she was not to do more than talk.

Was this crazy thing that was happening not just on her side? How could that be?

"She wants us to work together, and yet whenever I am near you … to be blunt, I become aroused. And I think it's the same for you. Desire, Maggie. Want, need, lust. Do you understand? We are feeling all of those things, are we not?"

She did understand, oh God, she did. She and Lorne were in lust with each other. He because he had been without a woman's touch for so long, and she because she was lonely and he was utterly compelling. Maggie eyed him with sudden suspicion.

"So, what is your solution to the problem?"

He was closer, he must be, because now she could smell the herby scent of his skin, and feel the heat of his body. His presence was overpowering. She could barely breathe, and she wanted … she wanted …

His breath was warm on her lips. "Resist?" he suggested with a breathy laugh. "How are you at resisting temptation, Maggie?"

Her eyes were almost closed, her lids drooped and her limbs weighed a ton. She felt the brush of his fingers down the side of her face, causing goose bumps to rise as they passed. Her groan was soft, but shocking to her own ears.

"Or we could capitulate," he went on, his own struggle evident in his voice.

"Capitulate?" she swallowed. "Would … would that sort things? I mean, would that put an end to it?"

"Put an end to it? I do not know, Maggie. Perhaps once is all it takes. Then again, once might just make matters worse."

"Worse?" she repeated. What did 'worse' mean? That she would have to spend every moment in bed with the wicked marquis? Their bodies fusing over and over again, until she no longer knew who was who? Until she lost the person Simon had loved? It was that thought that gave her the strength she needed.

Maggie opened her eyes. "No, I can't. I won't."

He stared back at her a moment longer. She saw the regret and the desire fading in his icy blue eyes. And then he closed his emotions down, just as she had, and all she could see now was the stranger.

"As you wish," he said, coolly polite, and stepped away.

She felt his loss immediately but refused to acknowledge it. Maggie told herself she could control this situation. She could work with him, but that was all it would be. There was nothing on this earth that could force her into the arms of the wicked marquis. She was her own person and always had been, and the only man she had ever trusted and loved, and been willing to share her bed with, was Simon.

Lorne was ignoring her, sliding food onto the plates and spilling some along the way, which Loki obligingly lapped up.

"We're going to bury the runes this morning," he reminded her, as if nothing had happened.

"I don't think—"

"That's the trouble. You don't. Think." There was a flash in his pale eyes, a hint of the man he used to be, and he turned away, carrying two plates into the other room.

Confused, she wondered if his anger was because she'd rejected him or because she'd dug up the runes? And did she really care enough to try to understand what went on in that two hundred year old head?

Maggie picked up the other two plates and followed.

Sutcliffe and Darlington were there and gave her and Lorne a fleeting look, but said nothing, beginning to hoe into their food as soon as it was set in front of them. Darlington was looking a bit brighter, the gray tinge gone from his face, and Sutcliffe's eyes weren't quite so bloodshot. Maggie sat down in the separate chair and wondered when she had begun to care about these strangers.

She was eating breakfast with three men who by all rights should be long dead, and there was a demon on the loose out there, killing for its own survival.

She swallowed what was an excellently fried egg, but it was suddenly tasteless.

"Delicious," Sutcliffe said with a full mouth,

passing Loki a piece of bacon.

That made her smile. She was surprised she could right now, but Maggie knew they were about to face a long and arduous day, and she didn't see any point in wrestling with issues that were beyond her ken. Not when she had no idea what might happen next.

Chapter Eleven

THEY SET OFF SHORTLY AFTER breakfast, Maggie driving the Land Rover. Lorne was beside her, with Sutcliffe and Darlington sprawled in the back. Loki lay panting between them, staring about with wild eyed excitement. None of her guests had seemed keen on being in the vehicle, but since her cottage hadn't come with a stable, let alone horses, they had no choice. Reluctantly— apart from Loki—they climbed aboard.

Lorne had taken the passenger seat. His closeness made her uncomfortable and he didn't seem all that relaxed himself. Was that because of what had happened between them in the kitchen? Well too bad. She reminded herself this was going to be a working relationship between her and the wicked Marquis, and going by the chilly expression on his face, he was doing the same.

She drove slowly through the dense woods toward the ford, trying not to see the demon in every shadow or behind every tree. The shotgun, she reminded herself, was in the back if she needed it. And beside it was the stone tablet carved with runic writing.

Burying their find was something that had to be done, she supposed, but she knew Owen wasn't going to be very happy about it—and how was she going to explain it to him? Just as well it was the weekend and the crew would be sleeping in at the village pub. She wasn't going to argue with Lorne about their decision. If someone were to accidently, or purposely, use it to call the demon—or summon *another* demon … they couldn't risk it.

Maggie reached the fork in the road, one way lead to Blackfriars Abbey and the other to the graveyard. She glanced at her companions but once again, apart from Loki's excited panting, they said nothing.

Maggie swung the vehicle toward the graveyard.

* * *

Lorne hadn't been aware of much last time he was here. He'd been too busy trying to save Maggie's life, and his own. In his mind's eye the graveyard had been as it was two hundred years ago, so seeing it now in the light of day came as a shock. Maggie and her team had created a terrible mess. The barrow was cut in half, with a trench running right through the middle, as well as various ruptures in the green grassy surface of the graves themselves.

Members of the immediate family had never been buried here—that was what the mausoleum was for. Rather this was a place for faithful retainers and more distant relations, as well as any villagers who'd requested it. There was a pet cemetery as well, in a clearing in the woods. Before the Reformation in the 16th century, when there had still been a working religious house here, the monks had been buried beside the abbey. In Lorne's day, those lowly graves had become part of the south lawn.

He remembered he and his mother and his grandmother taking afternoon tea on the lawn, and consequently on top of the dead monks. The thought of their bodies beneath his feet had made him uncomfortable, and he tended to wriggle about, much to his grandmother's annoyance.

"Your father never sat still either," the soft Scottish reproach echoed in his head. The Dowager Marchioness had stared at him, her face cold and hard, just as it always had been whenever she deigned to notice him. She had hated his father and now she hated him.

"Do sit still, Charles," his mother whispered, the lavender shadows under her eyes darker than they had been yesterday. Her hand trembled as she reached for her teacup. He knew she wanted to add the laudanum she kept in a little bottle tucked up her sleeve but, despite her need, could not bring herself to do it in front of the dowager.

Lorne tried to sit still but he was a little boy and boys were always fidgety. He wanted to race across the smooth green lawn, to roll down the slope into the woods, and lift his face to the sky to discover peculiar faces in the clouds.

Instead, he listened to the dowager insult his mother while she bowed her head and accepted every word.

At first he'd wondered why. He'd even asked her once, when they were alone. She'd hugged him close and whispered in his ear, as if the dowager could hear them from her own apartments. "Because I must, darling. We have nowhere else to go."

Surely, he thought, anywhere was better than here? This great big house with so many stern faces looking down at him from the portraits in the long gallery, and so many servants who bobbed him curtseys or bowed to him, and afterwards whispered cruel words as he passed by.

He'd hated it, but he had to stay. His father, tormented by the imaginary demons in his head, had hanged himself in a tavern in London and left his wife penniless and his son with nothing but his title.

Lorne remembered the bailiffs coming to repossess their belongings, even the little wooden soldiers his father had given him for his birthday. He'd loved those soldiers and when he finally inherited Blackfriars, despite having more money and possessions than he knew what to do with, he'd often thought of those soldiers and wished he had them still.

"Where should we bury it?"

Lorne shook himself from his memories. Just for a moment he thought it was his grandmother who spoke, but the voice was different. Younger, sweeter, and with a slight husky undertone. Maggie, he remembered with relief. She was holding the stone tablet.

The man who'd sold it to him was an Egyptian, the name given to members of the tribes of Gypsies who travelled about the countryside. He'd claimed that the tablet had come from a tomb somewhere in a vast desert and he'd had the translated words too, written down on a tattered scroll that Lorne was supposed to burn as soon as they were spoken.

Had he burnt them? He couldn't remember. He felt a moment of blind panic. Where the bloody hell was the scroll now?

"Lorne?" Maggie stared at him with a wary and slightly worried expression; the bones of her face seemed so much more fragile with her hair tied back.

He cleared his throat. "My apologies. I was … away for a moment." His smile was tight and probably looked sickly. "You were asking me where the tablet should be buried?"

"We found it near the barrow." She pointed at the area they had already excavated.

Lorne looked around for a moment and slowly he turned until he found a grave with a stone so old and covered in lichen that any words once carved into it were now illegible. He was relieved to see that Maggie and her team had yet to dig there.

"This time we will place it in the grave of my nanny, Mrs. Noakes."

Maybe the notion was foolish, but part of him still felt that Noakes would be able to tackle any amount of demons for him—as a child she'd kept him safe from his grandmother on more than one occasion. When Noakes had died he had insisted that everything possible be done to make certain she rest in peace. If the tablet was safe anywhere then it was surely safe here.

Maggie began to ask a question, took heed of his expression, and thought better of it. Good. He didn't want to talk about Mrs. Noakes. He didn't want to think about what had happened to her.

"All right. We'll put it there," she said. Sutcliffe was leaning against the bonnet of her machine and she called to him. "Get me the shovel from the barrow, will you, Aiden?"

Sutcliffe was so quick to do her bidding that Lorne's eyes narrowed. Maggie seemed partial toward the big man, and although he knew he had no right to be possessive, he couldn't seem to help it. The Marquis of Lorne, jealous? It was unheard of. Unthinkable.

And yet, as soon as the big man returned with the shovel, he took it before he could hand it to her. "*I'll* dig the hole." Maggie opened her mouth as if to speak but closed it without saying a word.

Lorne walked to the grave. For a moment he stood, waiting, half-expecting the past to rise up again and draw him into more uncomfortable memories. It didn't, so he slid the shovel into the soft earth and began to dig. He thought he should bury the tablet down only a few feet at most—he didn't want to uncover what was left of Noakes, grinning up at him.

The hole was soon ready, and he took the tablet from Maggie and placed it at the bottom before filling in the soil again, and patting down the surface.

"There," he said to himself. "Done."

When he looked up they were all watching him oddly, as if they weren't quite sure what to make of him. Had he been acting so strangely?

"Have I grown a tail?" he asked.

Maggie raised her hand. "Your hair …"

"It's changing back," Darlington explained.

"I looked away. Just for a moment. And when I looked again ..."

He reached up to touch it, and then realized how foolish that was. "Is it? Shame. I thought the silver suited me."

Sutcliffe gave a snort of laughter.

"I remember when the Sorceress put you in here." Darlington had limped over to the barrow and was staring down at it. "Sutcliffe and I knew we were next. We were shaking like leaves."

Maggie was looking over what she had called her dig site, when a musical sound came from about her person. All three men stopped and stared at her. Loki, who'd been busy inspecting the graves from a dog's point of view, gave a bark.

"Phone," she said, with a half-smile, as if that explained anything. She dug a thin flat object from her pocket. She flipped open the cover and it lit up. Smiling at their astonishment, she held it to her ear and spoke into it. Stranger still, judging from her reaction, the thing talked back.

"This world is most strange," Sutcliffe rumbled. "I feel as if I'm in a dream, only I can't seem to wake up."

Maggie finished talking to the object and fiddled with it a moment, listening again, before closing it and returning it to her pocket. "That was one of my team," she said, picking her way closer over the uneven ground. Lorne didn't even pretend he wasn't admiring her long legs in those trousers. The boots were a nice addition too, and before he could stop himself his thoughts went meandering down hot, lustful alleyways.

"Lorne?"

"Hmm?"

"*Lorne!*" She'd planted her hands on her hips. "Are you listening to me? Owen didn't return to the pub last night after he left me here, and he wasn't there this morning."

"Owen?" He scrambled for his wits. "The one who dug up the tablet? Perhaps he went to celebrate finding his treasure."

"He might have, but … I'm worried. I tried his phone and he isn't answering. No one knows where he is and no one has seen him." She chewed on her bottom lip, as if she didn't really want to voice her fears, before blurting them out anyway. "Do you think it has something to do with the Destroyer?"

Lorne looked past her to the dark woods under the leaden sky. If her Owen had come face to face with the demon then he was most certainly dead. He shot a glance at his two friends and knew that they were thinking the same thing.

"He was definitely going back to the pub after he left you yesterday?" he asked.

"I thought he was. I suppose he didn't actually *say*, but he had his tools in the back. Where else could he have gone? From here he would have taken the road to the Abbey, past the turn off to the cottage, to where there's another intersection. That's the only way to get to the village from the abbey grounds."

"Then we will hunt for him along that road," Lorne decided.

Maggie glanced at Sutcliffe and Darlington and chewed her bottom lip again. It was beginning to look quite red and swollen, as if someone had been sucking on it. His body responded to the thought, but Lorne forced himself to ignore it. He was starting to get used to his cock being semi-erect whenever Maggie was around.

"What is the matter?" He put his hands on his hips in a reflection of her own stance, trying to make her smile, but she was too worried to notice.

"It's just … This is an isolated part of the country and there aren't many people. If we find Owen or meet anyone else … It'll be difficult enough explaining away one strange man, but three? Maybe Aiden and Nicholas should stay here."

The three "strange" men exchanged looks. "We should search the woods anyway," Darlington said. "The Destroyer could be in there somewhere and Loki will find his scent if he is. With luck, we will have him bound and harmless by the time you get back from your search." He gave a competitive smirk to Lorne. "How much will you wager?"

Lorne reached into his pocket and pulled out a button, holding it on the flat of his palm. "A rare treasure," he scoffed.

Sutcliffe felt around in the lining of his jacket, but could only find a handful of soil left from his sojourn in the pet cemetery.

Darlington fiddled with his signet ring but seemed to change his mind. "I think, gentlemen, that wagering will have to wait until we have some funds."

Maggie shook her head in disgust. "We don't have time for this. I need to find Owen."

Sutcliffe brushed clean his hands and set off toward the woods, striding along with Loki at his side, while Darlington limped after them. They were already a dozen yards away before Lorne called out, "Take care, my friends!"

Sutcliffe raised a hand above his head in response. Neither of them turned.

Maggie waited by the Land Rover, clearly wanting to be on her way. And yet Lorne still hesitated. If Owen was dead, then what? The consequences of a meeting with the Destroyer were far worse than mere death, and although he had answered some of her questions about what it could do, he knew he would have to explain more fully at some point.

He felt as if it was happening all over again. Anxiety ratcheted up his spine as he remembered those awful weeks in 1808. And yet this time it felt different. Not for all the obvious reasons but because—

"Lorne, are you coming?"

He looked up and he knew why. It was different because after two centuries alone in the darkness, Maggie was here with him.

Chapter Twelve

THEY TRAVELLED ALONG THE ROAD to the abbey and Lorne was staring out of the window. Maggie glanced at his unwelcoming profile. Although the woods were too thick for a view of the house, she couldn't help but wonder what he would think when he saw it.

No doubt, he'd be disappointed.

And yet there was a frisson in the air around him, growing stronger the closer they got to his home. Maggie hoped she could head him off, for a while at least.

They hadn't spoken since they'd left the graveyard, but she was fine with that. She had enough to mull over without having to make polite conversation with someone she fancied so badly she might just go up in flames if he brushed his thigh against hers. The new dark streaks in his silver hair were certainly eye catching, and she found herself casting sideways glances at him, trying to catch the color change in progress.

Ahead of them was the hand painted sign that pointed towards the village. She swung around the corner onto the unsealed surface a bit more quickly than she meant to and heard a painful hiss of breath from Lorne. *Oops.* But any concerns for her passenger's ribs vanished when she saw the utility truck.

The woods grew close to the road all along here and the vehicle was half hidden. It must have slid across the verge and down into the culvert, so that the rear end was just below road level and the bonnet was pressed up against one of the trees.

"That's Owen's truck. He must have had an accident." Her voice was sharp with worry.

Maggie halted the Land Rover and jumped out. The air was colder now, and a sprinkle of rain came across, dampening her face as she ran to the ditched vehicle. Her heart was beating so hard that when she called Owen's name she could barely hear her own voice. The driver's door was wide open and one glance inside was enough to confirm that no one was there, although Owen's waterproof coat was still on the passenger's seat.

Lorne had been standing above her on the verge, but now he came down the slope, half sliding in his black dress shoes, to the edge of the trees. He crouched down, looking intently at the soft ground, before he straightened and stared into the depths of the woods. When he didn't speak she thought the worst.

"What is it? Can you see where he's been? Is he—is he—?"

"No." He frowned and took a few steps back up the slope to join her beside the open door. "I promise you, no. I see nothing."

"He was run off the road, Lorne. There must have been something."

For a moment he didn't answer her, still staring at the trees. Maggie followed his gaze, thinking this part of the Blackfriars' forest was almost impenetrable, as if the ancient trees were crowding in towards them, eavesdropping on their conversation.

"If his machine was broken, where would your friend go?"

Maggie gathered her scattered thoughts. *Be practical*, she told herself. *Forget about demons and runic spells and long dead men.* There could be a simple explanation for this, couldn't there?

"He'd walk to the cottage. Or call me on his phone to come and pick him up."

"But neither of those things happened. So what else might have occurred?"

Another scenario began to form in her head. One that was not so optimistic.

What if Owen had been on his way back to the dig and had run into the Destroyer as it wandered around the woods last night? What if the utility truck was in this position because the demon had stood in front of him, just as it had them? If Maggie's Land Rover hadn't stalled at that moment she may well have run off the road, just like Owen.

Lorne's voice interrupted her dark thoughts. "Might he have walked to the village?"

She turned to him and gasped. His hair! While she'd been looking the other way it had changed again, and now there was a great deal more dark than silver.

"Maggie?"

"I'm sorry. Y-your hair," she stammered, and then shook her head. "It's very distracting, Lorne."

He reached up to capture a strand and held it so

he could see it. She tried to read his expression but he seemed to be keeping his thoughts to himself. "You haven't answered my question."

"Your question? Oh. I don't know. He might have gone to the abbey. That's closer. And Mr. Stewart is very odd, so perhaps he hasn't thought to tell me."

"Mr. Stewart?"

"He's the owner of the abbey. I believe he's a distant relative of the … of you. He's an American and the end of your line, or so they say in the village."

He quirked an eyebrow.

"Apart from you, that is."

She knew they were wasting time standing here and she had to make a decision. Owen wasn't at the pub, she knew that, and it was unlikely he'd be in the village or one of the team would have seen him. And he definitely wasn't at the cottage or the graveyard.

"We'll go to the abbey. I suppose if Mr. Stewart thought Owen was an intruder or … or something, then it's possible he has him locked up and is refusing to let him make a phone call. Or perhaps he's hurt and unconscious and can't tell anyone—"

Lorne cut her short. "Enough, Maggie. That kind of speculation will not help your friend. Let us go to the abbey first."

But Maggie lingered a moment longer, gazing into the shadowy woods and still seeing nothing. With a sigh she shut Owen's door and locked it. Someone would have to collect the vehicle later, not to mention the tools in the back, but right now her main concern was her friend's safety.

Lorne tried to soothe her as she got back in the Land Rover and slammed the door. "Worrying will not make things better. We need to keep clear heads."

She glanced sideways at him, not sure if she was comfortable with the idea of Lorne being nice to her.

"You're right. Owen is probably walking into the pub right now, covered in mud and ordering a pint," she joked, trying for a smile.

Lorne smiled back, and for once his pale eyes were no longer icy. Her skin prickled, and his attention dropped to her lips and rested there for what seemed a very long time.

"Lorne …"

"I told you, I won't hurt you," he said softly. "I won't even touch you unless you wish it. But I can't pretend I don't want you, Maggie. Come, be honest. You feel it too, don't you?"

She shook her head, and, noticing his expression had turned skeptical, said, "No, I don't. Not even a little bit. Not at all."

His laugh was barely more than a breath but she ignored it. The Land Rover started and she pulled out, scattering gravel, before setting off to Black-friars Abbey.

———◆———

The state of the house was more grim than Maggie remembered.

She peered through the windscreen, already smeared from the rain, and wondered why anyone would want to live in such a pile. It looked like a sleeping monster; the many windows could be closed eyes, just waiting to spring open. And then she caught sight of a trickle of smoke from one of the chimneys and knew that someone must be home.

Relieved, she turned to point this out to Lorne, but the words died on her lips. He sat with his attention fixed on the house, and his clenched fists and rigid jaw made it quite plain that he wasn't happy.

This must be awful for him.

From the moment they'd reached the stretch of drive that led up to the front she'd felt the change in him. From excitement and anticipation to a smoldering fury.

The abbey was his home, or it had been. She tried to imagine going back to her tenement flat in Govan after two hundred years but the situations were too different. She'd be surprised if her building was still there in ten years, let alone two hundred, and quite frankly she'd be very pleased if it wasn't.

"Down in the village," she said, "they say it's a pity the National Trust didn't take it on. I don't suppose they'd want to now. The cost of repairs would be astronomical."

"National Trust?" he repeated, not taking his eyes from the crumbling grey stone facade.

"It's an organization that cares for old buildings of national importance. People pay to walk through the interiors and picnic on the lawns."

He barely let her finish. "Are you saying my home wasn't *important* enough?" And he shot her such a look that it took her a moment to find her voice again. He was awfully intimidating. She could imagine him as he must have been back then …

"Eh, no, I didn't say that. I believe the estate was in limbo for decades while they tried to find a descendant to take it on. Mr. Stewart was a distant cousin of the last person to live here, and by the time he took up residence it was in such a mess."

By now his stare was making her so edgy that she found herself prattling on just to fill the silence.

"Besides, why should one man have so much because of an accident of birth? Monuments to wealth and privilege, like this, should be shared. Not reserved for a fortunate few."

Maggie knew she'd made a gaff. This wasn't the time to inform the Marquis of Lorne of her social-ist leanings, which were rather mild according to Simon, but nevertheless probably pretty radical for a nineteenth century Marquis. With luck he hadn't heard her, or hadn't understood. But when she peeked him a glance sideways she realized it was a yes to both.

She wasn't a coward, but she was very tempted to climb out of the vehicle and run away. Mag-gie turned to face him. At least arguing with her would take his mind off the state of his ancestral home.

"I suppose you think I should have been sent to the guillotine?" he said with haughty precision.

"I didn't say that …" She sighed. "Lorne, I really didn't mean … I was just blathering because you were upset."

"So you're not a Revolutionary?" he mocked.

"No, Lorne, I'm an archeologist … eh, antiquar-ian," she retorted, "but I have my own views on the distribution of wealth and property. When you're as poor as I was as a child it leaves its mark. I'm sorry if I upset you. I truly didn't mean to."

He wasn't completely mollified, but some of the stiffness had gone from his bearing. "The abbey was in excellent condition when I left it."

There was a strained silence. This time Lorne was the one to break it.

"This Stewart fellow," he began curiously. "You say he's related to me? And he inherited the abbey? I don't understand, Maggie. Why has he allowed the house to continue to fall down around his ears?"

Maggie lifted her hands in the air. "I don't know if he inherited any money with the estate. If he wanted to make a profit he could have sold it off, but he hasn't. Maybe he just wants to live here alone. He's definitely a recluse. He rarely sees anybody, apart from his cleaner, and she collects everything he needs from the village shop. Simon, eh, my husband Simon," her eyes skittering to him and away again, "wrote to him and I've spoken to him by phone. The only reason Stewart allowed us to go ahead with the dig is because he's obsessed with—"

She stopped, looking down now, anywhere but at Lorne.

"Obsessed with?" he repeated.

She may as well tell him. He was going to find out anyway.

"He's obsessed with *you*, Lorne," she looked him in the face. "He thought we might find out something about the Hellfire Club by digging in the graveyard. Stewart talked about the murders you were blamed for all these years, and Simon let him think that was our aim when it was actually the barrow we were interested in."

He really had the most amazing eyes. They were so expressive. A moment ago he'd wanted to tear Stewart to pieces for his neglect of the abbey and now his vanity was stroked and he was trying to pretend not to be rather pleased that even after two hundred years he was still famous.

Well, *infamous*, anyway.

And she was not, under any circumstances, going to blurt out his current status as the village bogey-man.

Once she'd parked the vehicle on the over-grown carriage drive at the front of the abbey, they walked across the weed infested gravel towards the front door. A pair of raddled-looking stone lions watched them climb the shallow stairs leading up to the formal entrance. The doorknocker sent an echo rolling away inside the building—it sounded eerily hollow, as if there were acres of empty space in there.

"Come on, come on," she muttered under her breath. *Please don't let Mr. Stewart play his hermit games, not now.* She just wanted to find Owen.

Lorne reached past her to knock again, only louder. Again the sound echoed into nothingness as they waited.

"You're not going to say or do anything to give yourself away, are you?" Maggie asked him for the tenth time since they'd left the Land Rover. "If you think you are then maybe you should wait for me outside. Things are awkward enough without ..."

"Without me suddenly taking up residence in

my own home?" he replied calmly. "I have said I won't, Maggie. You must learn to trust me."

"Mmm, I must, mustn't I?"

He let his gaze rest on her face for a moment and she was sure there was a lurking smile in those pale eyes. Then he reached past her and gave the doorknocker another hammering. But no one came.

"Enough."

Impatient now, Lorne turned and strode down the steps before setting off along the building's facade. Maggie, taken by surprise, scuttled to catch up.

"Where are you going?" she asked, trotting along behind him.

"Stewart's probably in the kitchen. You say he lives here on his own? And his cleaning woman brings him food? Ergo, he must cook for himself."

She tried to keep up with Lorne's impatient strides. "And the kitchen is …?"

He stopped abruptly and turned around to face her.

She gasped as they collided but he steadied her, his hands on her hips, while hers seemed to gravitate to his chest. The unexpected contact sent a tremor through her that was as pleasurable as it was shocking.

If Lorne felt it then this time he ignored it. He was looking at her so intently she had no doubt of the importance of whatever he was about to say. "Listen to me," he said. "If Owen is here … it would be best if you do not go to him. Do not touch him."

"But …"

"It would be best, Maggie."

His intensity, the keen way he was looking at her, got through to her despite his lack of explanation. It was against her principles to agree to anything without first thinking it through, but she sensed this time the answer was too important. She had to trust that Lorne knew more about this world than she did.

"Okay," she said shakily. "I'm sure you're over-reacting, but I won't touch him."

He nodded. "Good." He released her, and quickly spun on his heel to resume his march around the abbey. It took a moment for Maggie to recover herself enough to follow.

There were other buildings back here, and in far worse condition than the abbey. Stables, she supposed, as well as barns and all the extras a wealthy estate would have to supply their wants and needs. Lorne didn't pause; he knew the way. Now they were crossing some uneven flags, punctuated by dandelions, and she saw a set of unprepossessing and muddy stairs going down to a door set below ground level.

"This is the kitchen?" Maggie peered through some narrow windows but they were opaque with grime, and in front of the door was an area slick with a build-up of leaves and other debris. Her nose twitched.

"I can smell toast burning," she whispered. Someone was at home after all.

Lorne barely paused to give her a triumphant smile before pounding so hard on the door it shook at the hinges. "Open up! Open up, I say!"

Maggie caught his arm before he could do any more damage. "Will you wait? If you frighten him he'll never open up. Stand over there, so he can't see you."

"I want him to see me."

The look on his face boded ill, as Jane Austen would have said. "And I want to find Owen. Now please, do as I say."

He hesitated, gave a sigh, and stepped out of sight, leaning back against the wall and staring into space.

Since they'd arrived at the abbey, Lorne seemed to be reverting to the man she'd heard about in the tales of the Hellfire Club—the wicked marquis. And he wanted her to trust him? Surely he could see why she might find that a little difficult.

Maggie took several deep breathes, to calm herself, before she gave the door a more gentle tap. "Mr. Stewart," she called out in what she hoped was a friendly voice. "I'm sorry to bother you, but it's Professor McNab, eh, Maggie McNab. Something important has come up and I need to—"

The door opened.

Mr. Stewart stood there. At least, she *supposed* it was Mr. Stewart. He wore a Led Zeppelin t-shirt, jeans that were ragged at the hems, plaid slippers, and a khaki overcoat. He held a spreading knife and a jar of marmalade. It wasn't until he opened his mouth that she was sure this was really him. He sounded like one of the Kennedys—which meant it was a Boston accent, she told herself, feeling clever.

"You've found him," he said. His hazel eyes blazed with excitement. He was shorter than Maggie, solidly built, and right now he reminded her of a terrier quivering outside a rabbit's burrow.

"Found him?" she repeated, trying to see around

him and into the room.

"The 4th Marquis of Lorne," Stewart said impatiently. "He's missing from the family mausoleum. I knew he must be in the graveyard somewhere. I *knew* it."

The thought of him rummaging through Lorne's mausoleum threw her for a moment. While her mind diverted down that weird side street, Stewart's eyes went past her and widened. His mouth dropped open. Maggie turned to see what the problem was, although she was very much afraid she already knew.

Lorne had decided to step into view behind her.

She began a hasty introduction, "Mr. Stewart, this is—" she didn't have the slightest clue how she was going to explain Lorne's identity.

But it was a moot point. Stewart's face had drained of all color. His eyes rolled up in his head and he fell backwards in a dead faint.

Chapter Thirteen

THEY'D HAULED MR. STEWART UP into a chair, his head tucked down between his knees. Maggie didn't appear to take Lorne's suggestion to slap the man back to full consciousness seriously, and instead found him a glass and filled it with water. While she helped him to sip, giving little murmurs of encouragement, Lorne looked about.

The kitchen was relatively clean and tidy—apart from the broken jar of marmalade by the doorstep. Assuming the makeshift bed beside a huge wood fueled oven was where Stewart slept, then he probably spent most of his time in here.

Was it the only habitable room in the entire abbey?

He gave an involuntary shudder, knowing this was nothing like the homecoming he had been hoping for.

But then, what had he expected? Without him, the abbey and title would have passed through a cousin's line, a cousin he had never even met. He should have thought of that before he brought the Destroyer from the underworld. The unfortunate truth was he hadn't been thinking of anything but his own selfish amusement and pleasure. And although such behavior was inconceivable to the man he was now, it was all too late. There was no going back, only forward, no matter how much he wished it were otherwise.

Stewart was now leaning back in the chair, wane faced, but his eyes were open. He stared at Lorne. "You look," he gulped, flinching as Lorne took a step toward him. "You look like him. In the painting."

He knew immediately what the man meant. There was a portrait in the long gallery which was said to be a very good likeness. It must still be there. He'd begun to wonder if there was anything left from his time, and he prepared to pepper Stewart with questions.

Maggie shot him a warning glare and promptly made her voice all syrupy. "I am *so* sorry, Mr. Stewart. This is Mr, eh, Rice. He's my sponsor for the dig and he just happens to also be a relative of the Marquis of Lorne. *Bar sinister*, I'm afraid. Bastard son and all that. The family resemblance is quite striking."

I'll throttle her, Lorne thought. *Call me a bastard … of myself?* How could he desire a woman so much it made his body ache and his heart pound, and at the same time find her completely infuriating?

Stewart had regained his senses. "Amazing. There's a portrait of him upstairs and Mr. Rice here is the spitting image." He stood up and reached for Lorne's arm. "May I?"

He didn't wait for permission before turning Lorne toward what little light was coming from the open door and the grubby windows. And then he simply stood and stared. Lorne waited impatiently, allowing himself to be looked over like some artifact in a curiosity shop and wondering if Stewart might guess the truth. But how could he? The truth was beyond most people's wildest imaginations. The American seemed harmless enough, but all the same … there was something about him, a simmering excitement beneath his unprepossessing exterior, that Lorne didn't entirely trust.

Then again, it was unlikely he would trust anyone who had allowed the abbey to fall into such appalling disrepair.

"Forgive me," Stewart said at last, and cleared his throat. "The resemblance really is astounding. There." He smoothed down the sleeve of Lorne's borrowed jacket and gave him an apologetic smile. "So sorry for the dramatics. No harm done. Could I offer you some coffee? Tea?"

"Eh, yes, thank you," Maggie moved swiftly to turn Stewart's attention away from Lorne and toward her. "Tea, please."

So much to do and Maggie wanted to stop for tea? He shook his head at her but she gave Stewart a big warm smile and pretended not to notice.

The other hesitated, eyes on her face, as if he'd suddenly realized she was quite something. Lorne slipped his hands into his pockets and clenched, telling himself he must let Maggie take charge of the situation. She understood this world better than he did. Besides, she would never trust him if he continued to go against her wishes … let alone let him climb into her bed.

Stewart began to bustle about, pouring some

boiling water from his kettle into a couple of ceramic mugs. He even had some cake in a clear sided container which he put onto a plate.

Maggie gave Lorne a quick glance, shrugging her shoulders as if to question Stewart's behavior. Lorne agreed that he didn't seem like an eccentric recluse. Rather he was behaving like a normal man who was quite used to visitors and knew how to entertain them, though he certainly didn't dress like one. And yet Maggie had said he was a hermit, and the bed here in the kitchen seemed to confirm it. The American was a mystery. One that needed solving.

"I bought your husband's book," Stewart said. "*Secrets of Moyle*. It's around here somewhere." He looked about as if expecting to see it.

Lorne could tell Maggie was pleased. "Have you read it yet?"

"Dipped into it. He was a clever man, your husband."

"Yes, he was," she replied quietly, glancing away. "Very clever."

"One day I think I will have to visit Moyle," Stewart mused. "Tell me, Professor McNab, how do you get to so isolated a spot?"

Lorne left them to their tea and conversation and began to prowl around the room. A large dresser was heavy with dining plates and other crockery, and there were rusting pots and pans hanging from hooks on the wall. He didn't recognize anything, but then he'd rarely had need to come down here. Usually his servants brought food to him, although there had been one or two occasions when it was late and the Hellfire Club was sitting, and they'd all trooped up from the tunnels beneath the abbey looking for something to eat.

An image filled his head, of Sutcliffe gnawing on a bone left over from the previous night's roast, under Loki's watchful gaze, and Darlington sipping tea from a china cup, while a half-naked girl sat on his knee and fed him crumbs of sultana cake. He could hear their laughter in his head but it was fading, being replaced by the voices and images of this new time and place.

It occurred to him that Darlington had also changed. His friend was acting rather strangely, and he wondered if the Sorceress had been visiting him in his sleep as well. Sutcliffe … well, he seemed to be just the same as he'd always been.

Maggie was smiling at something Stewart had said. *She had wiles, no doubt.* Prickly and opinionated as she was, she also held a great deal of charm. Was that why he was so attracted to her? He wasn't sure.

And what about Sutcliffe and Darlington? And now Stewart? They all found her far more appealing than Lorne felt comfortable allowing. Despite his determination to be a better man it seemed the old egotistical habits had crept in when it came to Maggie. He wanted her, therefore no one else could have her. Which was nonsense, he knew.

He'd just have to do better.

He wandered over to a door that led into the rest of the house. His fingers itched to open it and walk through but he knew he couldn't. Not until Maggie was ready. They were the rules by which he was prepared to live his life now.

Lorne feared the worse where Maggie's friend

was concerned. He suspected that her reunion with Owen wasn't going to have a happy ending, but he hadn't wanted to go into detail. Not yet. He knew all too well what the Destroyer was capable of because he'd seen it with his own eyes.

Mrs. Noakes stumbling toward him, so familiar and yet changed into something horrific …

They needed to search the house.

He caught Maggie's eye. There was a crease between her dark brows as she tried to read his mind. Eventually, she seemed to understand they were wasting time, and she reached up to tuck some stray curls behind her ear.

"Mr. Stewart," she said, "I actually called in to ask you if you'd seen a colleague of mine. Owen Edwards? He seems to be missing. His vehicle was in an accident and I'm worried he's been hurt."

Stewart turned with two mugs in his hands and set them on the table, slopping milky liquid as he did so. "Owen? Why yes, he's here. Came by this morning. Was a bit shaken up. Asked if he could rest a bit before getting help. He's here somewhere." He waved his hand. Then his face fell. "Wait. Is that what you came to tell me? So you haven't found the 4th Marquis of Lorne?"

Maggie turned to Lorne. "Owen is safe!" Her relief and happiness made her look very young. "Oh, thank goodness. I was worried that—anyway I am very glad he's here. Can you take us to him?"

Lorne felt some confusion. If Owen had been possessed by the Destroyer then why was Stewart unharmed? Perhaps Owen was safe and untouched after all, perhaps … But he had a sense that there was something wrong and he had learned to listen to his feelings. Maggie was already heading for the door and he had no time to warn her. Instead, he took her arm and she stopped.

"Remember to take care," he said.

She gave a little nod. *She understands*, he thought, relieved

Stewart watched them, bemused. "You want to find him right now?" He looked down at the freshly made tea and slices of cake, and cleared his throat. "Very well. Let me show you the way."

Once again, Lorne sensed no reluctance on Stewart's part as he let them through the door, nor any sign that he wasn't willing to comply with Maggie's request. So why didn't that put paid to Lorne's niggling doubts?

The stairs up from the kitchen were plain and bare, as befitted an area of the abbey given over to its servants. Once through the door at the end of a short corridor they found themselves in the main part of the house, but with the shutters closed and the curtains drawn, Lorne could only make out gloomy shapes and dusty draperies.

He was home, and yet he had the strangest feeling that the abbey was in mourning, and had been since the Sorceress put him into the ground.

"Why did you decide to sponsor this dig?" Stewart asked him, panting slightly as he tried to keep up with them on the grand curving staircase.

"Curiosity," was his clipped reply.

"Curiosity. As good an answer as any. But about what?" The American made an effort to get in front of them and nearly succeeded, but a second staircase thwarted him.

"I may come from a bastard line, but they're

still my ancestors, Mr. Stewart." He gave Maggie a bland smile.

They'd reached the long gallery now and Lorne's heart gave a strange sort of hitch in his chest. The portraits were still there, all of his ancestors going back to Tudor times, staring down with long dead eyes. He noticed Maggie shoot uneasy glances up at those aristocratic faces and tried not to smile.

He hadn't expected a woman who believed in wealth being shared out to the masses to be intimidated by such things, and yet he remembered his own first sight of this place. A little boy pressed to his mother's side and gazing up at all of these strangers while his grandmother pointed them out one by one, and named them like it was his duty to memorize each and every one.

Impulsively, he reached for Maggie's hand and gave it a squeeze.

"Mr. Stewart," he called over his shoulder. The American was clearing his throat just beyond the head of the stairs. "I don't see anyone you resemble. Where do you fit into the family tree?"

"Distantly, I'm afraid." The man gave a self-effacing smile and his voice echoed around them. "There was no one left to inherit but me. I was surprised when they tracked me down. Although I had heard about my grand ancestors and the abbey, of course. I just never expected to become part of its history. I almost sold it off without bothering to make the journey, but when I learned about the wicked 4th Marquis, well, I was hooked. I had to come to see for myself."

Lorne quickened his pace and there she was, his grandmother, the Dowager Marchioness, staring down her narrow nose at him with her hooded eyes. Clasped in her arms was, of all things, a small furry dog. The dog had been long dead by the time he came to live at the abbey, and the portrait had never seemed quite real to him. In his mind she'd always been old and crotchety.

Next to her, his father was painted as a young boy, fair haired and reclined romantically against a pillar. He looked as if he wasn't fit to face the real world, which was rather how things had turned out. Of his mother there was no official portrait, although he fancied there'd been a miniature in a drawer somewhere.

Ah, and here he was.

Lorne stopped and stared up at himself with an odd mixture of pride and disgust. The face before him was so full of arrogance it really was as if he was looking at a stranger. Maggie was behind him. At some point she'd tugged her hand from his, but when she saw what—or who—he was looking at she grasped his arm and spoke in a harsh whisper.

"You're giving yourself away!"

He turned to face her. "So, you think there's a resemblance?"

Maggie looked from him to the portrait and back again, and groaned. Lorne was enjoying himself immensely.

"You don't think I've aged well, then?"

She sighed.

"Do try to be objective." He leaned forward to murmur in her ear. "I am well aware that you believe all titled gentlemen should be sent to the guillotine."

She shivered as his warm breath tickled her. "I've

already apologized for that." As if she couldn't help herself she looked again at the portrait, and asked curiously, "Why are you sitting outside with the abbey behind you?"

"Because I am showing the world how wealthy I am. It's a statement, Maggie."

"Certainly not an *under*statement," she muttered.

He laughed and she looked at him, as if uncertain whether he was genuinely amused, before she smiled. She really was a most attractive woman. Not beautiful in the traditional way, yet he didn't want to take his eyes off her.

"Remarkable." Stewart arrived at that moment, also looking at the portrait, his face filled with wonder. "Although your hair isn't quite …well, you're going grey, Mr. Rice. The Lornes were always dark, apart from the 3rd Marquis. He was a very sad case. Hanged himself in a London tavern. Mentally ill, you'd call it today. And his mother, the 4th Marquis's grandmother, was a bit of a dragon. *Everyone* was afraid of her."

Lorne stood frozen, unable to prevent his family secrets being exposed by the American. He turned to Maggie, his head pounding as if he were standing on a field with a dozen cannons firing simultaneously, and still Stewart's voice was clear and ringing and he couldn't blot it out.

"Did you know that the 3rd Marquis left his wife and son virtually penniless?" Stewart asked Maggie in his diffident manner. "They had to return here to Blackfriars Abbey to live with the grandmother. She blamed them for her son's death and made their lives a misery, I understand. Eventually the wife overdosed on laudanum, the gentlewoman's drug of choice in those days, and left her son to the tender mercies of his grandmother."

"Oh dear …" Maggie shifted away from Stewart towards Lorne, giving him a distressed look. "Perhaps we should find Owen now and—"

"I mean, it's no wonder he went off the rails later on, with the Hellfire Club and the rest of it," Stewart continued his history lesson with obvious relish, enjoying himself like the worst sort of ghoul. "You'd think the English aristocracy in those days would be better behaved, am I right? But in reality they were more like some of our modern day celebrities. Spoilt, selfish and totally dysfunctional."

Lorne swallowed. His throat was thick and dry. He wanted to argue the point, because this was *him* they were discussing. His life, his unhappy childhood and his selfish excesses. He may no longer be that person but it was still his life and he felt a strange sense of loyalty to that poor misguided fellow. And yet he couldn't speak—it was as if his voice had been taken away from him and all he could do was stand and listen.

Maggie squeezed his hand and he stared at her, knowing his face was white and shocked. Her dark eyes were glistening, close to tears. And then she turned to Stewart and took his arm and drew him away, saying, "Please, show me where Owen is."

As they left, Maggie gave his portrait one last look before she turned her back on it. He wondered what she was thinking. Waster and scoundrel, perhaps? And yet there had been tears welling in her eyes.

Was it pity then? A woman's softness for a mistreated child?

He didn't want pity. Not from Maggie. He wanted her heart and soul, and her body. Oh, he most definitely wanted those long legs wrapped around him in the night, and her soft breath gasping out his name.

Lorne shook his head in self-mockery. That was the old Lorne peeking through again, and it was unlikely that Maggie would ever consider any such thing in any case. She might want him, though she denied it, but she was fighting that desire with every bone in her body.

Lorne ran a hand over his face, feeling his whiskers rasp. He was over two hundred years old and for the first time he felt like it.

Chapter Fourteen

MAGGIE WASN'T PAYING MUCH ATTEN-TION to where Mr. Stewart was taking her. It suddenly felt very warm here in the gallery. She wished she could strip off her sweater, but it didn't seem appropriate to ask him to stop while she undressed. The story she'd just been told was tragic, and although she'd heard worse it had struck a chord with her. Her own childhood had been far from perfect, but at least she'd had her sister Linny to watch out for her. Although she was only a few years older than Maggie, Linny had taken on the roles of mother and father.

As a child, Lorne seemed to have been very much alone. No wonder he was so screwed up. Not that it excused his actions—Maggie could just as easily have turned into a delinquent, yet she hadn't—but it still explained a lot.

The abbey, the portraits—his in particular—made her more aware than ever of just how large the gap was that stretched between them. Not in years, although there was that, but with who and what they were.

And yet he'd held her hand because he thought

she needed encouragement. He'd smiled at her, he'd laughed at her joke, and he'd looked at her in a way she wasn't sure she had ever been looked at before.

Maggie wiped another drop of perspiration from her cheek. The portrait really was something though, no denying that. She'd had to have a last look at it. Lorne standing before the abbey in his posh clothes, with his rakish dark hair down to his shoulders and his haughty expression, and his blue eyes so very, well, *blue*. Arrogant, was how he looked. And very, very hot.

That was probably how he managed to get all those women to come to his Hellfire Club. They'd hardly need any encouragement to start swooning over a man like him.

Maggie pulled a face, wiping the back of her hand across her brow. She could just imagine it. Running around half naked, drinking too much and chanting half-baked spells he didn't really believe in—because it had all been for a laugh until they found out it worked, hadn't it? She'd bet they even dressed up as monks and nuns—a sort of thumb-your-nose to the original inhabitants of the abbey. Very childish behavior for grown men.

She was so busy disapproving she didn't notice that Owen was right there in front of her. He was peering into a glass-fronted display cupboard, and was so intent on whatever was inside, he hadn't noticed her either.

"Owen?" Her heart gave a thump. "Owen!"

He started and straightened up. There was something awkward and stiff in his movement. Her first thought was that he must have been hurt when his vehicle swerved off the road.

"Mr. Edwards, there you are," Stewart called out in a cheerful voice. "Your friends have come to look for you."

Owen turned to face them then and Maggie could see at once he hadn't had any sleep. He looked pale with dark shadows under his eyes and there was a bruise on his cheek. Owen was a little overweight but today he seemed thinner than she remembered, as if he'd sprung a slow leak. He looked like he'd had a tough night.

"Owen, are you all right?" Maggie said, starting forward. At first she forgot Lorne's warning, but after a couple of steps her feet slowed of their own accord and stopped. A few yards still separated them, yet she couldn't seem to make herself close it. That ancient part of her brain was screaming at her again.

Run, run, run.

Owen was her colleague and her friend. He had been one of Simon's oldest friends. He'd been with her when she was at her lowest ebb and she trusted him completely.

"Maggie." He nodded, smiling at her. It was Owen's voice and Owen's face. It had to be Owen. So why did she feel as if it wasn't? "I came to see Mr. Stewart," Owen said. "I was coming back for you and my truck went off the road."

"Oh. I-I know. We found it. I was worried about you. Are you hurt? I'll take you to a doctor. Why didn't you come to the cottage? Why haven't you answered your phone? Everyone's wondering where you are."

He paused, then he gave a funny little shrug of

his shoulders. He was hurt, Maggie decided, he must be.

"Owen?"

The voice at her shoulder startled her. An iron grip on her arm held her in place even though she wasn't going anywhere. Lorne had crept up on her again.

Owen tipped his head in Lorne's direction.

"We've been concerned for your wellbeing," Lorne went on in an expressionless voice.

"Oh yes, sorry. I was just …" He waved a hand about him. "There's so much to see and Mr. Stewart has let me look around."

"I still think a doctor—" Maggie butted in.

"No, no, I'm fine. Copacetic."

Copacetic? That wasn't something she'd ever heard him say before. Where did that come from?

Maggie looked at Owen's smiling face, his grey hair falling over his brow as it always did, his short sighted eyes squinting into hers.

"Where are your glasses?" she asked.

"Lost 'em," he replied. "On the road."

Stewart was getting impatient. "I really don't mind if Owen stays a little longer." He patted Maggie's shoulder, the one Lorne wasn't hanging on to, and she winced. It was still tender from the night before. "I promise to keep an eye on him."

She didn't want to leave him. She felt woozy and she couldn't think straight. Owen was a grown man and she could hardly force him to come with her. Could she?

"Owen, are you sure …?"

That nodding head, like one of those dogs people had in the rear window of their cars. Vacant and grinning as it bobbed up and down.

"I thought we were going to play a game of whist?" Lorne said in that same friendly tone. Maggie turned to goggle at him. Whist? Owen wouldn't even know what it—

"Oh yes, so we were," Owen grinned at Lorne as if he'd known him all his life.

It was too much for Maggie. "Owen, you're coming with us."

She shook off Lorne's hand and took a step forward. Lorne moved with her, saying, "No," at the same time Stewart shouted, "Look out!"

Owen spun away, knocking heavily against another display case to the accompaniment of breaking glass. He didn't even pause, but began to walk away in a strange jerky manner.

"I have to stop him," Maggie groaned. "He's hurt. He's ill."

"*Listen to me!*" Lorne sounded as if he'd completely lost his cool. Maggie glared at him but Lorne only glared back. He looked to Stewart, who was clucking around the display case, no longer showing any interest in any of them. Lorne looked back to Maggie, dropping his voice to an urgent tone. "When it feeds, the demon takes the form of mortal men and women. Do you hear me, Maggie? Are you listening now? That may look like Owen on the outside, but inside I fear it is not Owen at all."

She turned to stare at Owen's receding back. Something cold and heavy filled her heart. "We have to stop him. We have to know for certain."

Lorne hesitated before he nodded with a sigh. "Leave it to me," he said. He quickened his stride to catch up to Owen. "Halt!" he shouted. "Halt, I say."

Owen took a couple of wavering steps and stopped. For a moment he stood still and Lorne stopped too, watching him. Maggie edged closer, but her legs were still shaking and her head was still reeling.

Owen turned as if he found it difficult to coordinate his body. *He's injured,* Maggie told herself again, *that's all. He had an accident and he's hurt.* But by now she was trying to convince herself of something she knew wasn't true.

Owen took a step toward them, and then another, a sort of a running-hopping step that made Maggie stumble backwards, even though Lorne was in front of her.

"Maggie," Owen said and smiled. But it wasn't Owen's smile, and it wasn't giving her any sense of familiarity. This wasn't the Owen who had held her in his arms when Simon died, and promised they would work on in his name at the abbey no matter who tried to stop them.

Lorne edged closer. Maggie saw him reach for a solid brass ornament. "What are you doing?" she hissed.

"If we can drive it out of Owen's body then it will be vulnerable. We can capture it."

And he took off, fast, closing in on Owen, with Maggie running after him.

One moment Owen was standing watching them and the next he spat at them. To Maggie's horror she saw the long fangs of the Destroyer in Owen's mouth.

"Surrender." Lorne's voice was deadly serious.

"There's nowhere for you to run."

"Oh no, little man," it mocked. "*You* are the one who should beware. I will have you, and your woman, too."

Maggie couldn't take any more. All her strength deserted her and only Lorne's arms prevented her from collapsing. Some far away part of her brain noticed that her shoulder was throbbing, but this wasn't the time to worry about that.

"Are you all right?" Mr. Stewart had come up behind them. He seemed puzzled, as if he'd missed the entire thing. "Where is Owen?"

Maggie pulled out of Lorne's arms. Part of her had been overwhelmed by just how nice it was being pressed next to his body. The room whirled around her and she tried to bring it back into focus. Stewart wanted to ask her a question, but before he could speak Lorne claimed his attention.

"Thank you for your hospitality, Mr. Stewart, but Owen had to go and I fear so do we." Lorne grasped Maggie's hand, giving her no option but to hurry along after him, as he rushed toward the ornate staircase.

Stewart panted as he followed behind. "But … What about the … 4th Marquis? He still needs to be found." He sounded bewildered, an innocent bystander in all this, oblivious to what was actually happening around him.

Maggie called back. "If we find his remains we will tell you, Mr. Stewart." It wasn't entirely a lie but she was glad they were too far away for him to read her face.

A moment later they were outside the abbey.

The rain was heavier than before and the weather

bleaker. Lorne stopped and looked up at the sky. He was still holding her hand and she pulled it away and folded her arms with a shiver. She was surprised to find herself cold when a moment ago she had been feverishly hot.

"Lorne, you have to answer me." Maggie stumbled over the questions but she had to know, no matter how painful the truth. "Where is-is Owen? What happened to him?"

The rain fell upon Lorne's upturned face and it was a moment before he gave her his full attention. He looked very much like the portrait she'd seen and she thought his hair must have gotten darker again. He was getting stronger, and that was a good thing. But then, if he was, so was the Destroyer.

"He's dead, isn't he?" She spoke for him, because standing in the rain, staring into Lorne's eyes, she knew exactly what he was going to tell her.

"When the Destroyer takes over a mortal there's no room for the two of them in that body. I'm sorry, Maggie. Owen is dead."

She curled her arms tighter about herself. There was an ache in her chest and another in her stomach. Her legs shook, and she was having trouble staying upright, but when the tears sprang to her eyes once again she refused to let them fall.

"Where is it now?" Her voice was rough with emotion.

He shook his head and his expression was bleak. "There are plenty of places to hide at the abbey. The tunnels underneath run for miles. It could be anywhere."

She looked over her shoulder, and took a hasty step to one side as the movement put her off balance. "Shouldn't we warn Mr. Stewart? He's in danger."

Lorne took her arm, steadying her. He looked to the brooding bulk of the abbey as he mulled this over. "Stewart was with the demon all this time, yet nothing happened to him. There's something peculiar about the man. When he cried out, as if to warn Owen about the cabinet … I had the impression he was actually warning the demon, telling it to run."

"You think he knows? That he's part of this?"

He seemed to consider his answer. "Perhaps Stewart is an innocent but it seems unlikely. There are things happening I don't understand yet and I think we need to be very careful."

"Owen." Her eyes welled up, but she didn't want to cry; she wouldn't cry, and she wiped the tears away before they could fall.

"He was your friend," Lorne offered in a quiet voice.

"He was Simon's friend, and he was mine. He wanted to make sure Simon's last wish came true. Now I feel as if I've lost Simon all over again."

The wretched tears wouldn't stop coming, no matter how she wiped at them, and her head was beginning to ache.

"Maggie." The Marquis of Lorne took her into his arms as if it was the most natural thing in the world to do. She clung to him in the rain, taking his comfort, and perhaps giving it as well. Even the sense of attraction, awakened by their close contact, felt good. It reminded her that she was alive.

It would be so easy to completely let go right now. She could sob into his shoulder and she knew he'd look after her; she was certain of it. But this wasn't the time for such weakness. She'd cry, yes, and probably take to her bed, but she'd do that when this was over.

She took a deep breath and stepped back. Doubtless she looked like hell, but at least she was alive. Owen wasn't. Not really.

"We need to go," she said. "We need to find your friends. That creature must be caught before it can hurt anyone else."

Lorne watched her closely. He nodded. "Yes. We will come back here with Loki. He can track the Destroyer down to its lair. If it's still inhabiting a mortal body we can surround it and force it to reveal itself. That was what we did last time. The bodies don't last long—they get weaker until they are no more—so it has to move on to another. Occupying our skin is the only way it can continue to live in our world. Once it's been driven out it is vulnerable."

"Whose skin was it occupying when you caught it last time?" she asked.

He didn't look away. She had the impression he was about to give her his secrets in return for hers. "Mrs. Noakes, my old nanny. She was the only person who showed me any kindness after I came to live here as a boy."

"Oh," she said. Maggie thought it was probably her turn to hold him, to give him comfort as he'd given her. "I'm sorry."

He nodded and the moment passed. He seemed to be trying to make up his mind and when he spoke she could hear the urgency in his voice. "There's something else I haven't told you. Last time we captured the Destroyer the door to the underworld was closed and that was why the Sorceress sent it to sleep."

"With you to guard it?"

"Yes. This time the door is open and we have the chance to do it right, Maggie. This time we can send it back to Hell."

She wanted to ask him what would happen after the Destroyer was dealt with. Would he stay or would he return to the chaos awaiting him in his own time?

But he had turned and was already heading back to the Land Rover.

"Come now," he called impatiently. "We have plans to make. We must capture the demon before it harms another and then …"

"And then?" she said, shakily, following after him.

"If we come out of this alive …"

If?

"We celebrate. I haven't thought beyond that, to be honest."

She surprised herself with a laugh. Who'd have thought she'd get to spend what might be her final hours in the company of a Marquis from the 1800s and his aristocratic companions?

And who'd have thought she'd wish for nothing more?

Chapter Fifteen

LORNE HEARD MAGGIE TAKE A deep shaky breath and turned his head to look at her. She blinked, hard, as if to focus, before giving a shiver. Her hands were clenched on the wheel so tight her knuckles shone white. He could see it was getting more difficult for her to keep control of the machine, and he was beginning to wonder if they were going to get back to the cottage without crashing into the trees at the side of the road. Like Owen.

"You are unwell." He put the back of his hand to her forehead and held it there until she shook him off. "You have a fever."

"Probably just the flu." She forced a laugh and gave another shudder. "That's all I need now, a wee dose of the flu."

He didn't think it was the influenza. This had come on too quickly, surely, unless the influenza in this modern world was different from the one he recalled. Where was the sneezing and coughing? And there was something about the way she kept blinking to clear her sight. A memory stirred and a warning bell tolled.

They were nearly there. The machine shot through the water of the ford and climbed back out. The weather had set in now, the rain much heavier, and two wipers on the window moved laboriously back and forth, trying to keep up with the downpour. When Lorne saw the blurred image of the cottage ahead he was more relieved than he let on—in her present state he doubted Maggie would have been able to take them much further.

She turned off the engine and all he could hear was the falling rain. When she didn't move to open her door and get out, Lorne climbed out his side and went around to open the door for her. She still didn't move, staring forward through the window. Frowning, he looked at her, trying to remember something, something important, but he was tired and his memory was two hundred years old.

"Maggie." Worry overrode his urgency to set off after the Destroyer. "Please, come inside." When she didn't move he reached in and took hold of her. She staggered once she was outside the machine and he kept his arm around her as they struggled toward the cottage door. Her long legs didn't seem to know where they were going or what was expected of them. He was unpleasantly reminded of Owen's strange hopping run. *The demon,* he corrected himself, because Owen was surely dead by now.

He'd hoped Darlington and Sutcliffe would be back, but the cottage appeared deserted. They must still be on the hunt. Perhaps they had picked up the Destroyer's scent, where its path crossed with Owen's, and were even now following it back through the woods to the abbey.

Maggie whimpered. She reached out a hand toward the wall but misjudged and almost fell into a potted plant.

He hauled her back up again. "Door key?"

When she didn't answer he dug his fingers into her pocket, the place where he'd seen her put them. Through her clothing her body felt warm, far too warm for a day like this. He slid his hand further into the pocket, searching, trying to ignore the intimacy of the action. Despite all they had been through today his body was taut with sexual desire, but this was hardly the time or the place.

He'd promised not to touch her unless she asked him and Lorne intended to abide by that.

"We could be dead tomorrow," she said, her voice husky.

His hand stilled, forgetting the keys a moment. "We could be. Let us hope not."

"What if we are, though, Lorne? What if we're dead tomorrow? We should make the most of this moment, right now, shouldn't we? Shouldn't we?"

She was rambling, delirious.

"And how would you make the most of this moment, Maggie?"

She touched the side of his face, definitely a caress. Startled, he looked up and saw that she was smiling—a wicked tantalizing smile that made him think of warm bodies and soft beds. She brushed her fingertips across his mouth, albeit clumsily because her hands were shaking.

"I'd like to spend it kissing you, Mister Marquis," she said.

He thought he'd like it too. He bent his head, thinking that was an invitation if he'd ever heard one, just as his fingers found the keys.

"That kiss will have to wait," he said. With one arm still holding her up, he opened the door.

The residual warmth inside was enough for perspiration to appear on Maggie's forehead and she began to sink at the knees. He heaved her onto the sofa and propped her up with cushions.

Simon's book, *Secrets of Moyle*, caught his eye. It was on the table, and Maggie's husband's smiling face stared up at him; he was distracted into wondering what it was about the man that had captured Maggie's heart. Kindness, probably, and belief. Women like Maggie who had come up the hard way weren't used to the men around them being considerate. Nor were they used to being treated as if their opinions mattered.

Lorne couldn't remember being particularly kind in his day. Ennui was fashionable when he was a young man and he'd played the part of the bored gentleman without requiring practice. *Well,* he told himself wryly, *it's never too late to turn over a new leaf.* Self-righteously he went to the kitchen to fetch a glass of water and brought it back for her.

She was trembling too much to hold it steady so he put an arm about her shoulders to help. She cried out, throwing up her hands and spilling water over them both.

"What? What is it?" he asked, irritated and worried in equal measure. "Maggie?"

She looked up at him and with an effort focused her dark eyes. They looked enormous, the pupils almost swallowing the irises. Curls of her hair were stuck to her face and before he could stop himself he reached to push them back, leaving his hand resting on her head. This time she didn't shake him off.

"Eh, there's something I should probably tell you," she said. She sounded more lucid than she had a moment before. "In the graveyard, before you stopped the Destroyer … It grabbed my shoulder. It racked me with its claws. I think, maybe …"

The memory came back to him, with all the suddenness of a thunderclap. A servant the Destroyer had mauled, one they'd saved—*thought* they'd saved—tossing and turning, wracked with fever, blinking as though he was no longer able to see. He'd gone mad in the end, screaming and sobbing in agony.

Lorne went cold. He'd been incredibly lucky when he fought the demon that he hadn't been clawed himself—but then he had known to avoid those talons. The thought of Maggie going through such travail, burning up, sobbing in pain, her clever mind turning crazed, her lovely face a mask of terror. A long, agonizing death. He would do anything to stop that happening to her. He had to.

"I need to see," he said in a rough voice, and reached for the bottom of her sweater.

She pulled away, only just staying upright. "If I have to strip down I'd rather do it upstairs," she said. With an effort he had to admire, she got to her feet and began to make her wobbly way to the staircase.

He followed. Halfway there she began to slide down the wall. He caught her, swinging her up into his arms. Her head flopped back and she groaned; her hands reached out for support and found a grip on his coat.

He carried her up to the bedroom and placed her on the bed, where she lay with eyes closed, her skin pale as snow. "I feel sick," she whispered.

"There isn't time." It was true. There wasn't time for anything if what he thought was happening was happening. He stared up at the ceiling. "Sorceress?" he called. "Where are you? I need you now. Maggie needs you!"

Nothing. No stirring of the air; no sense of a storm approaching.

He pulled off her sweater, slipped it from her arms and tugged it over her head. She wore a tight fitting shirt beneath and he pulled that off as well. It came away awkwardly, as she seemed to have no strength left to help him.

Perhaps it was just as well. She would be fighting him if she was properly conscious. Her eyes would be flashing with temper and insults would be spilling from her mouth. Despite himself, he longed for a return of the Maggie he felt he already knew.

She wore one of the unfamiliar undergarments he'd examined earlier—a strip of apricot satin about her breasts with straps over her shoulders. Remembering the chemises and stays and the long frustrating moments it took to undress a woman, Lorne thought Maggie was very nearly naked already.

"Like what you see?" she slurred, as if she had drunk too much wine.

He reached out and stroked a finger over the curve of one firm breast. It was small but perfect and he couldn't help himself. "Yes, I do." There were goosebumps on her skin and her nipples were tight hard buds showing through the satin.

She chuckled, gazing up at him through half closed eyes, and the sight of her filled him with a lust so powerful he wanted to fling himself upon her like the most callow and impatient of youths. It was something he hadn't done since he was thirteen with the dairy maid, and the memory of that shocked him back to his senses.

There was a gold chain about her neck, with a medallion attached. He took it gently to see what it was, anything to distract his thoughts from what he really wanted to do.

"That's Mary," she said, and gave another chuckle.

"The Madonna?" It didn't look like her.

"Queen of Scots, if you please. I bought her the day I started at university. She's my lucky charm."

"Did you need luck?"

"Oh, aye, I did. I was young and in classes where everyone was years older than me. I was lonely and awkward and out of my depth. Most of the kids were from posh families, too. I was there on a scholarship."

He smiled. "Posh? You mean like me? Maggie, you're far cleverer than me. I can just about sign my name."

"What? I don't believe you."

"I'm no academic. You'd no doubt run rings about me at a university."

"But you'd have them all eating out of your hand, wouldn't you? And I'd still be alone in the corner, swatting up for my exams."

"I think I'd rather be in your corner than anywhere else."

She gave a shaky smile. "You're a good man, do you know that? I like you, Mister Marquis." Her smile faded and she drew a shallow breath. "Okay," and she patted the mattress beside her. "Sit yourself down and let me tell you the story of my life."

"Maggie, we don't have time! I need to see how far the demon's poison has spread."

But she either wasn't listening or she preferred not to.

"It won't take long," she said with a grimace. "And it's not the whole story, just one little bit of it."

He gave a groan, but he sat down beside her.

"When I was at university I was very young. Too young. I was clever and that was why I was there, but I was still a child, really. Everyone else was so much older and I desperately wanted to join in." She looked at him through her lashes. "There was a boy."

His fingers had been stroking hers and he had to force himself to continue in the same calm manner. "He hurt you?"

"He asked me up to his room. He was very good looking, and I was flattered that someone like that would even notice me, so I went." Her voice began to drift, as if it was all unfolding before her eyes. "He had a camera hidden in the bookshelf. Like a-a photograph, like the one on the book, only they can move. Afterwards he laughed and said everyone was going to enjoy watching it. I think it's still around somewhere, though I suppose what we did is pretty tame compared to others. Of course, that wasn't the point. The point was to embarrass me. Hurt me. Take my virtue, I guess is what you would say. Use his power to diminish me."

Lorne understood, although the concept of a

moving photograph was quite strange. It was the pain in Maggie's voice that affected him, and the idea that someone could betray her trust so maliciously.

"What was his name?" he demanded.

She blinked. "Why do you want to know?" A smile lit up her wane face. "Oh, are you going to challenge him to a duel?" She smiled, and he wasn't sure if she was mocking him or not.

"Well … I … I simply meant that he deserved a thrashing for hurting you."

"Oh Lorne, I wish you could but he's long gone. But thank you." She then gave a shudder so violent it made the bed shake.

There was no time for this. Lorne knelt on the mattress and flipped her over onto her stomach, ignoring her feminine curves and creamy flesh with its sprinkling of freckles. He went still when he saw what he had already feared and yet hoped not to find.

The mark the Destroyer had left upon her. The claw marks stood out, swollen and puss filled, the redness spreading out as its corrupting poison crept relentlessly into her body.

He rested his fingers on the discolored wound and she was hot, so hot. Was it too late? He cursed the demon and the Sorceress and then he cursed himself for bringing the creature into the mortal world in the first place. If this was anyone's fault then it was his own, and if Maggie died then it would be because of him.

Chapter Sixteen

"DID YOU JUST SWEAR?"

Lorne was so angry and upset it took a moment for him to hear her, her dreamy voice muffled by the quilt.

"I didn't realize they knew those words back in eighteen hundred and eight."

He closed his eyes and tried to steady himself. Things were very serious, it was true, but nothing would be accomplished by carrying on like a beardless boy. He needed to stay in control.

"The best swear words have been with us for centuries," he said in a mild voice.

When he opened his eyes again he didn't look at the Destroyer's mark. He noticed instead the raised vertebra of her back and the shape of her bones and muscles beneath her skin. She was much slimmer than he normally liked his women, and yet there was that lust again, rising like a tide up inside him. He wanted her desperately.

This state of affairs held a certain irony.

There was a time when he'd begun to find women's attraction to him tiresome. He'd become bored with the lot of them, just as he'd become bored with most things. Now he'd found one he wanted more than all the others put together, and he may never have the chance to lie with her, let alone live with her.

"You're very quiet," she said. "Do I need a doctor?"

"You need more than that, I fear."

With an effort she lifted her head. "Hospital?"

Her wild curls were damp and tangled about her face. He helped her sit up and eased her back to lean against the pillows. She looked young and vulnerable, just like the girl in the story she'd told him, who had been taken advantage of.

"I do not think your physicians have seen anything such as this."

He tried to make her comfortable, but he could tell from her gasps of pain that he wasn't very successful. He pulled the bedclothes up, tucking them around her, and she watched him with eyes that were dark and round and shadowed beneath.

"It's serious, isn't it?" She barely spoke above a whisper.

He should lie but she would know it. Besides, Lorne was a man who preferred the truth, no matter how dire, and he thought Maggie was cut from the same cloth.

"You may die, Maggie, but it's worse than that."

"Worse?"

"You may first lose your mind. I've seen it happen. Only the Sorceress can heal you. I need to call her into the mortal world."

He moved to climb off the bed, intending to go to the door, but she stopped him.

"Lorne."

He looked back and she was holding out her hand. Even though he knew he shouldn't, he reached to entwine her fingers in his.

Once again the reckless longing to hold her caught him in its grip.

"I know you are trying to save me, but if-if you don't, do you think you could let my sister know what happened? Her name is Linny. The thing is she may already know, but all the same, will you tell her?"

He moved closer. "Maggie …"

A tear rolled down her cheek and she was too weary to brush it away. He did it for her, using his thumb, and then, because he couldn't help himself, he leaned in and kissed the place it had been. She turned her face. Before he had a chance to think about it, her lips were against his and he was kissing her, just as he'd imagined doing from the first time he'd seen her.

She made a soft sound, pressing closer, her mouth unbelievably hot. He leaned over her, drowning in the taste of her, and the intimacy he'd been longing for. All he had to do was slide under the quilt and be on top of her. She'd welcome him, and it would only take a minute. He was so hard, the release would be so sweet.

His selfish thoughts shocked him back to cold rationality.

If he did that, wouldn't that make him just as bad as the boy who had lied and used her? She was vulnerable, and not herself. He sat up with a groan, rubbing his hands down his face.

"I'm sorry, Maggie." His voice shook with emotion. "So sorry. Please forgive me."

She lifted her long lashes and looked at him with feverish eyes. "Where are you going? What are you going to do?"

"I'm going to save you," he said, knowing how ridiculous that sounded. The Marquis of Lorne had never saved anyone. Even when he captured the Destroyer, he'd only prevented further harm from being done. He was no hero.

He could see his grandmother in his head, hear her scornful voice. "You are a weakling, Lorne, and I cannot abide weakness. Do you understand?" Of course he'd said he did, even though he didn't, because how could a six year old understand why he wasn't allowed to cry for his dead pony?

"I must find the Sorceress." He spoke quickly, before she could ask him to stay. She was frightened and alone, and of course she wanted him there, but Lorne knew it wouldn't be right, and it wouldn't help her. He was better than that now.

"Don't worry, Maggie. It will be all right. Sleep until I get back."

She gave him a shaky smile as he closed the door.

Immediately his confidence deserted him. He didn't know what to do. The Sorceress had always come to him before; he'd never called her. He went outside and stared at the rain-filled sky but he knew she wasn't up there. She was from the between-worlds. That was her kingdom, the place between the here and the underworld. Purgatory, some called it, where those caught in limbo waited while their fate was decided.

Just like him.

"Please, I need you!" He shouted his plea. "You said I had to work with Maggie to recapture the

Destroyer. If she dies, how can I do as you ask?"

Still nothing. He clenched his hands into fists. Maggie was upstairs and he should be with her, trying to comfort her. He should be doing *something ...*

"Please! I cannot let her die!" The words roared out of him. It seemed as if he heard them collide with the trees all around, flying off, only to strike them again and again.

He felt it then. The stirring. The air tingled around him. A bird rose screeching from a bough and flapped away. He stumbled backwards, overwhelmed by the power that washed over him, and came up against the wall of the cottage. It was only that wall that kept him on his feet as the Sorceress made her entrance into the mortal world.

"Lorne," she said, her voice was soft and yet it filled his head in echoes, to the point where it became painful. Colors shimmered about her and her long red hair curled and waved with a life of its own. "What do you want from me?"

He opened his mouth but she had already rummaged through his thoughts.

"You wish me to save the woman Maggie McNab? So that you can recapture the Destroyer and be released from your bonds?"

"Yes." And then he shook his head. "No, that's not why. I ... I don't want her to die like this. She doesn't deserve such a fate."

"I thought you believed this was all her fault for releasing the demon into the world?"

"No, no, I don't think that." He felt sick but he couldn't stop now. He had to speak the words that were hammering inside his brain. "It is my fault, all of this is, and I must make it right. I want to do that for her. I don't care what it takes. I only wish to save Maggie."

The Sorceress smiled her terrible smile.

"Ah, so you wish to be heroic, Lorne? I've been waiting for the real man to make himself known. You've hidden behind your mask for so long, but I knew you were there. Yes, I will save her."

She leaned closer and he could barely keep his eyes open, but he heard her plainly enough.

"But there will be a price."

Chapter Seventeen

MAGGIE THOUGHT SHE MUST BE asleep. Dreaming.

Through her half open eyes she saw the gloomy, grey light from the window change to a shimmering blue, before the air began to crackle as if there was electricity in it. A storm perhaps? But she was inside the cottage. When she reached out her hands she could feel the soft quilt covering her, so she knew she was still in bed where Lorne had put her.

Where had he gone? Why wasn't he here? He said he'd be back and that he was going to save her …

She trusted him, she really did, but she was a practical sort of woman. Lorne could do many things but she wasn't sure he could do this. And if he couldn't, if she was really going to lose her mind and die, then she'd prefer he was by her side now in her final moments.

"Maggie?"

The voice was soft and feminine and yet the power of it shook her senses. Her eyes sprang open.

A woman stood in front of her. She wore a white dress and a full length white fur cloak, and diamonds gleamed about her throat. She might have been an actress in a BBC costume drama, except that her long red hair snaked about her as if she was standing in a strong wind. Yet there was no wind, only that strange electrical buzzing in the air. And her eyes … They were a brilliant azure blue, unlike anything Maggie had ever seen before.

They weren't human eyes.

Shock raced through her. Her heartbeat quickened, blood rushed through her body as if pulled by a tide. She wanted to turn away and yet she couldn't, because that brilliant regard held her in place.

"Maggie," the woman said again. Now her voice echoed as if they were standing in a cavern with vast space all about them rather than a small, cramped bedroom. "I am called the Sorceress. I am the ruler of the between-worlds."

You'll know her when you see her. That's what Lorne had said, and now she understood exactly what he meant.

"You have been injured," the Sorceress said, getting closer, although as far as Maggie could tell she wasn't actually walking. "Lorne has asked me to heal you. Close your eyes, Maggie."

Maggie wasn't sure she wanted to. It was like one of those games where if you closed your eyes then your opponent crept nearer and nearer and …

"Close them. Now."

She closed them and for good measure squeezed them tight.

For a moment there was nothing, then she felt a sensation, wonderfully cool, against the wound the Destroyer had left. Followed by a jolt, as if something had been wrenched from her, and it made her scream.

"Rest, Maggie. Rest now …" Vaguely she was aware that the voice was fading.

Through her lashes she saw the brilliant light fade before the room assumed its normal dull shades.

Her shoulder no longer hurt. Her head no longer buzzed with pain. She felt better, just tired. So tired. She needed to sleep. She needed … *oh no!*

The memories returned to her in sharp focus. What had she done? She'd *kissed him!* Worse, she'd begged him to kiss her back, and it wasn't just that she'd wanted. What had she said? Maggie squirmed, her entire body flushed with embarrassment. How was she ever going to look Lorne in the eye again?

The door to her bedroom flew opened.

Maggie sat up, too shocked to speak, hoping it was not the Sorceress again.

Loki ran in, then seemed to do a double-take as he sensed what had just been in the room. He let out a terrible howl as he backed out again, his claws scratching on the floor in his haste. Maggie heard him pounding down the stairs.

She giggled, and then she laughed. Even a wolf was afraid of the Sorceress. Not that she blamed him.

More pounding on the stairs, this time three men crammed inside the small bedroom. Maggie groaned and lay back down. Nice as it was that they cared, she could really do without this at the moment.

"Maggie?" It was Lorne. The bed bounced as he landed on it and it was so funny she wanted to laugh again. This was becoming more and more ridiculous.

"Will you not leave me alone to rest? Don't you know how ill I am?" Her voice was muffled because she had her hands over her face.

He hesitated, but only for a second. Then he crawled across the bed and pulled her hands away so that he could peer into her face. She glared back at him, trying not to remember their kiss. Lorne seemed concerned, but he only needed one searching glance to know she was fine. He gave her a grin.

"She healed you," he said with satisfaction. "You're your grumpy Scottish self again."

Darlington peered over his shoulder while Sutcliffe lurked in the background. "Lorne told us you'd been attacked," the big man said. "I've seen what happens to those touched by the Destroyer, Maggie. You are most fortunate …" He looked sideways at Lorne and something seemed to pass between them.

Maggie let out a loud sigh and sat up. "I feel much better," she agreed cautiously. "I'm sorry I am being my grumpy Scottish self, but I've been through a lot. Did Lorne tell you about Owen?"

Evidently he had. They gave her solemn looks of sympathy and she could tell they believed the same as Lorne—that Owen was dead.

"Loki found a scent in the woods leading to the abbey," Sutcliffe said. "We followed it as far as we dared. We think the demon is hiding there."

"In the tunnels," Darlington added. "He knows them, after all. He hid there the last time, before we drove him out into the open."

Loki had crept back into the bedroom and now

he jumped onto the bed, turned around a few times, and flopped down with a contented groan. Maggie thought about ordering him off but couldn't be bothered.

"We must make preparations before we go back to the abbey," Lorne said to the others. "And this time we will not halt our search until we have the Destroyer in our hands. Are we agreed?"

The men nodded and turned expectantly to her. She swallowed. "Eh … aye."

Satisfied, Darlington and Sutcliffe moved to the door, and she heard the word "food" mentioned. Since she'd taught them how to use the tin opener they'd been eating their way through her pantry. Although it probably wasn't the kind of food they were used to, she'd discovered these Regency gentlemen weren't fussy eaters.

"Maggie?"

Lorne was still seated on the bed, watching her face. She'd been trying to ignore him, hoping he'd go away so she wouldn't have to remember their intimate moment. Did he expect her to apologize? Did he expect her to pick up where they left off? Maggie wasn't an expert on social niceties but she thought an apology would be a mite peculiar for something they had both enjoyed. And if he expected her to continue …?

If only she wasn't so tired she might be able to focus. Whatever the Sorceress had done to heal her had also wiped her out. She needed to sleep if she was going to help the others hunt a demon.

Again Lorne's voice interrupted her thoughts. "I'm glad you're recovered."

"So am I," she managed with a yawn. "Thank

you."

His smile was the mocking kind she so disliked, but this time she had the feeling he was mocking himself rather than her. He looked down at Loki and began to stroke his fur. Maggie had a sudden longing to have his fingers massaging her in that same slow, mesmerizing fashion. Oh, why didn't he leave before she said or did something silly?

"You know I was out of my mind," she said, feeling her cheeks heat up. "Before, I mean. When I … we …"

He said nothing but looked at her. Was he reading her thoughts? His eyes darkened and he smiled, and she knew then that he must be reading them.

"When do we go looking for the Destroyer?" she asked hastily.

He let her off the hook. "When you're rested and we've eaten and slept. I'll bring you some food later. You don't eat enough," he added with a frown.

He sounded like Linny. Linny was the only one who ever noticed she wasn't eating. "I'm afraid we've run out of bacon and eggs," she replied to Lorne with a smile. "I'll have to go shopping."

Lorne was still stroking Loki, the wolf-like dog now almost unconscious. Maggie shifted restlessly in the bed. She was too tired even to feel her usual tingles of lust around him.

Well, maybe not quite *that* tired.

Her eyes had become so heavy, they began to close, struggle though she tried to keep them open.

"I like you when you're out of your mind." His deep voice went straight to the parts of her she was trying to ignore. One corner of his mouth quirked, followed by the other. He stood. "Sleep," he said,

"I'll be downstairs." And then, apart from Loki, she was alone.

Maggie felt safe. Lorne made her feel safe. How bizarre was that? Simon had been the only man she had ever trusted with her intimate thoughts and emotions, and now the wicked Marquis had managed to fill that void he'd left behind. Two more different people she could not imagine.

Her thoughts drifted and she wondered whether after all Lorne would remain here after the Destroyer was caught. And if he did, what would he do? How would the remarkably handsome 4th Marquis of Lorne fit in to the modern world?

Her head hurt. Maggie stopped thinking and slept.

———◆———

The sound of the phone woke her. Loki gave a loud yawn and jumped off the bed, wandering out of the half open door. Maggie lay a moment, still sleepy, then reached into her pocket and dug it out. She wasn't sure whether it was day or night—Lorne had drawn the curtains before he left. She'd been planning to get down to the village before the shop closed and pick up some groceries, along with whatever they might need to track down and capture a demon.

"Professor McNab?"

"Eh, yes?" The voice was familiar, very familiar.

"Stewart here. From the abbey."

She blinked, trying to sort through her woozy thoughts, running a hand through her hair and wincing when she struck a knot.

"Mr. Stewart? I'm so sorry I … What was it you wanted?"

"You haven't seen Owen, have you?"

"Owen? Well no. I thought he was there with you." *Whatever now inhabited Owen's body,* she thought with a shudder.

"I can't seem to find him. He's wandered off. I thought he might have met up with you."

That makes one of us.

She was out of bed now and collecting her clothes, which seemed to be scattered all over the place. Where were her boots? Lorne must have taken them off and put them somewhere. Ah, there, under the bed.

Stewart didn't wait for her answer. "Someone else has gone missing. I have a woman from the village who comes in and cleans for me, and does a bit of cooking. Mrs. Green. She was due to come this afternoon and when she didn't turn up I rang to see if she was ill. Her husband said she'd set out as usual on her scooter but she hasn't arrived here. She hasn't returned home either."

Maggie went still. Everything tied together, and not in a good way. How much did Stewart know about what was really going on? He'd seemed so utterly harmless that Maggie was finding Lorne's suspicions about him difficult to accept.

"What does she look like? I'll be going down to the village soon and I might bump into her."

"She's short and chubby with short grey hair and rimless glasses. She usually wears beige. You know, now I come to think of it, she looks a bit like Dustin Hoffman in *Tootsie.*" He chuckled at this. "I'm not too concerned. I think she might have gone off to London. She was talking about it last week. Some play or other she wanted to see and her husband wasn't interested. They'd had quite a tiff over it, or so she said."

"Right. Okay. I'll watch out for her anyway. And … and Owen."

In the silence she could hear him breathe, otherwise she might have thought he'd hung up. The moment stretched until finally he spoke in a reflective voice. "How strange, professor, that people are vanishing now just as they did in the days of the 4th Marquis. Do you think there's a connection? Do you think your digging in the abbey grounds has stirred something up and brought it back to life?"

Now it was her turn to let the moment stretch. What was he suggesting? What did he know? Her heart quickened as she considered whether she should ask questions or let it slide.

"I can't think what, Mr. Stewart," she finally answered. "You said yourself, Mrs. Green probably went to London, and Owen is probably meeting up with the rest of the team now." She really hoped *that* wasn't true.

That silence once more, and again the sound of him breathing.

"Mr. Stewart? Are you there?"

"Thank you. Goodbye, Professor McNab."

Abruptly the call ended. Maggie stared at her phone as if she expected it to explain itself. She slipped it back into her pocket and made her way to the bathroom. She pulled a face at the sight that met her in the mirror. *That* was a mess that needed some work.

Her hair was better for a good brush and the cold water splashed on her face sharpened her wits. She wanted to properly mourn for Owen but there didn't seem to be enough time to do that right now, not if they were to capture the Destroyer and send it back where it belonged. Mrs. Green missing was a worrying thought. Lorne had said that the creature had to keep moving from body to body in order to survive in this world. Was that what had happened to Mrs. Green? Was she its next victim?

She realized how easily she had put aside her doubts and disbelief. Everything that was happening now seemed perfectly logical.

Well, perhaps logical was the wrong word. There was nothing logical about the Sorceress or the Destroyer. And Lorne, what was logical about a 19th century aristocrat who'd been dead for two hundred years?

She caught her eyes in the mirror.

There was a gleam to them and a flush to her cheeks. It was a long time since she had felt like this about a man. Simon had been her dearest friend and her beloved husband, but she could not remember hungering for him the way she did for Lorne. She felt like a teenager again. Actually, she felt like the teenager she had never been. Other girls had swooned over pop stars, but Maggie had been too busy studying and staying out of trouble, and the one time she had fallen for someone they'd made her life a misery.

"Are you going through a late form of puberty?" she asked her reflection sarcastically.

Linny would have laughed at that. Linny had had far more boyfriends than Maggie, although she always seemed to choose the wrong men like some kind of creep magnet. Men like their father, with an unpredictable and sometimes brutal streak, who would not only break her heart but shatter it into pieces.

She wondered if their father was still in prison. Not that she either knew nor cared. She and Linny had cut him from their lives a long time ago—physically, anyway—but you couldn't entirely excise the damage he had caused them psychologically.

That was one reason Maggie always played it safe when it came to men. She supposed that, if she were honest, Simon had been safe. The father she'd never had?

No, that was going too far. Simon had been her mentor and her friend, and without him she often wondered whether she could have gotten where she was now. She was smart, sure, but there was more to success than passing exams.

"And how does that account for Lorne?" she grumbled to herself, pushing away from the wash basin and drying her hands. "He's the least safe man I've ever met."

She needed Linny here to explain it all to her.

Maggie stopped the thought stone cold dead as soon as it entered into her head.

She and Linny had always shared a bond. If one of them was in trouble then the other would intuit it. The connection between them was freaky but she knew it was real. Linny's sibling sense must be going haywire right now. The last thing she needed was to have her sister thrown into this mess with the Destroyer. Maggie didn't want her anywhere near Blackfriars Abbey.

Right now Linny was safe in Glasgow and as far as Maggie was concerned that was where she was going to stay. In fact … She reached for the phone again, calling her sister to tell her as many lies as necessary to keep her far away from here.

The phone rang out so she left a message to say she was fine. It was only when she was done that she wondered if that would only make Linny, probably already feeling anxious, doubly so.

Chapter Eighteen

BY THE TIME MAGGIE GOT downstairs the living history exhibit had already eaten. Again. And Loki was busy with the leftovers. There couldn't be much remaining in the pantry now. Maggie knew she really would have to do that shopping in the village if she was going to have a hope of keeping up with their appetites.

Outside the window she could now see it was late afternoon, not yet dark, although the freaky weather didn't help. Surely summer wasn't over yet? But there'd still be time to get things done if she hurried.

The three rakes sat around the table, and there was a large sheet of paper spread out before them that they'd gotten from somewhere. When she looked more closely she could see they'd drawn parallel pencil lines like streets onto it, and each street had its name printed neatly.

A map. But of where?

"The tunnels under the abbey," Lorne explained, seeing her puzzlement.

"You remember them that well?"

He looked at her from head to toe, a thorough

examination that left her breathless. "You're looking better." He smiled, perfectly aware of the effect he had on her, and obviously enjoying himself, then answered her question. "We've spent a great deal of time in them. That was where the Hellfire Club held their meetings."

"Okay. But why are you drawing a map of the tunnels under the abbey?" she asked. "Is this to do with capturing the Destroyer?"

"We're working on a plan of attack," Sutcliffe rumbled. "To contain it, and prevent its escape."

"When it's properly dark," Darlington added.

She could see an area marked 'the crypt' on the map, with the tunnels radiating outwards. They all had names appropriate to the Hellfire Club—Devil's Way, Fiery Furnace Street, Virgin's Walk, and so on. The sort of stuff used to scare children. She wondered if the current owner had ever wandered about down there in his tartan slippers, and could not imagine it.

"Mr. Stewart just called me," she said. "He thinks someone else has gone missing. Mrs. Green, his domestic. Although he then said she may have just sloped off to London to see a play."

Well, she certainly had their full attention now. She tried not to feel unnerved as they stared at her. Lorne's pale eyes were assessing, while Sutcliffe's dark eyes were thoughtful and Darlington's eyes … well, who knew what Darlington was thinking?

"You think it was the Destroyer," she said heavily. "Don't you?"

"What does this woman look like?" Lorne asked. She just realized his hair had gone completely dark. He looked exactly like his portrait now, and her perfect fantasy.

There, she'd admitted it. Maggie the Socialist dreamed of having a rich, spoilt rake in her bed.

Except Lorne wasn't spoilt and he was no longer rich. Now that she considered it, apart from the outer handsome shell, he wasn't anything at all like the man in his portrait.

"Hmm?" Maggie had lost the thread.

He grinned at her in that cocky way of his, rot him. "I asked you what she looks like?"

"Oh." She tucked a curl back, pretending she hadn't been devouring him with her eyes. "Short, plump, grey hair, beige clothing, but like I said Mr. Stewart thinks she's just having a little holiday."

"And I do not trust your Mr. Stewart," Lorne said dryly.

"Technically more like *your* Mr. Stewart," said Maggie. "He's your relative. Anyway, I need to go into the village before the shops close. While I'm there I'll check in at the pub, and tell the team not to bother working tomorrow. They're safer there. I don't want anyone out at the site until this is over. What can I get to help you capture this demon?"

"Rope," Lorne said. "Strong rope. Chain if possible. Something to use when we capture it in the tunnels."

"Right," she nodded. "Chain and rope."

"A sword," Darlington added.

"Any sort of weapon at all, really," said Sutcliffe somberly.

"I'm afraid the village store doesn't run to swords, but I'll do my best. Anything else? Aiden? Nicholas?"

Sutcliffe gave a deep sigh. "Food. We seem to

have run out. Can you purchase more of that apple pudding with the crumbly top?"

"Dry crackers and cheese." Darlington put in his request.

"Apple pudding, crackers and cheese." Maggie pretended to make a mental list. "What about you, Lorne? Anything you fancy?"

He looked thoughtful. Did she blush? Oh God, she hoped not.

For once he didn't use it against her, or perhaps like the rest of them he was just too focused on the thought of food. "Eggs and bacon. And bread for toast."

She smiled. "Your signature dish."

He smiled back at her, although she doubted he completely understood what she meant by it.

Loki looked at Maggie pitifully. "You too? I know what you want. Stew and lots of it. Actually I think there's one tin left that I hid from the others."

She left the men to their map and went to feed the dog. In the kitchen she found the tin she'd slid behind some jars of freeze-dried coffee. It was vegetable, but the dog didn't seem to mind and soon gulped it down, his tail wagging the entire time.

"He'll eat anything. Not unlike Sutcliffe," said a voice.

Lorne had followed her into the kitchen. He glanced down at Loki in fond disgust but then turned to Maggie.

"I should come with you."

As well as his hair being completely dark now, his face seemed younger and less drawn. He'd also shaved—probably with her razor, she thought, trying to find any reason for resentment and failing.

She was sorely tempted to let him accompany her to the shop, but she knew she couldn't. In the other room, when she'd asked about the tunnels, she'd felt the suppressed excitement in them. Lorne and his friends were getting ready for the hunt, ready to seek out the demon and return it to the Sorceress. Ready to get their lives and freedom back.

There was a great deal at stake, and it seemed somehow less than courageous of her to agree.

Maggie shook her head. "I can manage. I won't be long. And if you're there people will only be asking questions. You're rather conspicuous, you know."

"Then take your shotgun," he said, propping himself up against the bench and folding his arms. "And use it if you have to."

"I will." She nodded. "I will."

He watched her with the sort of concentration that made her all too aware of the two of them being alone in the small kitchen. What was it about her that the Marquis found so fascinating, because he clearly did. She could no longer pretend it was the only woman syndrome. Perhaps it had something to do with her being a woman in the future? Someone very different. And, she reminded herself, he had probably never met a woman archeologist (or antiquarian) before.

"Maggie …" The name seemed to rush out of him but he stopped and shook his head. There was something in the way he stared beyond her, as if he was struggling for words. Had the infamous Marquis ever been at a loss for words?

But Maggie knew now that the cold and arrogant aristocratic she'd heard of wasn't the real Lorne.

He'd worn a mask and behind it was a man who had been hurt and ill-treated. A man who carried a lot of damage inside and was too proud to let it show. The true Lorne was capable of depths of feeling, even if he rarely displayed them.

Perhaps it was time he did.

She took a step closer until she was near enough to feel the warmth of his body. "What?" she dared him. "What do you want to tell me?"

———◆———

She was too close and when she leaned against him Lorne could no longer resist her. He wrapped his arms about her waist and drew her even closer. That felt good. It felt even better when she lifted her face and kissed him.

Maggie kissed him. It seemed like poor manners not to kiss her back.

Her eyelids fluttered and she made a cross between a groan and a sigh. She encircled his neck with her arms. She tasted sweet, her mouth warm and welcoming. So welcoming that he knew if he kept on he wouldn't be able to stop.

He came back to his senses and lifted his head, breaking their contact. She still had her eyes closed, her lips slightly parted, and a faraway expression on her face.

"Tonight we'll capture him," Lorne said, committing her face to memory. "Then it will be over."

Her eyes snapped open. This was the moment to tell her. Before she could ask him any questions or see the truth written in his face, he pulled her closer. But the words stuck in his throat.

"You must return to the past and face whatever pun-ishment is meted out to you, Marquis," the Sorceress had said. *"Mortals have died and you allowed it to happen. It matters not that you failed to understand what you were dabbling with."*

"And if I refuse?" Lorne had asked her, the wall of the cottage against his back and her shimmering light in his eyes.

"Then Maggie will die. It is her life for yours, Lorne. So what is it to be?"

He'd given Maggie her life. Now it was only a matter of time before they found the Destroyer and returned him to the underworld, or died in the attempt. Either way Lorne knew his life was over.

"Lorne?" Maggie pressed her palms against his chest and leaned back in his arms so that she could see his face. She knew something was wrong and yet he prevaricated. Foolishly he told himself that if he didn't tell her then it might not happen. Perhaps he could stay here in Maggie's world and be the man he longed to be. With her he was a better man. It was as simple as that.

She gave him a tentative smile. "I'm not very good at this … this … whatever it is we have going on here. I accept that. But when you say 'over' I have to ask myself exactly what you mean."

He didn't answer her. He could see the worry clouding her eyes and that little crease between her brows he'd come to recognize.

"When you sent the Sorceress to save my life," she began, and he knew she was working her way toward the very thing he did not want her to know. Not yet. *Just a little longer,* he told himself, *and then*

I will tell her. But not yet.

"Maggie, the world would be a tedious place without you in it."

"Simon used to say I was a force of nature." She spoke quietly, but he could see her clever mind searching, searching, looking for the loopholes.

"I'm not Simon."

"No. No, you're definitely not Simon." She was leaning into him again, teasing him with her warm breath on his lips. "Kiss me," she said. It was half request and half command.

He was happy to obey.

Lorne's mouth claimed hers and the heat between them shot up to boiling point. Maggie tangled her fingers in his hair, her body writhing against his, her breath coming in soft moans. He fed on her with a passionate need that rocked the floor beneath their feet, desperate to forget what the Sorceress had in store for him, for just a little longer.

⬤

For someone who didn't consider herself very good at this sort of thing, Maggie was doing marvelously well. In fact, she was fast losing control. She wanted him, she'd wanted him since the first moment she saw him, and that urgency was greater than any awkward self-consciousness or doubt or even care for the future. When he'd said "over" she'd felt as if all the color had gone out of her world and it was just bland. Just ... nothing.

In the short time since she'd known him, Maggie admitted she had fallen completely under his spell.

His hands slid down to cup her bottom and he groaned in her mouth. She felt the hard shape of his arousal in the notch of her thighs, right where she wanted it. Her body was more than ready and she felt alive in a way she could never remember having felt before.

"Maggie." Lorne was breathing hard. "I want you. I want to stay with you."

"Then stay." She held his face between her hands. "Stay here with me."

His mouth covered hers again and she kissed him with a desperation she didn't attempt to hide. Her breasts ached and the swollen flesh between her thighs ached more, and she wanted so much to drag him upstairs to bed.

"I know it won't be easy," she said when she came up for breath. "But I have some ideas. We could work it out."

There was a stillness about him. Something was wrong, she thought, and he wasn't telling her. Didn't he know that the worst thing for Maggie was dishonesty? She had been lied to before. She could not be lied to again, especially not by him.

He reached up and gently removed her arms from around his neck and stepped out of their embrace. "I could die tonight, Maggie. We can't get involved."

Was he being noble? The wicked 4th Marquis of Lorne was playing the hero again, damn him.

"I *want* to get involved," she said, her voice filled with emotion. "Come to bed with me."

There, she'd said it. Oh God, she really had said it.

Passion flared like blue fire in his eyes. "Maggie," he said softly. But she knew that he wanted to say yes. He might even have weakened and done so, but at that moment Sutcliffe walked in on them.

The big man took one look, muttered something, turned on his heel and walked out again.

Maggie put her hands over her face with a groan. When she peeped through her fingers Lorne looked beyond frustrated. He tilted his head back and glared up at the dingy ceiling and cursed in his usual fluent manner.

Then he followed Sutcliffe back into the other room, saying over his shoulder, "Take the shotgun with you, Maggie." Those eyes of his bored into hers a moment longer, and he was gone.

Maggie took a deep breath. She was sure he wanted to stay with her. She might be wrong; it was possible, but she thought he very much wanted to stay. So what was wrong? What wasn't he telling her? Well he couldn't keep silent forever.

Meanwhile she couldn't stay here cogitating.

She needed to set aside her rioting emotions and concentrate on the practicalities. Her visit to the village for supplies. She had to admit it would be good to get away for a while. It was rather intimidating having the Hellfire Club constantly looking over her shoulder.

She fetched her bag, coat and gloves upstairs. Tugging her pink hat down over her wild curls she came into the sitting room to collect the shotgun.

The three men were gathered around the table, still talking in low voices. There was a definite tension in the air, as if they'd been arguing. In fact, as Maggie stepped into the sudden silence, she was sure of it.

She looked about at them, hoping for some clues

to the cause, but they avoided her eyes and said nothing.

"I'll be back soon," she said, picking up the gun and holding it with the barrel pointed toward the floor, finger off the trigger.

"Watch out for the Destroyer, Maggie," Sutcliffe warned.

"Don't be taken in by his tricks," Darlington added with a meaningful nod. Then, with a quick glance at Lorne, "By *anyone's* tricks."

Lorne ignored him. "I should come with you," he said, and started to get to his feet.

Maggie lightly touched his shoulder. "We've been over this. I'll be back in no time. Stay here and plot."

Lorne seemed to be on the verge of insisting before he dropped back into the chair. He reached up for her hand just as she removed it and their fingers brushed. She turned away, knowing her face was flushed, and that the others were watching.

Loki wagged his tail from his place by the fire and she bent to rub his head before heading to the door.

"Well, um, see you soon then," she said, a bit too awkwardly.

They nodded, their faces as gloomy as she'd ever seen them. Whatever it was that had soured their mood, Maggie was relieved to close the door and leave them to it.

Chapter Nineteen

LORNE LISTENED TO THE SOUND of Maggie driving away. His two friends were silent, their faces closed, but he knew them well enough to understand they weren't pleased with him. Reluctantly, he realized he needed to have this out with them before they could hunt the demon. Once on its trail there could be no disharmony to distract them.

"Say what you're thinking."

Sutcliffe cleared his throat. The way he looked at Lorne was almost apologetic. "You won't like it."

"I'm sure I won't, Aiden. But I would hear it anyway. Nicholas?"

Darlington placed his hands flat on the table. There was a flush along his cheekbones. He was angry, and struggling to stay calm.

"Maggie has become a friend to us. She didn't have to. She could have run or sent us away, but she stayed to help."

Sutcliffe chimed in. "She's courageous and a genuinely good person. I'd forgotten what one looked like."

"And your point is?"

"That she isn't one of your Hellfire Club whores, Lorne. She doesn't need you buggering up her life."

Lorne's mouth tightened into a hard white line. He was furious, but not for the reasons they were thinking. "Is that what you think I'm doing?"

"I don't know what to think," Darlington said, shaking his head. "Perhaps you believe you have feelings for her. You've both been through a lot in a short time ... I would give you the benefit of the doubt, but I've seen the way you charm women into loving you and then discard them. Too many times."

There was a gleam in Darlington's eyes, as if he genuinely hated his friend, and it seemed to startle even him. Darlington rubbed a hand over his scar, fingering the length of it, reminding himself of a time in his past that he did not enjoy visiting.

Sutcliffe finished for him. "Even if you do have feelings for her, and I suppose there is a first time for everything, she's too good for you, Charles. You would only hurt her, and she does not deserve that."

Lorne fought with his anger. He told himself that his friends' concern for Maggie was a good thing, and that their assumptions shouldn't surprise him. It was exactly what he would have done, once upon a time. Yet despite all his rationalizing, he was hurt.

"Whatever lies between Maggie and me is none of your business. But because of the years of friendship between us, I will do you the courtesy of answering you." He tried to remain cool and rational, but couldn't stop the bitterness that leaked into his voice. "I have no intention of seducing

Maggie and discarding her. I don't intend to add to her misery. When you saw us a moment ago, Aiden, I was telling her exactly that. She's better off without me."

They eyed him with suspicion. "It didn't look like you were saying that," Sutcliffe said darkly. "It looked like you were about to ravish her."

"You've never said no before," Darlington added.

"Well I did tonight."

Loki came and sat between them, an anxious whine growing in him.

They all still seemed inclined to argue but Lorne had had enough. He could tell them about his bargain with the Sorceress, make excuses, try to explain how he had been forced to relive his mistakes for centuries while in limbo, to see the harm he had done to others. His mind and his heart had been opened. He was no longer the same man. But he didn't want to explain. He shouldn't have to. All of that was between Maggie and himself, and when he told her, as he knew he must, then they would know too.

"We could die tonight," he reminded them. "Die without hope of coming back. The Destroyer could finish us off. Why are we arguing? We need to focus on what we have to do to save ourselves and all the other poor souls in the demon's path. Agreed?"

As he'd hoped, the reminder of the immensity of the situation had a sobering effect.

Sutcliffe and Darlington exchanged a glance before they reached to shake his hand. "I apologize if I mistook the situation," the former said. "It was a simple mistake to make," said the latter.

Lorne was about to remark that neither Sutcliffe nor Darlington were perfect themselves when the sound of a machine approaching the cottage caught their attention. It was far too soon for Maggie to have returned and it didn't sound like Maggie's Rover. He went to the window and carefully lifted the edge of the blind.

The light was fading but he was able to see another horseless carriage outside, a small silver-colored one. As he watched, a door opened and a woman climbed out. She wore a heavy black coat, and her hair, under a dark hat, was fair and hung down her back in a long straight waterfall. When she began to walk toward the cottage, Lorne noticed she was wearing black boots with very high heels. They were hardly suited for the ground she walked on.

Loki had come up beside him and growled. Lorne reached down to soothe him without taking his eyes off the woman. "I agree," he said to the dog. "We don't need visitors."

"What should we do?" Sutcliffe stood behind them and was watching the woman as well. "Pretend we're not here?"

She was at the door and they heard her knock. She stepped back, tilting her head back to look up at the bedroom windows, rubbing her gloved hands together and blowing into them. After a moment she knocked again, louder and more insistently. Clearly she wasn't going to go away.

"We can't hide in here like virgins at a rogering ball," Sutcliffe whispered aloud.

Now the woman was pounding on the door, shaking the whole framework.

"Enough. I'll send her off." Darlington limped

over to the door and flung it open.

The woman jumped back in fright, her gloved hands going to her face. "Sweet Jesus!"

"Another bloody Scot," Lorne muttered, but his heart wasn't in it.

The woman was sizing Darlington up with a hard stare. "Who are you?" she demanded. She had dark eyes, like Maggie's, and there was a resemblance in her features, but she was shorter in stature and her straight hair was nothing like Maggie's wild, dark curls.

Darlington blocked her entrance and seemed momentarily lost for words, so Lorne stepped in. At the sight of him, her eyes widened and then almost immediately narrowed. She seemed unimpressed and looked back at Darlington.

"I *said*, who the bloody hell are you?"

"We're friends of Maggie," Lorne drawled in his most aristocratic manner. "Might I ask who you are?"

She made a puffing sound, which seemed to suggest she also wasn't impressed by his attempt to mollify her. That was definitely a Maggie trait. By now Lorne was certain they were blood relatives.

"If you're really friends with Maggie then you'd know who I am," she said, daring them to convince her.

Lorne smiled. "You're her sister," he guessed. "Linny."

Her expression turned wary but it confirmed he was right. So, not just another Scotswoman but another McNab. It was just what they didn't need right now.

"Excuse me." Linny pushed past Darlington, who

seemed to have lost his mental faculties, giving him a curious sideways glance as she squeezed by.

"Where's Maggie?" she demanded. Loki had come over to inspect her, and she reached down to ruffle his mane, unfazed by the presence of such a large dog.

What was it about the McNab sisters? Did nothing frighten them? But then again Lorne reminded himself that Maggie had been frightened of one thing—her feelings for him, and he had to admit that he was rather alarmed by them himself. They were so strong, so intense, and unstoppable. A pity there was no chance of anything coming of them.

Sutcliffe answered her question. "She went to the village."

"Good lord, there's *three* of you in here?"

Sutcliffe sat down on the arm of the chair, to reduce his size and make himself less threatening. "She left to get some, ah, groceries at the cash and carry. And to see her team at the pub." Only the roll of his eyes toward Lorne hinted at his discomfort with this strange conversation.

"Are you part of her team?" asked Linny.

"No, but you could say she is part of ours," said Lorne.

"She should be back soon." Darlington added, finally closing the door and limping toward her. "We have to leave soon. We have an appointment at the abbey."

"The abbey?" Linny turned to look at him. "I thought the nutter who owned it didn't let anybody in. That's what Maggie told me, anyway. What makes you three so special?"

She had that abrasive way of speaking, even more

so than Maggie, as if she wanted answers and meant to get them.

"We're *very* special," Darlington said, his thin lips curling in a smile. With the scar running down the side of his face and his brown hair tied back with a narrow ribbon, he had all the appearance of a pirate trying to look respectable. A ring in his ear and a cutlass to brandish and the cameo would be complete.

"Oh, I can see that. *Very* special." Linny looked over him, but there was a spark in her dark eyes that belied her mockery. Darlington's smile broadened.

Surprised, Sutcliffe and Lorne exchanged a glance. Darlington … flirting? Next the sky would rain frogs.

Linny turned her back on Darlington. "I need to talk to Maggie." Loki followed her across the sitting room as she took off her gloves and removed her coat. Without it she was slim, though not so tall as Maggie. Her boots probably gave her a good five inches more than she deserved.

Darlington followed her and Loki. "Maggie may be a while," he said, watching with interest as she removed her hat. Her hair shone in the firelight and she flipped a stray strand over her shoulder.

"You just said she'd be back soon," she countered, tossing her coat onto the sofa and flopping down beside them as if she intended to stay the night. "Very well. I'll just have to wait."

Darlington stood looking down at her, still smiling, again unheard of for the man. She stared back at him as if this was some sort of contest of wills between them.

Finally Linny turned to the fire and held out her hands. "I've driven all the way from Glasgow so I'm not about to turn around and go back without seeing my sister, now am I?"

Loki came and rested his head on her knee. She laughed and gently pulled at his ears. "Aren't you a sweetie? What's his name?"

"Loki," Sutcliffe said, as uneasy as Lorne at the way the woman had walked in and made herself at home.

"A Norse god, eh? Full of mischief, are we?" Her eye then fell on the hand-drawn map on the table and she leaned closer to see it, frowning. "What's this? Looks like the London Underground. You're not terrorists are you?"

Lorne wasn't sure what she meant by terrorists, but he got the gist. He could see that as soon as the words were spoken Linny regretted them. She cleared her throat as she waited for his answer.

"This is a map of the tunnels beneath the abbey," Darlington said, ignoring Lorne's warning look. "We're here to inspect them."

Linny nodded, but she didn't appear entirely convinced. "What for?"

Darlington had run out of ideas. He turned to the other two for assistance.

"We can't discuss it. We work for the National Trust," Lorne told her in his most authoritative voice, hoping that would be the end of it.

Linny was unimpressed. "So you're not archeologists?"

All three of them hurried to assure her they were.

She didn't seem to give much credit to their hasty agreement. "So what are you looking for that you can't discuss?"

"Bones," blurted out Sutcliffe. "Human bones."

The fire crackled. Outside it was darker than ever and Lorne glanced at the window. As soon as Maggie returned they needed to get to the abbey and begin their search—but now they had the problem of what to do with Linny.

"Tell me," she invited them in a voice that only pretended to be friendly, "*why* are you going to the abbey in the dark with a map of the tunnels looking for bones? Wouldn't it make more sense to do that in daylight?"

Lorne was getting impatient. "It doesn't matter down there. It's always dark."

"Yes, but with overtime it would be less expensive to work during the day. Or are you vampires? Lestat and all that?" Her dark eyes lingered a moment on Lorne in his black suit.

Maggie had mentioned that name and he had a good memory. "No, we're not from Anne Rice's novels," he replied, feeling clever.

Linny gave a laugh that was rather attractive. "Lestat was always Maggie's favorite. And then she went and married Simon, who was the least vampire-like man I'd ever met. This dig was for him, you know—for his memory anyway. But you must know that, you being her friends."

"Of course," Lorne sounded bored.

Linny's eyes narrowed. "So, how is Maggie? Is she eating properly?"

"I made her bacon and eggs this morning. She calls it my signature dish."

Suspicion filled Linny's eyes. He'd said too much. He glanced at the window again. Where *was* she?

It was nearly full dark now.

"There is nothing for you to be concerned about," he said, before she could find more questions to throw at them.

Linny tossed another lock of hair over her shoulder. "Look, maybe I'm totally wrong, but I get the feeling there's an undercurrent here. I don't know whether I believe all this talk of tunnels and bones and I don't really care. Maggie and I have … a connection, I suppose you'd call it. I always know when she's in trouble and she's the same with me. I had that feeling very strongly last night. That's why I'm here. Only she's not here, but three strangers looking over underground maps are. So you tell me, what am I supposed to think?"

Lorne reached for the map and used the process of folding it up as an excuse not to meet her eyes. "Maggie isn't in trouble. She'll be back soon. Then she can tell you herself. Please wait here for her."

Linny's mouth took on a mulishness reminiscent of her sister. "Oh, I will," she said. "I'll do just that. And if she isn't back very soon then I'll go out looking for her. Or maybe I will just call the police."

The three men exchanged alarmed glances.

"I *knew* it. There is something wrong."

"Are you always like this?" Darlington demanded, finally losing patience.

"Like what?"

"Like a dog with a rabbit."

Linny didn't seem to care for the comparison. "Maggie is my sister and I've looked after her since she was little. She might think she's grown up but I happen to believe her wellbeing is still very much my business. Don't you have brothers or sisters?"

Darlington frowned. "No," he said. "I only have Lorne and Sutcliffe. They are my friends and my family."

"Okay. Well, let me just ask you this. What was Maggie wearing when she went out?"

Did she think they had her sister tied up somewhere? Lorne sighed. This was growing tedious. "Her blue trousers and black boots, her blue coat and blue gloves. Her rose pink hat. And she took the brown bag she carries over her shoulder and her phone in her pocket." He felt it wise to leave out mention of the shotgun, under the circumstances.

"Anything else?" Her eyebrows went up.

He thought. "And Mary, she was wearing her pendant of Mary."

Linny's lips quirked up. "You do know her. Sorry, I just had to be sure. You must understand how weird this is, coming all the way down here and finding three complete strangers in her cottage."

"Maggie was generous enough to invite us to stay," said Lorne.

"Loki adores her," Sutcliffe added, giving his highest praise.

"And she has my undying gratitude," finished Darlington.

A smile split Linny's face. "Well I'm very glad to hear it. Now I have just one more question." She leaned forward and her smiles were all gone. "Who the fuck are you, really?"

Chapter Twenty

MAGGIE REACHED THE VILLAGE SAFELY. Not that she expected it to be otherwise—she was wise to the Destroyer's tricks and felt ready for anything. He wouldn't fool her next time.

It was getting dark, the rain clouds moving in again, so she hurried into the shop, threw whatever she thought they might need into a basket, and carried it groaning to the counter. The woman—Maggie had been introduced but the name escaped her—eyed her with amusement.

"Dog food? I didn't know you had a dog, Professor McNab."

"I don't really. It's a stray that just turned up." Actually four strays when you thought about it.

"Ah."

Maggie hesitated, wondering if it was safe to pry, but the assistant seemed friendly enough. "I heard there's a woman missing, is that right?"

She nodded and her smile vanished. "Word gets around. Mrs. Green. Her husband is beside himself. He's been looking everywhere for her."

"She cleans at the abbey, doesn't she?"

"Yes. He's rung there but Mr. Stewart hasn't seen

her either."

"Has he called the police?" Maggie knew that was the next logical next step but she also knew it would create all sorts of problems if the police came face to face with the members of the Hellfire Club.

"He has," the woman said, "but they seem to think it's too soon to panic. Want to wait until the morning, but they're keeping an eye out all the same."

"The morning?"

By morning it should all be over, the Destroyer recaptured and Lorne free from his bonds. Then why wasn't she smiling? Maggie tugged her hat further down over her head. Because there was something wrong, and whatever it was loomed like a dark shadow over their future.

Or was she fooling herself? Was she investing too much in what, to the wicked Marquis, had probably been nothing more than a brief flirtation? She was finally thinking with her heart, for the first time since Simon's passing, and of all the men she'd been drawn toward, it had to be a notorious womanizer who probably didn't understand the meaning of the word faithful.

"I hope Mrs. Green turns up," she said to the shop assistant, and heaved her groceries out to the vehicle.

Her next stop was the pub. Lisa was playing billiards in the lounge, and caught sight of Maggie as she struck one of the balls with her cue. Maggie had her story all ready—Owen was staying at the abbey and it was too good a chance for him to miss—but Lisa jumped in first.

"I got a text from Owen." She was beaming. "He's at the abbey. Says he's fine."

"Oh." Maggie tried to smile but perhaps something in her expression alerted Lisa.

"Is anything the matter, Professor?"

"Eh, no, no, nothing's wrong. I just … I'm glad to hear it. I was worried." Tears stung her eyes. Owen was dead and it wasn't fair. But who had sent the text? Could the Destroyer imitate his host to that extent? Dig into his memories, learn his skills? Maggie pushed away the thought, concentrating on what she had come to say.

"I've decided to give you all another day off, Lisa. Can you let everyone know? In fact, no more work until further notice."

"But why?" Lisa asked. "I thought we were up against it time wise? Have you heard from your sponsor? Is that why …?"

Maggie waved off the question. "We should be fine, but something else has come up. I can't explain, Lisa, I'm sorry. It-it's personal."

Lisa's face turned sympathetic. Maggie suspected the woman thought she was having an emotional crisis, possibly a delayed reaction to Simon's death. Best if Lisa believed it was something like that. In fact, anything would do, as long as she and the others didn't go wandering around the graveyard.

When Maggie left Lisa gave her a hug, making her feel uncomfortable for lying, and wishing this whole horrible mess was over. At the same time, and she knew this was a selfish wish, she never wanted it to end. Because she wasn't sure what would happen to Lorne once the demon was caught.

How could she have fallen so hard for a man

she had only just met? She'd heard of these things happening, usually in books or movies, and her practical self had always scoffed at the idea. She could hear her voice now, after seeing one such movie with Linny, holding forth about people with no self-control.

"But it was *Keanu Reeves*," Linny had explained patiently. "I mean, obviously Sandra Bullock was going to fall in love with him."

"Obviously?" Maggie had repeated, voice dripping with sarcasm.

"They went through a lot together in a short time. They faced death in each other's arms. It was falling in love on steroids, sis."

Linny was right, who'd have thought it? Being thrown into a dangerous and chaotic situation had stripped everything down to the bone. She'd fallen in love. There, she'd admitted it. She was in love with the Marquis of Lorne.

She didn't want to be without him. She didn't want to find herself alone again, her life stretching out before her, with nothing to look forward to. These past few days had been the most exciting she'd ever known. Of course, they'd also been the most emotionally wrenching, and although she didn't want a repeat of all that, she couldn't regret meeting the members of the Hellfire Club.

Who would have thought that a girl from the wrong side of Glasgow and a Marquis from the distant past would find they had so much in common? And who would have thought that their desire would give off enough sparks to light up the night sky?

Speaking of which, with a glance at the encroaching darkness, she realised she'd better get back to the cottage.

Maggie climbed into the Land Rover, switched on the headlights, and pulled away from the pub.

Almost immediately, another car pulled out in front of her.

Maggie slammed on her brakes, expecting to feel the thud of a collision, but the car—a Golf—sped off in front of her, only to slow down again.

"Are you drunk?" Maggie shouted.

Not that he could hear her, but he'd given her a fright. Maggie set the Rover in motion again, but the car in front had slowed so much that she knew she'd have to pass it if she was to get home before dawn.

Muttering a few choice words she pulled out to go around him. They had the whole road to themselves so she took her time, keeping a close eye on the other car. The light in the village was poor, there were few street lights, but there was something about the shape of the driver's head, something …

The shock was like a punch in the chest.

The man behind the wheel had his profile to her but even so she recognized him. Knew him as well as she knew herself. At the same time, she knew this could not possibly be true.

Simon was dead. He was *dead*!

He turned to her, staring straight at her, and she saw that he was crying, his face crumpled up with grief, tears shining wet on his cheeks. Before she could call out or do anything other than stare, he'd driven off.

Maggie didn't realize she'd stopped. Not until

one of the few users of this road had driven up behind her and tapped their horn. Hands shaking, throat tight, eyes stinging, Maggie raised her hand in an apology and slowly began to move again.

Far ahead she could still see the Golf, and the vehicle turned down the very road she was about to take. Was he going to the cottage, too?

She followed, staying back, her mind still trying to come to grips with a matter that was beyond her understanding. How could Simon, *her* Simon, be here now? But no answers came to enlighten her. His being here was unimaginable—another impossible thing to add to the rest. And yet the image of his face, his tears, wrenched at her heart in a way that left her feeling utterly lost and defense-less.

The Golf reached the intersection and slowed. Left would take it to the cottage, and right to the abbey.

It turned right.

Maggie slowed down, hesitating, torn. But this was Simon. The Destroyer could be involved, of course she'd thought of that, but how could the Destroyer have taken over Simon's body? Simon's ashes were scattered over the sea near Moyle. There was no body to possess.

But what if … what if those ashes hadn't been his body?

She felt a building urgency to see him properly, to speak to him and touch him. She had to know if he really was Simon, her Simon.

Fully aware that she was doing something reck-less and stupid, but unable to stop herself, Maggie turned right and followed the Golf.

Lorne had pulled up the blind and now stood at the window staring out. It was full dark. The trees appeared to be crowding around the cottage, as if they were playing that childhood game where he imagined them shuffling closer every time he turned his back on them.

Where is she?

Maggie should have been back by now. Why the hell hadn't he gone with her?

Behind him he could see the reflections of Sutcliffe and Loki, tucking into a cake they'd dug out of the cold box in the kitchen. It had been as hard as rock when they'd found it, and it had taken some time for it to thaw it out by the fire. Out in the kitchen, Linny was making herself a mug of coffee, and Darlington seemed to think he was helping. Or perhaps he just liked watching her.

They'd given her their real names, though without the titles. She'd made a sarcastic comment about "Chums of Biggles, are you?" and although Lorne didn't know who Biggles was he understood she was making an observation about their position in society. He was sure now that Maggie hadn't contacted Linny at all, and that Linny had arrived because she had an uneasy feeling. Part of their emotional bond.

"She should be back." Lorne said it aloud. He wanted to do something, and if he'd been in his own time there were many things he could have done. Saddled his horse and set out to find her, sent his men scouring the woods with torches … In fact, in his time she would never have gone at all. They had servants for that sort of thing.

But in this world he was powerless and he'd never felt it more than right now.

"She probably found she had more to do than she thought," Sutcliffe suggested, his mouth full of cake. He swallowed and gave Lorne a sheepish look. "My apologies for before. I don't think you would harm Maggie, at least I don't think so any more. That was Darlington's idea and although at the time he seemed to make sense, I can see now …"

Surprised, Lorne stared at him. "What can you see now?"

"You're worried about her. Genuinely. I don't think you've ever been worried about anyone before. Well, not a woman anyway. And when you look at her you have an expression on your face that I can't say I've ever seen you wear."

The urge to say something sarcastic, to retreat to his former scornful self, was almost overwhelming. Instead he said, "I would never hurt a hair on her head, Aiden. I would die myself rather than allow harm to befall Maggie."

His friend looked too shocked to answer at first, and then he grinned. "Good," he said. Loki nudged his hand, and he handed over another slice of cake which the dog snapped up greedily.

Darlington and Linny were laughing in the kitchen.

Sutcliffe raised an eyebrow. "Uhm, Lorne, have you noticed anything different about our ill-tempered friend?" he asked, dropping his voice. "He seems to have developed both a conscience *and* a sense of humor."

Lorne had been thinking more of his own transformation but it was true, he had noticed Darlington behaving in odd ways. Had something similar happened to him as he lay sleeping? And if so, what about Sutcliffe?

The big man was still watching him, chewing reflectively on the last piece of cake. "You and Darlington were always tricky fellows," he said. "I wasn't sure at first, I mean after we were all awoken by the Sorceress, but I think I'm right, aren't I, Lorne? You've changed, and so has he."

Relief flooded him. For a moment he wanted to throw his arms around his friend and hug him in gratitude, but perhaps that would be a little much for them both.

"It was two hundred years." There was so much else he wanted to say but the words jammed in his throat and refused to come out.

Sutcliffe seemed to understand. He nodded. "Don't feel much different myself," he said. "And Loki hasn't changed a bit. Maybe it was just you and Darlington."

Lorne smiled. "Perhaps." He turned back to the window and his smile faded. Where is she? He needed to see her before they left, in case …well, it might well be their last moment together.

He frowned. Had the trees actually moved closer? He shook his head at his own madness. That was a game he'd played when he was a child, a fantasy he'd frightened himself silly with. Mrs. Noakes had coaxed him out of it. After his mother died it had been his nanny who'd taken her place and loved him, giving him teacups of happiness in an ocean of misery.

He'd carried that pain with him into adulthood but it was time to free himself of it. There were far more dangerous matters to deal with than walking trees. If all went to plan and they captured the Destroyer, then he would just have to beg the Sorceress to let him say goodbye to Maggie before she sent him back, and hope that somewhere beneath that glittering awfulness she knew what it was to have a heart.

"We have to go," he said quietly. "We can't wait any longer for her."

"She'll understand. We must catch the Destroyer," Sutcliffe said with all the confidence he could muster. That was the thing about Sutcliffe; he was a relaxed sort, and took the good with the bad. A far less highly strung character than either Lorne or Darlington.

"Yes, she'll understand," Lorne murmured, and hoped she would. She had her life at least, and surely that was worth whatever happened to him.

"You don't think the Sorceress will send us home?" Sutcliffe asked suddenly. "Or back to the pet cemetery? Ye gods, anything but that!"

"Don't you want to go home?" Lorne asked curiously. "Don't you miss it?"

Sutcliffe shook his head. "You'd think there might be something back there I'd miss, but there isn't. The three of us are here together and I have Loki. This is a new world, full of new wonders to explore. Why would I want to go back?"

Lorne rubbed his ribs, though they no longer hurt, while he considered his next words. It seemed he had fully healed, far faster than he had expected.

"If I'm no longer here once we are finished," he said hesitantly. "Will you promise me something, Sutcliffe? Will you watch over Maggie for me? I don't mean you should touch her or hold her or—" He stopped, glaring, as the big man gave his deep laugh.

"Watch but don't touch?" With a frown as he took in what else Lorne had said, he added, "But why are you asking me that? Has the Sorceress told you something?"

"In case I die. Nothing is certain with the demon. It'll put up a fight."

Sutcliffe gave a grimace, unconvinced, but before he could question Lorne further the clock on the mantelpiece struck the hour.

Loki came to his feet, alert, tail wagging. Linny stepped in from the kitchen with a mug in her hands, smiling back over her shoulder at Darlington behind her.

He looked flushed, Lorne thought. And young and … could it be … *happy*? It was so long since he'd seen that expression on Darlington's face that he barely recognized it.

"It's time to go." Sutcliffe gave Darlington a meaningful look.

At once Darlington sobered.

"Yes, we have to go," Lorne agreed. Again he wished Maggie was here, but then he thought that perhaps it was just as well she wasn't. She'd want to come with them, and this undertaking was too dangerous for her. He wanted her far away from the demon, even if it meant that his promise to the Sorceress might mean he never saw her again.

"So, what do I do?" Linny's belligerent voice

snapped him out of his dismal thoughts. He realized she was probably worried and trying to hide it, just as Lorne hid his anxiety with a sarcastic tone.

"Stay here and wait for Maggie," he said in a voice gentler than any he'd used so far with her. "Tell her we're at the abbey, doing what we came to do, and that she should stay here with you until we return."

Linny considered this. "And if she doesn't come back?"

"Why shouldn't she? She's only gone to the village." He dared her to suggest otherwise.

She looked ready for a fight when Darlington came to the rescue. "She'll be back soon," he said, his voice also gentle.

She smiled at him. She was an attractive woman, but there was a toughness about her that spoke of difficult times in the past. The McNab sisters were not weaklings.

"All right," she said, turning to Lorne and narrowing her eyes again. "I'll wait here. But if she doesn't turn up in the next hour I'll be following you up to the abbey."

Linny sipped her coffee as if there was no more to be said on the matter.

Without Maggie's supplies from the village, they had had to make do with the rope and a length of chain they'd found at the back of the cottage, as well as some stout sticks to use as cudgels. The shotgun would have been helpful but they could manage without it. They'd collected together these items and left them outside, ready to carry them. If the Destroyer was occupying someone else's body—perhaps this Mrs. Green Maggie had mentioned—then it would only be a matter of time before it needed another victim. To do that it must return to its native state, and that was when it was at its most vulnerable. Lorne knew they could wait no longer.

They saw Linny peer out of the window, but now that it was completely dark she couldn't make out what they were doing. Just as well, or she'd be asking more questions. If luck was on their side they would be finished before Maggie returned and one or both of the McNab sisters came hurrying out to find them.

"Are we ready?" Lorne's breath puffed white as he turned to his friends.

"Aye," the other two answered.

"Then let us go forth, my friends. Tonight, we make things right."

* * *

The ground in the woods was soft as they wound their way between the trees. By avoiding the road they'd save time and miles, but the air was bitterly cold and the terrain more difficult than he remembered. Loki skipped ahead, excited by this unexpected outing.

"We could do with the Sorceress now," Sutcliffe growled, hunching his shoulders in his coat, which was too small for him but had been the best Maggie could provide from her wardrobe. "Why doesn't she come and give us a hand?"

"You know why," Darlington snapped. "This is penance. She wants us to deal with the mess we've made." His leg was hurting and his face looked pinched and pale, the scar standing out starkly in the pale smudge of moonlight that had managed to penetrate the clouds. At least it had stopped raining.

Regret filled Lorne. He wished this wasn't happening. It was his fault, the blame was his alone, and although they had been happy to go along with him, he knew Sutcliffe and Darlington would never have unleashed the Destroyer onto the world. They'd always followed him, and he had led them into very bad waters indeed.

There was a rough justice in the Sorceress's ways, insisting they pit themselves alone against the demon. Innocent lives would be lost in the struggle and it was up to them as to how many they could save. It was also up to them whether they ultimately triumphed or failed, and Lorne didn't want to fail. He was resolved to show the world that he was a different man to the one he'd been before.

He needed to show Maggie. What she thought of him was suddenly of paramount importance. Even if he never saw her again after tonight—and that was more than likely—he wanted her to know he had faced the challenge and did not falter.

The sound of Darlington's voice brought him back. "Ah, here we are."

There ahead, through the close growing trees, he could see the dark shape of Blackfriars Abbey.

He was home.

Chapter Twenty-One

SIMON'S CAR WAS NOWHERE TO be seen. Maggie pulled into the carriage drive in front of the abbey and slowed the Land Rover, looking for any hiding places. Nothing. Perhaps he'd parked it round the back? Maybe Mr. Stewart was using one of the old barns as a garage?

The darkness was warning her to get back to the cottage but she sat in the silent vehicle on the edge of the driveway, in full view of the house, uncertain how to proceed. Then she saw a shadow, someone striding along the front of the building, making for the main steps, guarded by twin stone lions, worn by age.

Simon.

She recognized the shape of him and the tilt of his head. Even his walk was so familiar. It *was* Simon.

Maggie's heart leapt. She wanted to rush out of the car and rush into his arms. She wanted it so much it physically hurt to stop herself. But deep inside there was no joy, just a terrible aching doubt. She knew this wasn't right, that it couldn't be real. Hadn't she sat by her husband's bed and watched him take his last breath? Sat through the service at the crematorium? And the final moment on Moyle, with the sea crashing on the shore, and his ashes falling into the swirling grey waters.

Whoever this was it was not, *could* not be, Simon. Could it?

Maggie gave a dry sob. Her fingers clenched on the wheel. She watched Simon walk up the steps to the door. He paused there a moment, his head bent, as if he felt her gaze upon him. She bit her lip, waiting for him to turn, but he didn't. A moment later he'd pushed opened the door and disappeared inside.

For what seemed an age she sat in the dark, silent Land Rover, her eyes fixed on the abbey. Lorne would be waiting for her at the cottage. They all would. She had the equipment they needed and they'd be eager to come here and hunt the Destroyer. She knew she had to tell them what was happening. She had to turn around right now and drive back.

But she also knew in her heart she wasn't going to do that.

Her mind was whirling with what-ifs and she seemed to have no control over them. What if this really was Simon and somehow the Sorceress had brought him back from the dead? She'd done it for Lorne, after all. What if he was alive again, and waiting for her? What if the Destroyer had taken his soul and copied his body, and her Simon had been wrenched from the peaceful place he should be and into some pit of hell?

She had to find out.

Legs trembling, Maggie climbed from the vehicle

and stood huddled in her coat in the chill night air. A sliver of moon rose over the roof of the Abbey and she stared up at it, thinking of it as a sign, beckoning her onwards.

All the same she reached back into the vehicle and found the reassuring shape of her shotgun. Keeping the barrel pointed downwards, just as Simon had taught her, she made her way along the driveway, before she cut across the withered stalks of the perennial border toward the back of the Abbey.

Walking in the front door might be quicker and more dramatic, but it made more sense to investigate the lay of the land first. She wanted to be the hunter, not the hunted.

And when you find him, what then?

Maggie didn't know, only that when the time came she would make that decision.

The three men paused at the edge of the woods, staring down at the dark bulk of the abbey. The moon that had lit their way had vanished behind the clouds, and it was only their familiarity with the grounds that kept them from getting lost.

"Do we go in the front? Find Stewart first?" Sutcliffe asked, his hand on Loki's collar to prevent him running ahead. The dog seemed to have picked up a scent, and they hoped it was the demon's.

"Or we could go straight to the back and down into the tunnels?" Darlington countered.

Lorne tightened his grip on the length of chain he had looped over his shoulder. "I think we need to know where Stewart is. I don't trust him. We don't want him wandering around behind our backs. We need to lock him up first, before we start searching for the Destroyer."

There was murmured agreement, and Lorne set out their strategy. "We go in the front door and search every inch of the abbey until we find him."

Maggie could see a glow through the grimy kitchen windows. Mr. Stewart was home then, and possibly Owen too, or the demon that had taken over Owen's body. Or was he now in Mrs. Green's body?

Maggie shuddered.

She started down the outside stairs, watching her step on the piles of wet, slippery leaves. The handle turned and the door opened smoothly and silently beneath her hand. Cautiously, carrying the shotgun, she peered around the door and into the kitchen.

The room was empty. It looked exactly the same as it had earlier, when she and Lorne had come here seeking Owen. There was still a smell of burnt toast in the air and the floor beneath the soles of her boots was still slightly sticky from the broken jar of marmalade.

She stopped to listen but there was nothing to hear. The abbey could have been empty for all she could tell. And yet she had the strong sense that somewhere in this vast space there were ears listening and eyes watching, following her every move. She was not alone in Blackfriars Abbey, Maggie was certain of that.

The door that took her deeper into the servants' quarters made a little creak when she opened it but Maggie kept on, determined, all doubts swept aside. She had her shotgun, and she would not hesitate to use it if she had to, but she needed to know first. She needed to know what her dead husband was doing here.

As she climbed the plain wooden stairs, up into the shadows, there was only silence, no matter how she strained to hear. When Maggie reached the top, only the final door into the main part of the house remained, and that opened as easily as the rest.

The chandelier in the entrance hall was fully lit, and its illumination allowed Maggie to see a lot more detail than she remembered from before. Muted tapestries hung on dark paneled walls, with fine furnishings set beneath them. In fact, the place looked immaculate, like a museum, despite no one having lived here properly for years.

The neglect outside had led her to believe she would discover the same inside, but Mr. Stewart had everything shining and clean. It was as if rather than the solitary Mrs. Green there was an army of servants about, just as there must have been in Lorne's day.

A sound came from upstairs.

Maggie stared up the curve of the grand staircase. A faint light spilled down, picking out the rich jewel colors in the carpet and the gleam of pointy weapons decorating the wall above. She wondered if she should take one of the swords, but the shotgun seemed more certain. At least she could fire that. She couldn't imagine herself wielding a sword properly—she'd probably injure herself by accident.

She began to climb, listening as the murmuring sound waxed and waned. Someone was speaking in a sing song voice. Could they be reading aloud? Reciting poetry? It sounded like poetry.

She pictured Stewart up there in the gallery, reciting Byron to Lorne's portrait. The absurdity of the image made her cover her mouth to stifle a hysterical giggle.

Unless it was Simon? That sobered her. Could Simon be murmuring to himself?

Now she'd reached the top of the main staircase and stood staring at the corridors running off into infinity, their closed doors hiding unknown secrets. The second staircase beckoned her upwards to the long gallery. The sounds were definitely coming from there.

Something rattled behind her, making her heart jump, and she turned to look back the way she'd come, bringing the shotgun up at the same time. The lights flickered on and off, and a moment later she realized it was just the wind outside, shaking the windowpanes and moaning down the chimneys. The weather was turning nasty.

Would Lorne and the Hellfire Club be here soon? Surely they wouldn't wait forever for her to come home? No, they'd have set off for the Abbey to complete their task by now. They might even be outside.

The idea felt comforting in the same way she had felt in Lorne's arms and thinking of him helped too. His pale blue eyes and the way his lips quirked into a smile, as if he was fighting it every inch of the way. Yes, Lorne would be here soon. Maggie kept telling herself that, as she set her foot on the first step and began to climb.

◆

They were at the front door. The wind had risen up, whipping around them, tangling Lorne's loose dark hair into his eyes. He ignored it, focused on what was before them.

"The house first. Find Stewart and incapacitate him. Then we go down into the tunnels."

Darlington leaned on the doorframe with a grimace, as if he needed the support—his leg must be paining him. "We'll hunt the bloody demon to the ground. Just as we did the last time."

Sutcliffe grinned. "What are we waiting for then?"

With a roar, they flung open the door, sending it crashing inwards.

Only to stand frozen to the spot, jaws agape.

The abbey was now brightly lit, in complete contrast to the gloom that had greeted Lorne earlier. Revolted, he stared about him. It was as if some awful disease had been let loose here, ravaging the rooms, eating through the wainscoting, and smashing holes in walls. It had torn at the regal beauty that lived in his memory. Huge ropes of cobwebs hung from the corners and there were horrific patches of damp everywhere.

Sutcliffe and Darlington were shocked speechless. Lorne stumbled forward, turning around, staring at the awful destruction of what had once been, and he believed still was, his home.

"This can't be." His voice was hoarse with emotion. "When Maggie and I were here this morning it wasn't like this. Everything was as it used to be. How can …?" The floor creaked dangerously under his feet and he jumped back as he felt it give, his heart pounding.

The abbey was falling down around him. He could smell the mold and rot. He could sense the painful groans of its approaching death.

"You're certain?" Sutcliffe's hand was heavy on Lorne's shoulder.

Lorne glared up at him in reply.

"Then it's magic. Isn't it? What we are looking at can't be real."

"Or perhaps what you saw before wasn't real." Darlington swallowed. "Come on, Lorne. We can't stand here like virgins on their wedding night. We need to find Stewart."

Lorne stumbled after them, his heart aching. Seeing this devastation gave him no pleasure.

On the wall of the staircase a few remaining weapons hung dangerously. He paused to reach up and remove a fine rapier. It was rusty but when he ran his hand along its edge he knew it could still cause considerable damage.

His muscles flexed in readiness. Just let him discover who had allowed this vandalism to take place and he would run them through.

Sutcliffe and Darlington had seen him take the weapon and did likewise, Sutcliffe choosing a heavy broadsword and Darlington a cutlass. They nodded at one another without humor, before making their way up the stairs, in search of their prey.

Simon stood alone in the gallery, his back to her, speaking aloud. The words he spoke made no sense, and she didn't recognize the language. It was like something made up, the sounds all running together, creating a rhythm, like singing.

She stepped closer, shotgun still cradled in her arms. A tear rolled down her cheek. Followed by another.

"Simon?"

He stopped. His head came up and she saw then that he'd been reading from a sheet of paper. Parchment. The edges were yellowed and torn.

"Simon? Is that you?"

He turned and it was indeed Simon. The same face, same hesitant smile, same shoulders and arms and hands.

She wanted to run to him, to hold him tight, and yet she stayed where she was. Even though her eyes and her heart were telling her it was him, there was something, that niggle at the back of her brain, that warned her to stay put.

"Maggie." He walked toward her. "It's really you. I've missed you."

She put a hand to her trembling mouth, the tears dripping freely now. "But how? How can you be here? I don't understand."

"'There are more things in heaven and earth,'" he quoted with a smile. He cleared his throat. "On the other side … you can't begin to imagine what I've seen. Worlds, beings, possibilities."

"But *why*? Simon, why are you here?"

"My dear girl, you must know why by now," he said with a gentle loving smile. But she didn't, she didn't understand at all.

He cleared his throat again.

Maggie froze. She recognized that little nervous habit. She'd heard it only recently. Her mind replayed the scene. Mr. Stewart trying to catch up with her and Lorne on the stairs to the gallery. The sound of him clearing his throat following them every step of the way.

Instinctively she tried to hide her knowledge but it was too late, he was close enough now to read it in her eyes.

"Oh dear," Simon spoke sadly, tilting his head to the side. "And here I thought I was doing so well." Simon's odd mannerisms made the moment even more appalling.

"Mr. Stewart," she said dully. "This is a trick, isn't it? A horrible, cruel trick."

"I don't know about horrible or cruel, Professor McNab. But it is a trick. I needed to get you here, alone. And it worked, didn't it? Was it the tears? Ah yes, women can never resist a man who cries."

"You're despicable."

He smiled and she gave a sob, because he used Simon's smile.

"Could I have gotten you into bed? I wonder. Would you have let yourself be persuaded? You're a most attractive woman, Maggie, and I've been celibate for far too long. I rather liked the idea of claiming my conjugal rights."

Sickened, she brought up the shotgun barrel but he was too quick. He grabbed it out of her hands and pushed her down onto a nearby chair.

"Now be good, Maggie. You're here for a reason. This isn't about you. It's about your friend, the Marquis."

"How—?"

"Oh, I've known all along. I hate him, you see, and I want him to suffer. I could have killed him long ago, but that would have been too easy. I wanted him to feel pain first, the sort of pain I've felt for the last two hundred years."

Maggie was getting used to hearing Stewart's words in Simon's mouth. *He's not Simon*, she told herself as she glared at him. "I won't be a part of that."

Stewart laughed. "But you will, Maggie. You have no choice. I'm going to show you a side of Lorne you haven't seen before. And after that … Well, I think you're going to go right off him."

He paced away from her. She watched him anxiously, waiting for her chance to run. She planned to launch herself from the chair, but before she could move he'd began to chant in that sing-song voice again. The words spun around her, like fingers brushing against her skin, tangling in her hair, tugging at her clothing, holding her in place.

"Don't …" she gasped.

It was too late. She was spinning, whirling through space, and hurtling toward an unknown destination.

Chapter Twenty-Two

ALL THE WAY UP TO the gallery the signs of neglect and destruction continued. The three men were silent, appalled by what they saw. Furniture had simply been left to rot, and ornate wallpaper was peeling in long strips. The ceiling bulged as though water had seeped in, and was just waiting to come cascading through to cause even more damage. On the upper landing there was a vase of flowers sitting on a table covered in thick dust, but when Lorne reached to touch one of the desiccated blooms it crumbled to powder.

The elements had wrought a terrible punishment upon the abbey and yet there was more to it than that. There was something about this that was personal. Someone had *wanted* this to happen. More than that, they had actively encouraged it.

At first the long gallery appeared to be empty. More dust lay on the floor and the portraits he had admired earlier were now marked by damp, some almost unrecognizable. Lorne felt sick. Violated.

"There he is," Sutcliffe hissed, his hand tight on Loki's collar.

The short stocky figure of Mr. Stewart was

already halfway down the gallery.

Cold fury undermined Lorne's sense of caution, and he strode toward the man, cutting the air with his rapier and enjoying the deadly sound it made. This was all the American's doing!

"Mr. Stewart," he called, the Marquis at his most aristocratic. "We have come for the Destroyer. Give him up now or it will be all the worse for you."

Stewart had turned to watch their approach, but didn't seem overly concerned by what he saw. Above him on the wall was Lorne's portrait, and like the others the paint was warped and streaked with dirt. But there were also patches of black mold growing where once there had been a vista of the abbey in the distance.

"Ah, it's Mr. Rice," he said, his voice full of derision. "Or should I say the 4th Marquis of Lorne?"

Lorne's steps slowed. He was feeling the same aversion to the American that he'd felt before. There was something wrong here, something very wrong indeed, and despite all their preparations he had the sensation that they had walked into a trap.

Seeing Lorne's expression change, Stewart looked gleeful. He looked like a child who had played a trick so clever he could barely contain himself.

Lorne rested the tip of the rapier on the ground beside him, stirring the dust. Behind him, he was aware of the comforting bulk of Sutcliffe on one side and Darlington on the other. Loki pressed his muzzle into Lorne's hand. He wasn't alone, he reminded himself, and Stewart was.

"So you know who I am. Full marks to you. Now I'd like to know who you are, *Mr.* Stewart."

Stewart seemed more than eager to comply. He

grinned, full of his own conceit, then paused to perform his habitual clearing of the throat, before launching into a speech.

"I knew if I found the Destroyer and it was awoken you wouldn't be far behind. Professor McNab didn't think I was aware of her husband's real plan, that he meant to dig the barrow. It pleased me to let them believe what they needed to; after he died I'd hoped Maggie would come back to carry out his final wish, and she didn't disappoint. She's turned out to be very efficient at her job, and at fulfilling my expectations." His gaze slid past Lorne, and rested briefly on the other men. "I didn't believe I would get three for the price of one. The Hellfire Club." His voice filled with an almost sensuous satisfaction. "How marvelous."

Lorne ran his rapier through the dust, drawing a pattern, watching Stewart at the same time. "Who *are* you?"

Stewart almost quivered with excitement. "Don't you know?" he mocked. "No, of course not. Why would the selfish Marquis of Lorne bother to think of anyone but himself? But I was there all along, Lorne. I watched you from afar. While my mother ran after you and soothed you when you wept and loved you so much more than she ever loved *me* ..."

Lorne must have made an involuntary movement, because Stewart smiled.

"Aah. Understanding begins. Can you guess now who I am?"

Lorne's brain seemed mired in dust and cobwebs, just like his house, as he struggled to conjure up faces from his past. His grandmother was easy to picture, and his mother, his poor father, Mrs. Noakes, and … The realization caught him by surprise.

Stewart had been closely watching him and now he nodded his head in agreement. "Yes. The miserable little bastard who was your shadow. Hoping against hope for a kind word or a crumb of affection. Oh, not from you," he added quickly. "I never liked you. From my own mother."

Was it possible? Lorne barely remembered him. Truly the child had been a shadow, unimportant and rarely acknowledged, certainly not by the family. Mrs. Noakes's bastard child, much younger than Lorne, living on the fringes of Abbey life. But how could he have become powerful enough to be here, now? Because if Stewart, or Noakes, was telling the truth, then it was *he* who had pulled the strings and manipulated Maggie, using her to bring Lorne out of his grave and back to life.

"The Sorceress," he began.

Stewart snorted. "That absurd woman? She thinks she knows everything, but she knows nothing. I have run circles around her for two hundred years."

Sutcliffe and Darlington exchanged glances.

"I don't remember you," Darlington said, a sneer in his voice, "and the abbey was my second home."

Stewart shot him a look of indifference then turned back to Lorne. "That Egyptian who came with the runes you needed to bring forth the Destroyer … do you remember him? It amused him to stick around, and see what chaos resulted—I don't think he had much faith in your ability to control the demon, Lorne. Why was that, do you think? But I must not deviate from my story. One afternoon he came across me in the woods, alone as usual, and saw my potential. And I his. It was I who persuaded him to cast a spell to lock the door to Hell. At first he was doubtful, but I played upon his conceit. I did not want you to escape, Marquis—the underworld was too good for you. It worked out well in the end though, didn't it?"

It was Stewart who had been instrumental in locking the door. Was he the 'other' the Sorceress had spoken of? Was Stewart his true nemesis?

The man was rambling on. "After my mother was killed by *your* stupidity the Egyptian took me with him. I like to think he was too afraid to leave me behind—afraid for his own sake, that is."

"Took you where?" Darlington demanded, gripping his cutlass.

Stewart waved an arm. "Everywhere. He taught me all he knew—he was lonely too, you see—and when he wasn't teaching me, he was beating me, or using me for his own pleasure. But I knew how to survive, so I was patient and I waited, and when I had learned all that he had to offer, I killed him."

Lorne felt an ominous chill. He wanted to scoff and call Stewart a liar, but this had the brutal ring of truth to it. He believed Stewart really had been waiting for two hundred years to tell his story.

As the man waffled on, none of them said a word.

"I have lived a long life. Mostly in America. I waited and plotted, and eventually the stars aligned, and I returned to the abbey. I had to lie about my history, of course, but finally this place was mine. And see what I have done." He waved his arm around them. "My great work. Of course I masked it at first, so as not to frighten you off, but now I want you to see it all clearly."

So this was his revenge? Lorne admitted it was truly dreadful, but he reminded himself it was just wood and stone. Did Stewart really believe someone like Lorne could be turned into a quivering wreck by an act of vandalism? If so, then the man still had a lot to learn.

"Oh, but I'm not finished yet." The man spoke quietly, and Lorne realized he'd been watching him again, reading his thoughts.

"I think you are," said Lorne.

"Oh no, not by a long way," Stewart assured him. "I still have my final act to perform. My piece de resistance, Marquis. Can you guess what it is?"

"All of this was because you were jealous of me?" Lorne's voice dripped with sarcasm, as cruel as he could make it—the wicked Marquis at his finest. "Because your mother loved me better? Well, who could blame her, really? I mean, just look at me. And look at *you*."

Stewart puffed up with fury, like some sort of furious toad. Yet Lorne did not feel the desire to laugh at him. There was power in the man, and Lorne could see it, sense it, taste it. The air had begun to crackle, just as it did whenever the Sorceress appeared, and surely that was not a good sign.

"You took my mother from me and then you killed her with your stupid Hellfire Club. You stole my childhood and any chance of a happy life I might have had. You were not worthy to live in a place like this, in comfort and beauty. You don't deserve to be happy or sleep at night with an untroubled conscience. And you most definitely *don't* deserve the love of a woman like Maggie McNab."

Lorne stiffened. His rapier stilled. He looked into Stewart's eyes and wondered what the other man saw. Fury, or fear?

"Maggie has nothing to do with this," he said, his voice emotionless, because to show he cared would only make matters worse. "Take your revenge on me if you must but she is innocent of any wrong doing toward you. She wasn't even alive when your mother died!"

He'd said too much. Stewart gave a quiet laugh. "Ah, have I found your weakness, Lorne? I had thought about capturing one of your friends and letting you watch him die an agonizing death, but that seemed too easy. Then you paid me a visit and I saw the way you looked at Maggie. You think of her as yours, don't you? You want her. You may even love her—if you're capable of loving anyone but yourself."

"You do not know me," Lorne snarled. What Stewart said may have been true once, but he had changed. "I'm no longer that man. You're wrong, Noakes, or whatever you wish to call yourself. You've wasted all these years for nothing."

"Oh, I don't think so. I've had long enough to study you and long enough to plot my revenge. I'm going to enjoy destroying any love Maggie might have had for you, or any chance of a future between the two of you. I want her to look at you with disgust and fear. I want her eyes to reflect back to you the sort of man you truly are."

His hand clenched on the handle of the rapier. "Leave her *alone*." More than anything he wanted to skewer Stewart through the heart and watch him die. But he couldn't. Not until he knew what the man had done to Maggie.

Stewart was smiling again, loving every moment of their encounter. "And what will you do to save her, hmmm? Crawl on your knees? I'd like to see that, Marquis. But I have a confession to make. Maggie has already paid me a visit." He watched Lorne's reaction. "You seem surprised."

"Maggie knows better than to come here on her own," Sutcliffe growled.

Stewart shook his head at the big man's stupidity. "Ah, but I tricked her. I took on the form of her departed husband—that photo on his book was very handy, by the way. I ordered a copy as soon as it came out. You can learn a lot about a man through the way he writes. Even better, did you know the good Simon Frazer was often on television? Oh, wait, you probably still don't know what that is. No matter. I was able to study his mannerisms and perform well enough to fool poor Maggie, at least for a while. She followed me all the way here and walked straight into my trap."

Lorne lost control then, whipping the rapier blade up, the point dangerously close to Stewart's throat. "If you've harmed her ..." Sutcliffe grabbed his arm to hold back.

"Don't kill him until we know where she is."

Stewart seemed unfazed by the threat. "Poor Maggie," he sighed again, feigning sympathy. "She's dazzled by your allure. But I'm helping her come to her senses. I've sent her back in time, you see. Back two hundred years for a visit to your Hell-fire Club. She's down there in the crypt. I wanted her to see *exactly* what sort of man she thinks she's in love with. That should do the trick, don't you think?"

Lorne pulled out of Sutcliffe's grasp, and now the tip of his rapier was pressed to Stewart's throat. To his satisfaction a trickle of blood ran out. But Stewart didn't even seem to notice the discomfort. He was too busy reveling in Lorne's pain, his eyes fastened on his face, almost as if he was feeding off it.

Lorne knew he was capable of doing anything to protect Maggie, but that wasn't what this was all about. If what Stewart said was true then after he'd captured the Destroyer and fulfilled his promise to the Sorceress, Maggie may not want his help any longer. She may not ever want him near her again.

"Bring her back," he said, his voice cold and deadly.

"Even if she hates you?" Stewart asked.

"I don't care if she hates me. I want her here. Safe." Not down there in the crypt. Dear God, not with the three of them at their worst.

Stewart's smile broadened. "But I've already brought her back. She's waiting for you down there."

"You really are a bastard, aren't you, Noakes?" Darlington said with contempt.

Lorne set off toward the stairs, the sound of his running footsteps echoing around the gallery.

"Good luck, Marquis!" Stewart called after him.

"Watch him," Lorne shouted back. "We may need him still. Don't let him cast any spells. Don't let him say a word!"

"Our pleasure," Darlington replied, who limped

toward Stewart as Lorne lost sight of them, leaping down the steps, no longer concerned whether he might fall through the rotting wood.

Maggie was in the tunnels. And if what Stewart had said was true—and Lorne believed him capable of anything—then she had been to the past, to the Hellfire Club, and by God he knew what that meant. The man had chosen his revenge to perfection.

Had Lorne been so transparent? He must have been.

Stewart had seen how Lorne felt about Maggie, and now Stewart had sent her to the past.

The knowledge was like a stone in his chest. Maggie had been to a meeting of the Hellfire Club. It wasn't a question of her hating him now. It was a question of how much.

Chapter Twenty-Three

THE AIR WAS COLD AND dank, and the heavy smell of being underground mingled with the faintest whiff of incense. Maggie tried to sit up, and groaned. Her head was swimming so badly that she had to hold it in place until the world stopped turning.

What had happened to her? Where the hell was she?

Slowly, jerkily, like flashes from a movie, the memories came back.

Simon … She'd seen Simon! Only it wasn't him. It was a trick. Mr. Stewart had cast some sort of illusion. Looking back, the man she had followed to the Abbey was Simon in his prime, the Simon whose photo graced the back of the Moyle book. It wasn't the Simon she had watched slowly waste away. But why had Stewart done it? Why had he turned himself into her dead husband?

As her mind cleared, another memory revealed itself. While Stewart was casting his spell over her, he'd spoken about Lorne. If she was right, this was all about revenging himself on the Marquis.

Maggie raised her head, tensing like a fox on hunt

day. She could hear sounds off in the gloom, voices calling, followed by raucous laughter. She seemed to be in a tunnel, hand hewn by the look of it—she ran her fingers over the rough stone, feeling the chisel marks. A torch burned sullenly over her head, throwing shadows against the floor and the walls. The ceiling was high enough to allow her to stand upright, but only just.

Using the wall for support, she pulled herself to her feet. That was when she realized that her clothing felt wrong, tight and unwieldy, and when she looked down at herself she gave a gasp of amazement.

What on earth was she wearing?

A dress that looked to be a vivid scarlet in the torchlight and made of some stiffened fabric. It molded her breasts, which were mostly uncovered, and nipped in just below them, before the skirt fell in a straight drop all the way to her ankles. There was a silly sort of train that hung down from the back and was attached to the high waist, while a ribbon of lace was fastened to the bodice and around the hem.

Maggie might have laughed if any of this had been remotely funny.

She looked like she was ready for a night at the opera, except that her hair was loose around her shoulders, as wild and tangled as usual. She pulled it back, out of the way, before she drew up the skirt to see why her feet felt so peculiar. Ah, that was why. Her boots had been replaced by what looked like a pair of flat satin ballet slippers. The toes were scuffed, as if she'd been dancing very vigorously in them.

Or running.

Maggie's heart sank. She was tricked out like the heroine in a historical movie—or maybe the villain, because what heroine would wear a scarlet dress? But this wasn't a movie. This was real and she was here. And she was beginning to think she knew where 'here' was. She just didn't want to believe it.

The noises came again, echoing down the tunnel. They sounded familiar. It was the sort of noise she used to hear in Glasgow on a Saturday night, when all the drunks spilled out of the pubs, ready for anything. She listened, and this time she was certain she heard the sounds of drunken revelers, only one of the voices sounded very much like Sutcliffe. Yes—he gave another roar of laugher— she was certain of it. Were they throwing a party?

A Hellfire Club party?

That was when she began to understand the nature of her position and the danger she was in.

Owen had read her bits out of the book he had on the Hellfire Club, and she'd let them slide over her head, because the truth was she hadn't been very interested. And she certainly had no desire to see any of their goings-on up close and personal.

She'd scoffed about it to Lorne, calling them silly boys, and she'd meant it. But it wasn't so easy to scoff when you were about to be confronted by the roaring bad boys deep in their element.

Yet what was the alternative? She'd seen the maps they had drawn and she was pretty sure the only way out was through the crypt, and that was where the voices were coming from.

Cautiously, she began to make her way forward. The dress hampered her and she tugged at the skirt, taking great handfuls of cloth and lifting the rest out of the way, so that her legs were more or less unimpeded. She didn't want to do this, she really didn't, but what else could she do?

After this you'll hate him. That's what I want, Professor McNab. I want you to hate him.

Mr. Stewart's voice repeated itself in her head like an old vinyl disc with a scratch in it. She understood well enough what he was about. He had sent her into the past because he hoped that what she saw there would be so abhorrent, so completely repugnant to her, that she would hate Lorne to the very depths of her being.

And there was a hollow feeling in the pit of her stomach, a gnawing kernel of fear, that he might be right.

Ahead of her, beyond the light of the next torch, someone was speaking in a sonorous voice. Deep and serious, and yet at the same time dripping with mockery. Maggie rather thought that someone was play-acting at being a monk at prayer.

Such a thing would have been considered blasphemy in 1808, surely? Even today in some quarters it would be frowned upon and heads would be shaken at such disrespect. She supposed it could be argued that just like modern miscreants, these Regency gentlemen were amusing themselves by poking fun at the establishment.

At least, she *hoped* that was all they were doing. Some harmless anti-social behavior was preferable to malicious intent.

Maggie had reached a junction in the tunnel. Ahead of her there were now two tunnels, one splintering off at a right angle and the other going more or less the way she was already walking. The right angled tunnel was darker while the other had one of the flickering torches fixed to the wall. That seemed the best option, even if it would lead her into the heart of the Hellfire Club.

I'm in the past. Two hundred years, in fact. Maggie shook her head in wonder. How was that possible? And yet, just like the Destroyer and Lorne returning to life in the barrow, it was true. As much as it went against everything she'd learned and knew and believed, Maggie had to accept it if she was going to survive.

Maggie paused, suddenly realizing the implications of that and what it could mean for her job. Imagine rocketing back through time to the Iron Age, or a Pictish settlement! Being able to confirm her theories about a certain dig by going amongst the people who once lived there? It was mind boggling. Exciting. It was …

A woman squealed, the shrill sound drilling into her head.

Maggie froze, her excitement replaced by dread.

She listened as Darlington cackled with drunken laughter, and Sutcliffe whooped as if he was chasing after something. Or someone. Maggie tensed as the woman squealed again before relaxing as she realized the noise wasn't one of fear. It was excitement.

Perhaps this wouldn't be so bad after all. Not that she wanted to see the three men she'd grown fond of at their most feral. In fact, she'd rather not, but maybe they really were just silly boys.

And yet, the Hellfire Club hadn't gained its reputation for nothing.

Maggie glanced back over her shoulder, hoping there would be some swirling light there that she could jump into and find herself back in her own time. But there was nothing to see but the tunnel winding on. She had no choice but to face Lorne and accept the fact he wouldn't be the Lorne she loved. That man with his wary eyes and hidden pain, the man with a laugh he used so rarely it sounded rusty, and the kindness to take her hand when he knew she was feeling out of her depth.

The man who had saved her life.

No, this was going to be a very different Lorne, and she was fairly certain she wasn't going to like him very much.

She tried to tell herself it didn't matter. Surely there was some small part of him she could connect to? She'd talk sense to him and he would listen and everything would be okay.

Holding on to that thought, she pushed her shaky legs onward as the voices grew louder and the sickly smell of incense grew stronger.

Soon the tunnel ended and a room opened up before her, everything painted white. Pillars supporting the vaulted ceiling, and braziers gave out heat, while more torches were set at intervals around the walls. The room was furnished with divans laden with cushions, tables piled high with dirty plates and goblets, and a crude looking altar complete with an upside down cross. A raven cawed and fluttered anxiously in a cage.

Darlington stood closest to her with his arms around a naked woman. He was upending a goblet of liquid into her open mouth and laughing as it spilt all over her breasts. Red, like blood. Perhaps it was blood? But Maggie was pretty sure it was wine—the Darlington she knew seemed a bit too fastidious to drink blood.

"Up, up!" Suddenly Sutcliffe came into sight, dressed as a monk and very drunk. He was holding a whip in his hand, one of those long tailed whips she'd seen in cowboy movies. He shook it at a group of several women who were lounging about on the pile of cushions, either drunk or sleeping. They didn't seem all that keen to get up.

"I want to see you dance," he shouted, but no one, apart from a plump girl with long fair hair wearing a white Vestal Virgin dress, seemed inclined to oblige. She clambered to her feet and did a few clumsy twirls. He flicked the whip and the tail of it wrapped around her waist.

As he began to reel her in she let him have it. "Keep that bloody thing away from me! I told you what I think of you and your whip."

Maggie bit her lip, fighting a hysterical urge to laugh.

"Oh-ho, I'll have to punish you for that." Sutcliffe sounded thrilled at the thought. "Come here."

The woman still struggled but she looked more irritated than terrified. Besides, Sutcliffe was far too unsteady on his feet to do much harm. He staggered and made a grab at the girl but she evaded him, scampering back to the cushions and collapsing upon them in relief. One of her companions raised her head, but they all looked too out of it to care what was going on.

Sutcliffe sat down on a stool, appearing crestfallen. "Lorne, she won't play," he whined, sounding like a thwarted child.

Lorne? Maggie squinted through the smoke and incense-laden fog of the crypt. Where was he? And then she heard his voice, its familiarity raising goosebumps on her skin.

"Do as you're told, wench, or we'll send you home to your wretched pig sty."

Maggie's heart leapt with equal parts of joy and dread. She saw him now, half hidden behind a pillar. When she took a step to the side he was right there before her. It seemed impossible that she could have missed him.

He was seated on a carved chair that was more like a throne, high backed with purple velvet cushions, and placed beside one of the braziers. Lounging, Maggie thought, was probably a more apt description. His booted feet stretched out before him, a black cloak spread over his legs, and he leaned back sipping from a golden goblet. His pale eyes gleamed wickedly in the torchlight and his handsome face was pale and aloof, as if he was holding himself apart from the degradation around him.

At least he didn't seem to be as drunk as the others. Surely that was a good thing? She had more chance of reasoning with a sober man, although what she was going to ask for she didn't know. How to get home probably wasn't going to work, nor was skulking in the tunnels for the rest of her life, listening to them cast half-baked spells and …

Wait.

She had a chance to stop them from bringing the Destroyer into the world! Stewart had sent her back for his own warped purposes but she could use it against him. If she was able to reason with the men, make them understand the consequences of their actions, then all those lives could be saved. Owen could be saved. She had to try.

Her excitement faded a little when she began to think of what success might mean for herself and Lorne. Would they still get to meet? Then again, if she was stuck here for the rest of her life she'd see plenty of him. He just wouldn't be the man she wanted. Maggie dropped the handfuls of crimson dress she'd been holding up and gave it a shake so that it all fell into place. Her breasts were threatening to pop out of the bodice, so she adjusted them as well, making herself as respectable as it was possible to be in such an outfit.

Ready or not, she had to face the Hellfire Club.

Maggie took a step closer, full of determination. Then she realized that the cloak spread over Lorne's legs wasn't a cloak at all but a woman's dress, and that the woman wearing it was kneeling between his thighs, face buried in his lap.

Sickness ate into her. And anger. And jealousy. And all the things a woman feels when she sees the man she loves with another. Because she did love him, and it didn't matter that this was long before she had ever met him, or that right now he didn't even know Maggie existed. She was still furious with him. She'd known about his past, but seeing it was an entirely different matter.

Before she could stop herself, Maggie strode out of the shadows and into the crypt.

One of the women stretched out on the cushions noticed her and stared. Her face was heavily made up, with red spots on her cheeks and bright red lips, and her eyes lined in black. Perhaps she wasn't as drunk as Maggie had first thought, because she called out a warning.

"My lord Darlington!"

Darlington looked up from tipping wine down his partner's throat, trying to focus his vision. Maggie noticed his scar was red and angry, as if the injury was fresh, and had yet to properly heal. His voice came out slurred. "And what have we here? One of yours, Sutcliffe?"

Sutcliffe had gotten to his feet and was divesting himself of his monk's habit, but now he stopped and swung around. The sudden movement made him stagger off balance, as he blinked blearily in Maggie's direction. She noted he was still holding the whip. "Mine?" His expression changed as he took her in properly. "My lords, beauty has come to visit. Should we make her welcome?" He looked across at Lorne. "What say you, Master?"

Maggie ignored them. It was Lorne she was concentrating on as she walked toward him, but it was tricky to move gracefully in such a costume, when you grew up in jeans.

"Lorne," she said, in her best no-nonsense voice. "You need to stop this. Stop before things get any worse."

The Marquis sat up. The woman slid off his lap and he made no move to save her from landing on the floor in an undignified sprawl. He didn't even seem to notice.

"Stop?" he drawled. "Why, we've hardly begun."

The throne was on a dais, raised a foot above the floor, as if he were a king surveying his kingdom. The woman staggered to her feet and made for Maggie, reaching out both hands as if to clutch at her, but like the others she was drunk and uncoordinated. Maggie shoved her away, not bothering to see where she landed.

She also realized that she'd been wrong in her assumption about Lorne's sobriety. He was as drunk as the others, if not more so, it was just that he was better at disguising it. He would see that as a matter of pride, she supposed, and at the moment he seemed to be trying to fight his way out of his befuddlement. He sat up straighter, his hair lank about his face, and his eyes slits of blue ice.

"A Scot?" he declared, enunciating his words carefully. "We don't allow Scotswomen into the Hellfire Club. How did you get in here? Are you my grandmother's kin?"

"Don't talk such rubbish," she retorted. "I'm nothing to do with your grandmother."

He laughed involuntarily. Good, she thought, at least now she had his attention.

She moved closer, avoiding a plate of half eaten food with a disdainful sweep of her skirt, until she was standing directly before him.

"Have you done it yet? Have you cast the spell to bring the Destroyer into the world? Do you still have the runes?"

Behind her Sutcliffe snorted. "What spell? Are you mad? Lorne, she's mad. Let me give her a taste of the whip."

Maggie didn't turn, couldn't take her eyes from Lorne's. This was too important. She just hoped that she wouldn't be caught up in the long tail of the lash, and trussed like a chicken.

Lorne held up his hand to halt his friend. "How do you know about that?" he asked in a soft and dangerous voice.

So he did have the spell. But had he used it yet? The others didn't know what she was talking about so perhaps not. At this stage he may just be exploring the notion. Maggie almost breathed a sigh of relief. She was in time then. She had to stop him. But if she did …

This was no time for selfish regrets. Maggie knew she could not put her own love before the devastation the demon could bring. Sacrifices had to be made.

She was close enough to him to notice the stubble on his jaw and the reddened whites of his eyes. His hair looked greasy, and his clothing none too clean, and he gave off an unpleasant aroma of wine and smoke and sex.

Anger gripped her, and repulsion at the futility of what he was doing. How long had he been down here, she wondered, passing the hours, the days, with this idiotic behavior? Using up his life a piece at a time in all this pointlessness?

"I've come to warn you," she said, but her throat was dry and she had to swallow to get the words out.

"Warn away," he muttered, his eyes dropping to her breasts.

Maggie looked down and saw that the bodice had slipped very low, and only her nipples were stopping it from falling even further. She wrenched it up inelegantly and he gave a soft chuckle.

"Please, don't bother on my account."

Maggie shot him a savage look. "Oh *stop* it. You don't even know me. Not yet. And yes, I have come to warn you. The spell you let lose will destroy you.

All of you. You'll be ruined by it." She turned to fix the others with a glare that they seemed unwilling to meet. They shuffled about like nasty school boys caught out in a misdemeanor. So much for the big bad Hellfire Club.

But Maggie had let her sense of superiority go to her head. Suddenly two strong arms slid around her from behind. Lorne had left his throne and now he dragged her backwards, lifting her clean off her feet. His breath was hot and unpleasant on her cheek and she wrinkled her nose in disgust.

"Don't fight me, my little Scot. You'll enjoy it once I start."

She gasped, struggling furiously. "Let me go, you … you *idiot*."

He'd fallen back into his chair now, dragging Maggie with him and plonking her on his knee. She jabbed her elbow back and heard a huff of breath as she connected but he didn't let her go. She was beginning to realize that the more she fought against him the more he enjoyed himself. He was simply waiting for her to run out of steam and Maggie knew that eventually she would.

"Lorne, you have to listen to me," she said, shoving away the hand that had suddenly clamped onto one of her breasts.

"Listen? I'd prefer it if you stopped talking." His mouth brushed her cheek, his whiskers scraping her skin.

"I'm not going to let you do this," she said in frustration. "You can't go around laying waste to everything and everyone, just because you're *bored*! You're not a fool, Lorne. Can't you see you're a damn sight better than all this?"

He stilled and she gave a silent sigh of relief. Now all she had to do was—

She was pushed roughly off his knee, landing in an ungainly sprawl on the floor.

"Ouch." She sat up and rubbed her bruised hip.

"You!" He leaned down, his face thrust toward hers, and his pale eyes glittered weirdly. He looked … well, he looked dangerous.

"Lorne, please, I only …"

He waited a heartbeat and then smiled. And because this was Lorne, and yet not Lorne, it was the most frightening thing she'd ever seen.

"Run," he said softly. "Run as fast as you can."

Terrified now, Maggie edged away, scrambling like a crab.

Sutcliffe cracked his whip so close that she felt the hiss of it on her cheek. "Run!" he took up the chant, leering at her.

Darlington staggered into sight, slopping wine down his shirt, his limp so pronounced he was almost dragging his leg. "Run!" he shouted. "Run, little rabbit!"

Maggie had managed to get to her feet. "Oh you big brave men!" she shouted back. Her heart was pounding and she knew running was the worst thing she could possibly do. If they saw her fear then they would hunt her down.

Lorne leapt to his feet on his chair, looming high above her. He stretched out his arms and lifted his face to the vaulted ceiling and screamed, "*Run!*"

Maggie turned and ran into the tunnel.

Chapter Twenty-Four

THE COTTAGE WAS VERY QUIET.

Linny had tried to occupy herself with the *Secrets of Moyle* book she'd found. Although Maggie had sent her a copy she hadn't read it properly, not right through. It was too textbooky for her tastes—she preferred a good murder mystery herself—but because it was Simon's she thought she should at least make the effort.

Maggie had loved Simon, there was no doubt about that, but Linny was glad she was healing from his death and finally looking to the future. She had a feeling Lorne might have something to do with that. Maybe he didn't know it himself, but his description of what Maggie had been wearing had been very detailed. In Linny's experience, most men would have forgotten what a woman was wearing the moment she left, unless they were focused on her for some romantic reason.

The room was so warm and the fire gave off a pleasant glow. She almost dozed off. She was tired after her long drive and if she hadn't been so worried about Maggie she might have curled up on the lumpy looking sofa and given in to sleep.

Where was Maggie? She hadn't come back from the village, and neither had the three men returned from the abbey.

Now there was a trio of trouble! Linny didn't know whether to drool or run for her life. They'd rattled off their surnames—Lorne, Darlington and Sutcliffe—like soldiers captured by the enemy. She didn't believe everything they'd said, not entirely, but she'd always had good instincts when it came to people. She had no doubt these three could be trusted. Where Maggie was concerned, anyway.

Her personal taste ran toward the one with the scar, Darlington, but then she'd always been a sucker for bad boys. It seemed she was running true to form then.

Linny shook her head impatiently. She was here for Maggie, not to get laid. Sure, it had been a while, but that didn't mean she should hook up with the first interesting man she met south of the Scottish border …

There was a noise outside. Linny looked toward the door, and right on queue there was a knock.

"Maggie?" She was on her feet and moving forward, propelled by the relief coursing through her. "Maggie, where have you been, hen?"

The door swung open, but it wasn't Maggie on the other side. Surprised, she stared at the unfamiliar figure of a stout, middle aged woman with grey hair and a beige colored raincoat. Her head was tilted oddly to one side, and her lipsticked mouth was fixed in a smile that didn't quite fit right.

"Hello there, dear," she said cheerfully, as if they were meeting over a cake stall rather than on a dark, rainy night in the middle of nowhere.

"Eh, hello …?"

"I'm Mrs. Green. I've been sent to fetch you."

"Mrs …?" Linny stammered, but Mrs. Green didn't wait to be invited in. She was already moving jerkily toward her.

———◆———

A torch flame flared and spluttered as Maggie sprinted by. She came to the branching of the tunnels and slowed, while her brain tried desperately to remember which one she had originally come from. But the three men were crowding up behind her, whooping and yelling, and she didn't have time to stop and think. She chose the one with a glimmer of light further down it, and took off as fast as she could in her scarlet dress and ridiculous dancing slippers.

Ahead of her the tunnel made another sharp turn, but her slippers had no grip, not like proper shoes, and she had to slow down or risk crashing into the wall.

Maybe Regency ladies didn't go out jogging …

She could hear the pack still in pursuit. They were laughing that drunken sort of laughter where the most insignificant thing seemed funny, and every now and then it was punctuated by Sutcliffe's whip. Darlington she could discount—he could barely walk let alone run. It was the other two she was worried about, and the one who frightened her most was Lorne.

Maggie set off again at a quick shuffle, though she'd begun to suspect with a sinking heart that it wasn't the right way. The tunnel was unfamiliar, and when she passed the last torch there didn't seem to be any more of them shining up ahead, just a blank wall of solid darkness. Soon she wouldn't be able to see where she was going, and her only hope was that Lorne and Sutcliffe couldn't either.

Or perhaps they'd lose interest and wander back to their harem? An image flashed into her mind, of Lorne with the woman across his lap and that expression on his face—bored out of his skull and hating himself.

He was wealthy and titled and yet had no purpose to his life. That was what led him to set the Destroyer loose into the world. Boredom and self-loathing. She could imagine how corroding those emotions must be.

"And he has changed, he has …" she muttered to herself in the darkness. "He's not that man. Not anymore."

Maggie was moving toward the pitch black when suddenly she came up against an invisible wall. It wasn't solid, though. It was oddly elastic, like a trampoline, and it flung her backwards. She landed flat out on the ground, shocked and winded, and lay staring at nothingness while she tried to get her breath back.

She realized then she was not alone. There was a presence here with her. She couldn't see what it was, but she knew it was moving. A mass of something, even darker than the space around it, was travelling toward her. She was being enveloped in something evil. Her heart sped up and her skin was suddenly drenched in a cold sweat. This was evil at its most absolute.

"W-what …" she croaked, trying to lift her head,

trying to see, but the blackness was opaque.

Far away she could hear Lorne's voice, still shouting '*Run*' and Sutcliffe's mad cackling, but they were no longer the real danger to her. Yes, Lorne might break her heart or her body, but this thing would take her soul.

A face appeared. It was Stewart's, but twisted so that it was almost unrecognizable. Gone was the slightly odd, polite American. This creature was utterly malevolent.

"Are you enjoying yourself, Maggie?" The voice seemed to be not one but many, intertwining and striving, each against the others.

She managed to drag herself backwards until she came up against the side of the tunnel, but the face followed and hovered over her, grinning.

"I could leave you here for the Marquis, Maggie, but I have other plans for you and your friends. So many plans. It doesn't end here. You'll see. So much more fun to come. And your sister. Lovely Linny. We mustn't forget her."

Maggie stared at him in horrified silence. Linny? What did he know about Linny?

The howling was getting closer. She took her eyes off the face to look back the way she'd come. She could see the glow of an approaching flame, with the elongated shadows of the Hellfire Club cavorting before it.

"Send me back," she begged Stewart. "Send me home."

"Poor Maggie. She wants to go home. You know that won't save you, don't you? Or your sister?"

She felt a tear roll down against her cold skin.

"Ah, Maggie's crying," the face said, in a terrible

parody of sympathy.

"Let me go, you fucking piece of shit!"

Laughter now. "*That's* more like it."

Lorne and the others were still coming and in another moment they'd be on top of her. Maybe they wouldn't hurt her. Maybe she could talk them out of whatever plans they had—she still believed they weren't as bad as they were pretending—but she never had the chance to find out.

There was a roaring in her ears and that sick spinning sensation she remembered from before. Her body seemed to dissolve into itself, and she screamed as she began to twirl around, every molecule stretched and hurting.

Everything went still. The vertigo drained away and she forced her eyes open. Where was she this time?

Chapter Twenty-Five

AT FIRST LORNE COULDN'T SEE her. Like the rest of the Abbey, the crypt had changed over the last two hundred years. The white paint was discolored and peeling, and there were boxes against one wall, piled up with broken pieces of furniture and rusting metal. He felt as if he was looking at it through a dusty glass, complete with old cobwebs hanging in ropes from the ceiling. The air was oppressive. No one had bothered to come down here in a very long time.

So much for the Hellfire Club standing the test of time.

There were no candles or flaming torches, but he did find a switch on the wall, just like those in Maggie's cottage. When he flicked it, dull light speared down from four bulbs. These, at least, had to have been recently installed.

"Maggie?" His voice echoed eerily. He was more afraid now than he'd ever been of the Destroyer. What was he going to see in Maggie's eyes when he found her?

"Maggie?"

There was a sound, like the scuff of a boot on the dusty ground. He followed it down one of the tunnels, the shadows growing thicker with every step.

He found her crouched low against the wall, her arms folded around her head, her hair a wild mass of curls. She was breathing like a trapped animal and when he moved closer she whimpered as if she expected to be struck.

The relief he'd felt at finding her melted away. There was a lump of fear in his chest, and although he wanted to go to her and take her in his arms, he stopped himself. If she'd just encountered the Lorne from the Hellfire Club she no doubt would prefer he kept his distance.

"Maggie?" he said, his voice quiet. Gentle.

She went still.

"Maggie, it's me. It's all right. You're back now. You're safe. I'm here."

He knew how ridiculous the words sounded. Why would she think being with him made her safe? He didn't know what she'd been through, but he could imagine. Surely when she saw him now she'd feel only loathing and revulsion, just as Stewart had wanted. She'd look at him with hatred, and he would lose the only woman he'd ever loved.

And yet the fact that she hadn't already started screaming gave him a glimmer of hope.

Maggie uncurled her arms and Lorne steeled himself for what was to come.

He could see that she'd been crying, her face streaked with tears, her eyes dark with shock and pain. His optimism began to leak away. He watched in silence as she wiped the back of her hand over her mouth, as if to take away a nasty taste.

"Lorne?" Her doubtful gaze took in his modern clothing, and yet she couldn't seem to believe it. Then, with that husky note in her voice that squeezed his heart every time he heard it, she asked, "Is it my Lorne? Or are you … the other one?"

My Lorne. He dropped to his knees in front of her, as if his outer skin had been stripped away and he was as naked as he had been the first time they met.

"Your Lorne," he said in a voice that shook. "Most definitely *your* Lorne."

She stared a moment. It was taking her a while to process his words, and then she gave a wail that made him wince. Maggie flung herself into his arms. He caught her, holding her so tight he wondered if he might be hurting her, but he didn't stop and she didn't complain.

"Oh Lorne, oh Lorne," she sobbed against his shoulder.

He stroked her hair, reassuring her that everything was all right, and all the time he was thinking that it wasn't and how he'd like to kill Stewart, the bastard who'd done this to her. Or perhaps what he really wanted to do was kill the man he'd once been.

"Maggie?" He eased her away so that he could look into her face. "What did he … What happened?"

She sighed. "Nothing happened," she said. "Not the way you mean. I don't know if something might have happened, if … Oh Lorne, I'm so glad you're here."

He kissed her lips, trying to be gentle, but she wasn't satisfied with that. She kissed him back with vigor, her mouth salty with tears, as though she couldn't get enough of him.

His body went hard. She was clinging to him and he could feel the softness of her breasts. He slid his hand under her sweater and cupped her, the jut of her nipple prodding his palm. Her mouth opened under his in a gasp.

"Yes," she said.

Lorne told himself to stop, but when he tried to move away she dragged him back, her hands holding his hips. The next moment she had her hands all over the front of his trousers, murmuring approval when she felt his erection. He kissed her again, at the same time fumbling at the unfamiliar fastening on her jeans, but she wriggled away.

"My boots," she said breathlessly.

He discovered the metal zip at the side, and removed one and then the other. She had her trousers undone by then, and they both pushed and pulled until they came off as well. She lay back, breathing fast, and he saw that she was wearing one of the thin satin garments he remembered from the trunk in her room.

Lorne reached for her, his fingers brushing the silky cloth, sliding down over the moist heat between her thighs. She was damp, ready for him, and by God he was ready for her. He caught the edge of the flimsy garment, planning to tear it from her body, but she caught hold of his wrist, stopping him.

His eyes flew to hers, thinking the worst, but what he saw in her face so threatened his control that for a moment he struggled not to climax right then and there.

"I want you inside me," she said in a low voice. "I need you, Lorne."

With trembling hands he reached down and unfastened his own trousers while she watched. It was her focus on him that almost finished him again but he gritted his teeth and held on. His cock was so hard it hurt, and when she wrapped her cool fingers around him he groaned and pushed against her.

"Maggie …" He tried to calm himself, but it had been so long and he wanted her so much.

She lay back, pulling him with her, and he let himself go, landing clumsily on top of her. No finesse, but after two hundred years what could you expect?

"Maggie," he said again, because in a moment he knew it would be too late to stop. "Do you really want me to … after what you …?"

She looked confused. Her thighs were cradling him and his cock was resting against the edge of her undergarment. He almost expected her to come to her senses, screech and push him away. Instead, she looked him in the eye and said with perfect clarity, "Yes, I really want you to," and pulled him down.

Lorne pushed his fingers beneath the satin cloth, stroking his way inside her. She pressed her hips against him, her arms were around his neck and she was kissing him wildly.

His cock followed his fingers and he was nudging his way to the core of her, the place he knew he needed to be. Along the way his body stretched hers, filling her, and they both groaned. She was his, he thought with a hint of his old arrogance, but at the same time he knew that he was hers, and always would be.

When he began to withdraw, Maggie met him

halfway, and they moved in a wild frenzy of relief and desire and affirmation.

He couldn't last long, but he held on until he heard her cry of ecstasy, her body arching, her thighs trembling as they gripped him. Then Lorne allowed himself to join her. Not exactly his finest hour, though the fact that he didn't care about that, so long as he'd pleased her, might be a more worthy ambition than playing to the crowd.

He realized he was laying on top of her, breathing hard, his heart pounding with exertion. He rolled onto his side, concerned he might be crushing her, but she rolled with him, their legs and arms still entangled, her damp cheek pressed to his.

He shifted his head to look at her. Her eyes were closed, her mouth pink and swollen, and he stared into her face, waiting. Because, he told himself, this could still go either way. She might still hate him. More than one woman had loathed him yet given into their desires. It had a certain intensity he'd enjoyed, but that's not what he wanted from her.

Maggie's lashes flickered but her eyes stayed closed. "That was pure magic," she said.

He grinned, so relieved that for a moment he couldn't answer. "I was afraid that after what you'd seen you wouldn't want anything to do with me."

At last her eyes opened, and he saw that she wasn't as happy with him as he'd hoped. "I can understand you thinking that," she said.

"Then why …?"

"I needed to exorcise him. The other you. Rather appropriate to do it in the Hellfire Club, don't you think?"

He didn't have an answer for that. She drew away

and began to pull on her clothing. Lorne did the same, then helped her to her feet, though they were both still a bit unsteady, still shaking from their passionate encounter.

"Maggie, tell me what happened?" He had to ask. He had to know the worst, whatever that was.

Her dark eyes slid to his. She bit her lip. "It wasn't very nice, Lorne."

Involuntarily he laughed at her understatement.

"Oh, very funny. You were *horrible*. Loud and sneering and nasty. And you were drunk."

"That about sums him up," he said dryly, refusing to refer to his former self in the first person.

"There was a woman giving you a blowj … you'd call it fellatio, and you didn't even seem to notice. Ugh."

He rubbed a hand over his jaw. "He was probably too drunk to know what he was doing. I don't imagine she'd get more than a twitch out of him, the state he was usually in."

Maggie gave him an unimpressed stare. "I tried to reason with you."

He frowned. "I don't imagine that went down well."

"No, it didn't go down well at all."

"So, how does this change what you think of me, now that you've met him?"

Maggie cocked her head. "Here's the thing. You keep saying *he* and *him*, because you know that man wasn't you. He looked like you and for all intents and purposes he *was* you, but he wasn't. Does that make sense?"

He tucked a curl behind her ear and stroked his thumb down her cheek. "Yes, it makes wonderful sense."

"Lorne …" He saw his reflection in her eyes, and knew if it was up to him then he'd want to see himself there for the rest of his life.

"Maggie?"

"I saw Simon. He wasn't dead. I-I followed him here and … it was Stewart. He was pretending to be Simon. Somehow he knows magic, and he seems to hate you. He's like a giant spider and we're all caught in his web. I saw him in the tunnel too, but he was different then. Immense. Terrifying. He said things …" She shuddered.

"What things?" he asked calmly, but inside he was anything but calm.

She told him, her voice in turn angry and frightened, and he didn't like what he heard. Stewart had bigger plans than he'd imagined and he meant to do more damage than Lorne had realized. But how could they stop him? Especially as it now appeared he could be in two places at the same time.

"Where is he?" she asked, as they walked toward the crypt.

"He's upstairs with Darlington and Sutcliffe. They have him prisoner, although from what you're saying …"

Her curls sprung as she shook her head. "He's not their prisoner, Lorne. He could escape if he wanted to. He's only letting you keep him because it suits him."

"You were right before. Stewart hates me, Maggie. This all began as a way for him to punish me, but now he wants to go further. Hurting me is no longer enough."

"Linny," she said in a shaken voice. "He knows

about my sister. He said that it was too late to save her. Please tell me Linny isn't here? Lorne?"

She must have read the truth in his eyes because she gave a cry.

"Linny is safe," he quickly assured her. "She came just after you left for the village. She's at the cottage. She did not come with us."

"How do you know she's safe? Stewart can be anywhere he wants to be. We have to go to her."

"Come then, we'll get the others."

Upstairs, when Maggie saw the state of the house, she was as shocked as he had been.

"What … what happened?"

"This is part of my punishment, it would seem. Somehow he'd hidden its true form—some sort of masking spell—so we couldn't see the true state of the place until he wanted us to. Our friend has many clever tricks, Maggie."

"I need to find Linny. I can feel there's something not right. I need to find her."

He pulled her to him and kissed the little frown between her brows. "You will." Then he was climbing the stairs, pulling her along by her hand in his.

When Maggie reached the final landing she could see Sutcliffe and Darlington halfway down the long gallery. As they got closer she knew they were beneath what had once been Lorne's portrait. It was an awful mess now, though she barely had time to take it in. Sutcliffe had Stewart by the scruff of his neck and was shaking him hard while Loki seemed ready to snap at his heels. Darlington had a cutlass in his hand and was prodding their captive with it.

They all looked up at the sound of Lorne and Maggie's approach.

She was flattered to see the expression of joy on the two men's faces. It made up a little for her experience with their counterparts in the Hellfire Club. Loki came bounding over and tried to jump on her but Lorne caught him by the collar.

"Maggie! You're not hurt?" Sutcliffe had a big hand on her shoulder, and was trying to read the expression on her face. "We … we didn't hurt you? Back then?"

She shook her head, thinking it was probably best not to go into too much detail at this point—like asking him about his whip—though she planned to get everything off her chest later.

"We weren't *that* bad, old chap," Darlington sneered, but spoiled it by giving her a worried glance. "Were we?"

"No," Maggie said, trying to sound truthful. "You weren't so bad. Just a bit, eh, silly. And I'm back." She jerked her head at Stewart. "He looks rather the worse for wear."

Sutcliffe gave an evil smile. "We've been trying to get him to tell us where he's hiding the Destroyer."

"Set him down," Lorne said. "I need to speak to him."

Sutcliffe dumped him back into his chair, and Maggie saw the trickle of blood that ran from Stewart's nose, while there was a red mark on his cheek which would probably become a bruise. His glasses were askew and he took the opportunity to straighten them.

Maggie refused to feel sorry for him. This was all just play acting. She had seen the real Stewart down in the tunnels. She was sure of it.

Stewart brightened at the sight of Lorne. "Ah, the Marquis." His gaze slid to Maggie. "Well, well, Professor McNab. Tell me what you think of your friend now?"

Maggie shrugged as if the subject bored her, knowing it would annoy him. "I saw some silly boys misbehaving, Mr. Stewart. What else was there to see?"

He frowned. Obviously not the answer he'd been hoping for. "Oh? I think you're telling a fib so as not to hurt his feelings." His face cleared and he forced a laugh. "Or maybe I underestimated the power of your attraction to our Marquis. Or per- haps your own damaged nature …"

But despite his efforts to hide it, Maggie could see his disappointment that his great plan had fallen flat.

"You're an evil man," she said. "I saw you down there. I saw you and I know what you are."

He looked mildly amused. "I doubt that very much."

"How can you be here and there at the same time? How can you travel through time and yet still be here?"

"I can do anything and be anywhere I want to be," Stewart retorted. There was an arrogance about him now, as if he believed himself far superior to any of them. He smiled up at her, a glint in his eyes behind his glasses. "How is your sister, Professor?"

Maggie's heart skipped a beat. She clenched her hands to stop herself from hitting him. "Don't you *dare* hurt Linny," she said, her voice trembling. "I'm warning you."

"Warning me?" he repeated, and gave his little throat clearing cough. "Well, consider me to be duly warned. Although …" He cocked his head as if he was listening to something only he could hear. "I do believe your sister has a visitor at the cottage."

Maggie's face went white.

"Oh my," he went on, eyes fixed on hers, feeding on her pain, "I do believe that dear Mrs. Green has come calling."

"You *bastard*," Sutcliffe shouted in his face. "I'll throw you out of the window!"

Stewart's eyes flicked to the windows and back again. It was a long way down. "Well, you could try, my brawny friend," he said without emotion, "but I fear it will take more than that to finish me off."

Darlington limped closer, and rested the curved blade of his cutlass against Stewart's neck. "There's only one way to deal with filth like you." It was touch and go whether he would run it through to the other side.

Sutcliffe growled and pulled the smaller man back. "No."

"We need him," Lorne reminded them. "I wish we didn't, but we do."

Maggie had been watching them in silence, too shocked to speak. She had been through an awful lot tonight, and now her sister was in danger. She pulled herself together. "We need to get to the cottage," she said, "I need to find Linny."

She began to walk down the long gallery, quickening her pace.

"Bring him with us," Lorne called, starting after her.

"You had better hope that woman is unharmed." Darlington sounded unhinged as he dragged Stewart behind him by a length of rope. "Or I *will* find a way to finish you off."

Sutcliffe and Loki brought up the rear, and the ruined faces of Lorne's ancestors stared indifferently down upon them.

Chapter Twenty-Six

OUTSIDE THE RAIN WAS SHEETING down and they ran through it to the Land Rover parked on the driveway. Maggie felt as if she had left it here weeks ago rather than hours. So much had happened her mind should be in complete chaos, and yet her thoughts were crystal clear. She had only one objective—to save Linny.

So often when her sister had needed her she had felt it, and earlier in the crypt there had definitely been a sense of Linny being in trouble. Now … there was nothing. A big blank nothing. And that in itself was worrying.

Lorne climbed in beside her and the others pushed Stewart into the back between them. His hands were bound with rope and his glasses were so splattered with raindrops that he could barely see, but nothing appeared to worry him. Even Loki, puffing in his ear, he barely noticed.

Maggie knew that Stewart's state of unconcern was a bad sign, but she couldn't let herself think of all the horrible things that might have happened to her sister.

She drove like a mad woman back to the cottage.

There was more water streaming through the ford now, and it made a huge splash as they shot through and up the other side. The woods closed in upon them, dripping and dark and threatening, but all Maggie could think of was Linny's face when she opened the door.

Please let her be safe …

Linny had been everything to her when they were young. Parent and friend as well as moral support. When it was discovered that Maggie had outstanding talent, Linny had fought to see that her sister received the very best help with her schooling. Eventually it had paid off, but there had been bumps along the way and plenty of them. Yet Linny had pushed through, never for a moment letting her sister give up on herself, even when the going got tough.

Maggie owed her so much and she'd tried her best to repay. When things went sour with that loser Keith, she'd helped her sister pack and leave the house she'd tried to make a home, and found her another one. When Maggie married Simon, Linny was there at her side, beaming with happiness.

If anything happened to her sister, Maggie would blame herself, and rightly so. If she hadn't dug up the demon, if Lorne hadn't saved her life and she hadn't fallen in love, making her a target for Stewart's revenge … Now all of that was spilling over to ensnare her sister. Linny couldn't be made to pay for Maggie's mistakes.

She pulled up beside the cottage, still hoping, still praying. But as she jumped out and ran for the door, she could see light shining from the house and the door was wide open.

Lorne caught her before she reached it, holding her back. "Wait," he warned her. "We need to see what's in there."

Maggie didn't want to wait, although she knew he was right. She tried to force herself to be still but being patient just wasn't possible and she anxiously shifted around.

Loki and Sutcliffe went first, while Darlington dragged Stewart behind by his roped hands. She saw the big man kneel down just inside the cottage and after what seemed a very long time, he called out to them.

"There's an old woman here. Or, I should say, what's left of her."

Mrs. Green! Maggie felt a guilty spurt of hope— if Mrs. Green was here then perhaps Linny was still alive? But that hope died just as quickly when she realized what that meant.

"Oh God, it has Linny's body."

———◆———

Mrs. Green lay near the doorway to the kitchen. She looked diminished, deflated, and her skin was horribly mottled. The demon had sucked the life from her.

"It seems the Destroyer has moved on to fresher meat."

Stewart spoke from behind them, his voice reflective and emotionless, as if he were a mere observer to this tragedy. Maggie turned on him, her nails crooked, but once again Lorne caught her and turned her into his chest, holding her tight.

"You'll be punished for your crimes, Stewart." She heard the cold fury in his voice. "Evil like this does not go unpunished."

"It does if you're clever," was Stewart's reply.

Darlington, Sutcliffe and Loki had set off to search the cottage but they soon returned. "No one," Darlington said, and bent over to rub at his lame leg, as if he wished to hide his face.

"The woods then," said Lorne. "She can't have gone far. The … It is never very quick when it takes on a new …" His voice trailed off.

Maggie lifted her head. "When it takes on a new host, you mean?"

He didn't lie to her, but his eyes held hers. "We'll find her," he promised. "We'll do everything we can, Maggie."

"I know you will, Lorne. Everything except bring my sister back alive."

Darlington tried not to wince when his leg began to ache, as it always did when he'd used it too vigorously. He wanted to take Stewart by the throat and squeeze until the bastard's head popped off like a dandelion. He understood why he couldn't, but that didn't stop him longing for the satisfaction.

Maggie's sister was out there somewhere, her body inhabited by the Destroyer. She was more or less dead. No, she *was* dead. All this talk of finding her, of saving her, it was just talk. She was dead and it was too late to do anything but mourn and prevent further tragedy.

He didn't pretend to feel as Maggie must be feeling right now, but Linny's death left an emptiness in Darlington.

She'd been special. A diamond of the first water. He replayed the brief moments they'd spent together and knew it in his bones. He'd liked the way she'd showed a genuine interest in him. In the past there'd been women who used him to get to Lorne and he understood that. He accepted it. Lorne was handsome and compelling, and women were drawn to him as if they had no will of their own. It was the opposite for Darlington with his scarred face and shattered leg. Women sometimes found him repulsive and he didn't blame them—there were days when he found himself repulsive.

And yet Linny McNab had seemed more interested in him than either of his friends. She'd even made him laugh, a rare quality. How could she be gone? It wasn't fair; it wasn't just. During his two hundred years buried in Lorne's family mausoleum, he'd begun to understand how important justice was—an eye for an eye and all that.

Linny was dead and someone would pay. He would drag the Destroyer to the underworld himself if need be.

When they'd been in the kitchen together, he couldn't help but notice the way her fair hair fell forward as she made her coffee, or how the light shone upon it like gold. Her nails had been painted different colors, like a rainbow, and she glanced up at him, smiling, whenever he made some remark, focusing her attention on him. It had been a long while since Darlington had felt that good about himself.

"What do we do now?" He looked at Lorne

and Maggie, standing close together. They were a couple, he realized bleakly, and wondered why he hadn't seen it before. It made him feel more alone than ever.

———◆———

Lorne tried to think. They all looked to him for leadership. Well, why wouldn't they? He'd always shown them the way, even when it was the wrong way.

"Oh, um, you can still save her, you know. Just FYI." Stewart's matter-of-fact statement broke the silence.

Maggie turned on the man. "What do you mean?" she said, her voice trembling with hope. Then the optimism washed out of her, and she shook her head. "You're lying."

"No, Professor, I'm not. Her soul, her essence, whatever you'd like to call it, is still living. At least, it will for the next hour or two. If you can catch her and bring our mutual friend out of her before that, then there's no reason she won't survive the experience. But after that …" He twiddled his fingers and sputtered as if mimicking her melting to the ground.

Maggie was desperate to believe him. Lorne could tell she was struggling to keep her emotions in check, not to get her hopes up. She knew as well as he what Stewart was capable of. Deception was in his very being.

His fingers closed over hers, holding firm, and he felt her respond. He sensed there was some truth to what Stewart said. They had to play along, even though he'd begun to understand the other man too well. Everything had a price, and Linny's life would require an exceptional payment.

"What do we have to do?" he asked.

Stewart grimaced, pretended to ease his hands in their bonds. "It works both ways, doesn't it?" he said. "A two way street, if you will," he added, using words that Lorne was sure he thought meant nothing to men from his time. "First, I'll need you to let me go, and then I will tell you what you must do."

"Let you go?" Sutcliffe roared, but Lorne spoke over him.

"How can we trust you?"

"Oh, you can't. You really can't. But you don't really have a choice, either. Now give me the keys to Linny's car and—"

"No," the three men spoke as one.

Stewart's smile was one of someone who knows that he is going to win. "Now that's a shame. If we can't trust each other, if we can't come to some agreement, then I'm afraid I won't be able to help you."

Lorne glanced at Maggie and saw she was biting her lip again. If she didn't stop soon it would be raw. He was procrastinating, pretending to think over Stewart's offer, but he already knew he would agree.

He couldn't be sure this was going to work, but if there was the slightest chance Linny could be saved then they would take it. There was also the question of the Destroyer and their task of capturing it and returning it to the underworld. Their very survival hinged on completing that task.

"Do it," Darlington spoke before Lorne could. The other man rarely took the lead but now he seemed adamant. "Give him the keys." He gestured at Stewart. "Let him go. If it means we can save Linny then we have no choice."

Sutcliffe was more cautious. "And what about the Destroyer? The Sorceress won't be overjoyed if we just let it go on its merry way."

"Did I neglect to mention?" Stewart looked shocked. "My friends, I would not see you sent to the underworld." He gave a shudder, play acting again. "No, no, certainly not. You can capture the Destroyer if you follow my instructions. Isn't that what you want?"

"Yes." Maggie spoke up, her voice tight with emotion. "We agree. We have to agree."

One by one the others murmured their consent.

Stewart's ropes were removed. He rubbed his wrists, not bothering to hide his amusement. Maggie found Linny's car keys and handed them to him.

"Now tell us," she said. "You gave your word."

"I did, didn't I?" He tilted his head and smiled at her. "I'll miss you, Maggie. I wish you could see that you are far too good for the Marquis here, but they do say that love is blind. I just didn't realize it was deaf and dumb as well."

He moved toward the car and for a moment Lorne thought he was going to climb inside and drive away, leaving them with nothing. He'd reached the car door before he turned to them.

"The runes."

Lorne watched him click a button and a light came on at the front of the car, followed by the sound of the doors unlocking. A moment later, he was inside with the engine started. He let the window down and stared at Lorne. There was hatred there, bubbling and boiling, but only for a moment and it was gone. Stewart's face resumed its usual polite expression.

"The original tablet that my master gave you. Read the runes backwards to bring the Destroyer into your power and force it from its host. Then Maggie's sister will be free."

"Wait!" Lorne strode forward. "I cannot read the runes. The Egyptian gave me a translation."

Stewart had begun to roll the car out of the driveway, but paused long enough to throw something out of the open window. It fluttered through the air, drifting almost out of reach, but Lorne managed to catch it.

When he held it up to the light from the cottage door he recognized it. This was the same scroll the Egyptian had handed him. He hadn't destroyed it after all. Stewart had possessed it all this time. When he looked up his nemesis was driving off into the night, the sound of his engine fading into silence.

Maggie rested her hand on his arm.

"You know we can't let him go free," he said. "We'll have to go after him."

She shook her head. "Right now I don't care. There's Linny to think of. We have to save her and bring her back."

"And for that we need the original tablet. The person who is reading the spell has to hold it in their hand. That was what I did before."

Her face was unfathomable but he knew she must be thinking about what he'd done. If he hadn't cast the spell in the first place none of this would have happened. Maggie would be working on her "dig" and Lorne and his friends would be long dead and dust. They never would have met and formed this unlikely attachment.

Lorne couldn't be sorry, but he suspected she was.

But Maggie didn't accuse him of anything. She turned and headed for the Land Rover with Loki bounding along at her side. "Let's get to the graveyard then," she called out over her shoulder. "Come on!"

Chapter Twenty-Seven

EVERYTHING WAS SO VERY QUIET. Swathes of white mist drifted among the graves and covered the barrow where this had all begun. Maggie tried not to let herself hope for too much, but it was difficult not to pray for a happy ending.

If this was a movie they would save Linny, send the Destroyer back, and all end up dancing and singing a song before the credits rolled.

Unfortunately, real life tended not to be all tied up in a big pink bow like that. Real life was messy, and sometimes people were left with their dreams unfulfilled and their hearts broken.

Sutcliffe retrieved the spade from the back of the Rover and hoisting it over his shoulder, set off toward Mrs. Noakes's grave. Darlington followed, dragging a pick by its handle, while Loki gambled about them as if this was an everyday outing.

Maggie looked beyond them at the dark trees, ghostly in the mist, and wondered what was hiding within them. Was the Destroyer in there some-where? What would happen when Lorne read the spell backwards? Would Linny suddenly appear?

She shivered and wrapped her arms about herself. The three men gathered about the grave, and she watched them dig into the soft earth and toss it aside. It only took a moment before Lorne called out that they'd found it, and she made her way over to the grave.

Lorne dusted the parcel free of damp soil and unwrapped it. Maggie thought the tablet looked the same, but whereas before she'd been drawn to it, now she found it repulsive. For a moment Lorne said nothing, and she knew he was remembering the last time he had spoken these words.

She knew he felt this was his fault, but she also knew that he was doing his best to make things right. If he thought she was going to walk away from him because of his past then he was wrong. After he had come to find her in the crypt, Maggie knew she could trust him completely.

Raising her flashlight, she illuminated the markings on the tablet and the scroll in his other hand. She knew he was watching her but she didn't know what to say. "Good luck" seemed too frivolous given the gravity of the situation.

"Shall we begin?" Lorne said, with just the right somber note.

There were nods of agreement.

At first he stumbled—reading backwards was not a simple task—but soon the words began to run more easily off his tongue. The language sounded strange, archaic, and she recognized the same musical resonance she had heard when she came upon Stewart pretending to be Simon, in the gallery.

She wondered what he had been doing at that moment, what spell he had been reciting, but then she was distracted.

Somewhere in the woods an animal screeched. Maggie's head snapped up and she stared once more into the opaque shadows. Lorne continued to read and when he got to the top of the scroll he started over again.

He had the sort of voice that was perfect for this, Maggie thought, feeling a little light headed. If he needed work in her time he could make a living doing voiceovers for commercials, for posh brands of men's products.

The screech came again, louder now, or perhaps simply closer. Loki growled, and it was only Sutcliffe's grasp on his collar that kept him from running off to investigate. Lorne had reached the end of the scroll again, and for a moment paused. The silence throbbed like an ache before he began yet once more, louder now, and with every ounce of his authority.

Something was coming.

Maggie could see the shape of it, stumbling out of the trees as if dragged by an unseen force and down the slope toward them. It tripped and almost fell, only to right itself again. As it drew closer she felt the skin prickling on the back of her neck and her heart began a rapid beat.

Linny.

Her sister's long hair glowed pale like moonlight, and she had that same awful jerky movement Maggie remembered from Owen. There was no point in approaching what had once been Linny. Instead her hand clenched hard on the flashlight and she looked down at the tablet.

"She's nearly here," Darlington said. "Come on, my lovely, just a bit further."

At last Linny stumbled to a stop and despite herself Maggie looked up.

Linny was wearing her favorite high heeled boots, and her face was the same as always, but there was a strangeness about it. Maggie knew in her heart that her sister was no longer her sister.

Please, please don't let it be too late ...

Lorne kept reciting the spell. Linny threw up her arms and gave one of those awful shrieks they'd heard coming from the woods. They all jumped. The sound was like a knife blade down Maggie's spine. Her sister's face twisted and her lips drew back in a snarl, disclosing the long yellow pointed teeth of the Destroyer.

Loki struggled against his master's hold but no one else seemed keen to get any closer. Linny took another wavering step, then sank to her knees. For a moment it was as if her shape blurred out of focus, as if there were two Linnys. Then one of them flopped onto the ground and the other one was crawling away, shifting, changing.

"Keep reading!" Maggie cried, excitement making her voice squeak. "It's working."

Darlington limped toward the fallen woman, and knelt down at her side, his hand against her cheek. He looked over his shoulder at Maggie, and she could see the sorrow in his face.

"I don't think she's alive," he said.

Maggie ran to her sister, refusing to believe it. Linny looked ashen and very, very still. Maggie grabbed her hand, trying to feel a pulse, but the skin was cold and lifeless.

She barely noticed the Destroyer, now returned to its old demonic shape, dragging itself across the ground away from them, growing weaker with each moment. Lorne was following, continuing to read. He seemed to know the words by heart now.

"Linny, please, please," Maggie sobbed. "Don't die. Please don't die."

At first she thought the flicker of Linny's eyelashes was nothing but her own wishful thinking, but then it happened again, and her sister gave a little gasp.

"She's alive," Darlington said it for her, and for a moment his face was full of emotion, before he closed himself down.

Linny's eyes opened and she peered about her. "Wha …" she slurred, before she swallowed and tried again, while they awaited her first words after returning from the dead.

"What the hell is going on, Sis?"

The Destroyer had run out of strength. It couldn't live in this world without a body to protect and nourish it. Now it lay curled on its side, chest rising and falling, each breath an obvious effort, and a keening sound coming from its throat. Lorne kept repeating the words, over and over again.

He was aware Linny was alive, and felt grateful he got to see Maggie's reaction to her sister's resurrection. Now there was only this last thing to be done and all would be finished.

Time to go home.

As if the thought had brought her forth, the air began to crackle and spit, and a strange blue radiance enfolded them. The Sorceress appeared from the light, her terrible beauty making Lorne's knees quake.

The Destroyer raised its head one last time and the Sorceress pointed her finger at it. The creature crumbled into tiny fragments, hovering a moment in the air, only to be sucked into the blue vortex behind her. It was done.

Linny clung to Maggie, staring at the Sorceress, while Darlington stood guard over them. "And just who the fuck are you?" she demanded in a belligerent voice.

The Sorceress could have ignored her, Lorne fully expected her to, but instead she turned her terrible regard upon Maggie's sister.

"I am the ruler of the between-worlds. The place where those who have transgressed receive their punishment."

Linny's mouth fell open. "Sorry I said fuck …"

The Sorceress turned back to Lorne and he forced himself to stand and face her. It was a matter of pride that he had never shown her how much he feared her, and soon pride would be all he had left.

He had made a vow and now he must abide by it. He might wish he could have had more time with Maggie, but at least she was alive. Lorne reminded himself that he could find comfort in that.

"You made me a promise, Marquis." The Sorceress's voice had dropped to what, with any other woman, might have been a caress. Lorne felt as if she was scraping her nails across his unprotected skin.

"And I will honor it, madam."

The Sorceress nodded her head in acknowledgement. Her azure eyes gleamed and she turned them to Maggie. "What do you think of his promise, Maggie? It was your life he saved, after all. Are you glad to see the back of our handsome Marquis?"

Puzzled, Maggie gave Lorne a look which he avoided, and proceeded to get shakily to her feet. "What promise?" Linny tried to hold on to her, but Darlington took her in his arms instead.

"Of course, he hasn't told you. He has become very noble of late, has he not? Lorne made a promise when he asked me to save your life. I am sending him back to his time, where he will accept the consequences of what he did. He brought the Destroyer into the mortal world and lives were lost. He must take responsibility."

Maggie's eyes widened and Lorne, glancing at her, could see she was shocked by this news. Then she shook her head violently, her curls falling into her face so that she had to brush them back again.

"No. I don't want that. I didn't know he'd promised … If I'd known I wouldn't have let him. Please, you can't send him back."

"Maggie …" Lorne spoke quickly, before the Sorceress could take exception. "It is a matter of honor."

"No," she said, still shaking her head. "Lorne, please …"

Impatiently, the Sorceress waved her hand and caused the leaves in the forest to rustle. "Do you love him, Maggie?"

"Yes," Maggie gave him a defiant stare. "I do love him."

"And Marquis, what say you?"

Lorne gave a shaky laugh. "Oh yes," he said, "I

love Maggie with all my wicked black heart."

"I don't think your heart is wicked." Maggie went to his side, fighting the imposing presence of the Sorceress every inch of the way. By the time she reached him her face was very pale.

He caught her to him, breathing her in, telling himself he would remember this moment for the rest of his life. However short it may be.

The Sorceress smiled her terrible smile. "As much as I want to send you back, Marquis, there is still the matter of Stewart. He is far too dangerous to be allowed to roam free in this world. You must confine him first. And afterwards … unlike the Marquis I make no promises."

Lorne couldn't believe his ears and then Maggie gave a cry of joy. "Yes, yes, let him stay and find Stewart," she said, her words tripping over themselves.

"It will not be forever," the Sorceress reminded her.

Maggie's face fell but she straightened her back and lifted her chin. "We'll have to cross that bridge when we come to it."

The Sorceress ignored her. "When you find him you will place this upon him." She was holding something in her palm. A ring that dazzled and shone. "Once you do that, he will be trapped in this world and I can destroy him."

Lorne shaded his eyes. She threw the ring into the air and he instinctively caught it. The metal was hot, just for a moment, before it cooled and the dazzling ring dulled to grey. There were markings on it, but it was too dark to see them clearly.

"It will be my pleasure, Madam," Lorne said.

Sutcliffe cleared his throat. "Ah, madam, what happens to me? And Darlington? And Loki?"

The Sorceress turned to him and he took a step backwards before he could stop himself. "I would not think of splitting up the members of the Hellfire Club," she said in a way that in anyone else might have been called a joke. "There is more to be done, gentlemen. A great deal more."

"Thank you," Lorne said to the Sorceress. "We will not fail you."

"You had better not, Marquis."

She began to fade, the crackle of the air intensifying briefly and then fading, until once more the cold misty night enclosed them.

As Lorne held Maggie in the circle of his arms he knew this happiness was bittersweet. He could stay, but only until they captured Stewart. Then he must leave her. A promise was a promise after all, but at least, for a time, they would be together. Maggie lifted her head from his shoulder, reaching up to place her palm against his cheek. "We won't think about the future," she said determinedly. "We'll only think about right now."

"Yes. This is our time and we will make the most of it." He smiled and turned his face to kiss her fingers, then he bent and kissed her lips.

Epilogue

THE ROOM THEY WERE IN was sumptuous—there was no other word for it. The four poster bed was hung with green silk and tassels of gold, and in the flickering firelight she could see the dark gleam of Georgian furniture and muted Turkish rugs upon the floor. Candles burned in sconces.

They might have been in Blackfriars Abbey back in Lorne's day, but they weren't. Such a thing wasn't possible if Lorne was to stay alive. Nor were they truly safe in her time, not after the two unexplained deaths—Owen's body had been found in the abbey grounds—and Stewart's disappearance. The authorities would be looking for the culprits and it seemed sensible to remove themselves from the situation.

They'd had no choice but to allow the Sorceress to hide them away somewhere safe until Stewart made his presence known again and they could chase after him. Because he would appear at some point, they all knew it. He wasn't finished with Lorne and wouldn't rest until he had revenged himself upon his enemy.

Maggie, who had seen Stewart at his most malevolent, suspected it wasn't only Lorne he planned to destroy. His kind of madness would never truly be satisfied, no matter how much power he gained.

Lorne sat at a desk by the window. He wore a white shirt with lace falling over his hands. He dipped his quill in the pot of ink and began to write on the paper before him. The firelight shone on his dark hair, tied back with a ribbon this evening, and for a moment he paused, pen raised, considering his next word.

"Who are you writing to this time?" Maggie asked. She was sprawled on a divan, half asleep, her body warm and relaxed after their love making. Lorne had that effect on her.

"The Duke of Portland, the Prime Minister," he said. "Might as well go right to the top. When I go back to my time I want him to look favorably upon me."

"*If* you go back," she corrected him.

He turned to look at her and she thought he was going to warn her, just as he always did, that matters may not end happily for them. But he didn't. He smiled instead.

"Come here," he said.

Maggie had wondered, when she first agreed to live here with him, whether she'd get bored and miss her life outside. She did miss Linny, but as for the rest who knew how long they had or what might happen? She was making the most of him.

She got to her feet. The dress she was wearing was of the Regency style, a rather pretty blue, with a low neckline and long sleeves. When she arrived she found her wardrobe stuffed with clothing more suited to Jane Austen than Maggie McNab. She'd been doubtful at first, until Lorne explained it had been the Sorceress's little joke.

Hard to believe the Sorceress had a sense of humor.

They were living in the between-worlds. If she walked out of this door she would find herself in Sutcliffe and Darlington's apartments, and beyond that again … well, she didn't go out there. Lorne said it wasn't safe and the one time she'd peeped over his shoulder and seen for herself there had been darkness and things moving, and sounds such as she'd never heard.

No, it was much safer with the door closed.

He took her hand and set her down onto his knee. His warm breath tickled her nape, and then he nipped her gently, making her gasp. "Perhaps you should finish your letter first?" she suggested, trying not to smile.

"Perhaps I can finish it afterwards." He turned her so that he could run a fingertip over the mounds of her breasts above the low cut bodice. "Very nice. My compliments to your modiste, my lady."

"Would you call the Sorceress my modiste?" she asked, catching her breath as his lips followed his finger. "She might not be pleased, although I think she has a soft spot for you."

He laughed—he laughed a lot these days. "I'm not sure what terrifies me more, the Sorceress having a soft spot for me or her wanting to punish me."

Maggie smoothed her palm over his face and leaned in to kiss his mouth. "How much longer do you think we'll be here?"

She could see the doubts in his eyes. "If you are unhappy, Maggie, we can go. You know that. We will do whatever you wish. I am completely at your disposal."

Completely at your disposal.

And he was, in every way, and he'd proved it over and over again. She linked her arms about his neck and rested her brow against his. "I don't want to go anywhere. I was just wondering when Stewart will appear again. He can't stay hidden forever."

"No, he can't. He'll want me to come after him so that he can hurt me." Lorne's eyes narrowed. "And soon, I think."

Her body was heating up and his caresses were growing bolder. In a moment he would carry her back to their bed and make slow, enchanting love to her on the cool silk sheets. They could never get enough of each other and she could not bear to think of losing him.

"My love." Her wicked Marquis reached to touch the frown between her brows. "You mustn't worry. We are together, and that's all that matters."

"Yes," she whispered. "We are together."

For now.

Excerpt of
HELLFIRE CLUB—DARLINGTON
AN IMMORTAL WARRIORS NOVEL

Present Day, Glasgow

LINNY SMILED ABOUT AT THE circle of expectant faces. Her group was assembled and she was ready to lead them into the night, and hopefully scare them witless. Well, she had some experience of that, at least.

"Everyone ready then?"

Heads nodded and a youngish girl in a long knitted coat gave an elaborate shiver.

"Do you think we'll see any ghosts tonight?" she asked with an American accent.

Linny shrugged but raised her eyebrows at the same time, a bet either way. They would be walking down some of Glasgow's oldest streets, the ones spared destruction after the bombing of the Second World War and the bulldozers of the nineteen seventies. Who knew what they might find? Although in her experience anything ghostly had more to do with the over active imaginations of her tour group rather than having any basis in reality.

But who could blame them? It was dark and chilly, and the stories she told were designed to frighten people. She wouldn't be complaining if someone said they saw a ghost.

"This way then!" she called, and set out, digging her gloved hands into the pockets of her jacket.

"Do you believe in ghosts?" The middle aged man, who had been giving her the eye ever since he arrived, was at her side. He was lonely, probably. A stranger in a strange city looking to hook up. Shame he'd chosen her--shame for him, that was.

"Of course," she gave the standard reply. The company she worked for insisted they all be believers. What they didn't know was that Linny believed in far worse things than ghosts. She'd seen them first hand, and come close to dying when a demon took over her body.

Afterwards, Maggie had wanted her to stay with Lorne and the others—even take up residence in the between-worlds. But Linny had refused. What had happened to her had terrified her. It was very nice seeing Maggie happy with her Marquis, but Linny wasn't going near the Sorceress or any of her pals.

This job as a ghost walker had been a way of exorcising the past, and so far it was working. With all these 'believers' around her she no longer felt like such a freak.

"Ms McNab?" The American girl was tugging her sleeve. "Is that … who *is* that?"

Linny looked up with a smile, expecting to see some homeless person with a bottle in a brown paper bag. It happened. Or else some joker who had a bet with his friends that he could get the tourists to run.

But it wasn't either. A man was leaning against the wall of the building, in the shadows of the laneway, almost invisible, and yet …. there was something about him. He was looking down, hands jammed into the pockets of what looked to be an old fashioned great coat, and as they approached he lifted his head.

Linny caught her breath.

She knew that scar and that dark watchful gaze. She didn't realize she had stopped until he began to walk towards her, using an elegant ebony cane to assist with his leg.

The girl at her side gave a little cry and stumbled back. "Are you-are you dead?" she asked, eyes enormous in the light from the street lamp above them.

Darlington considered the question. "Yes, I suppose I am," he said.

They turned and fled, the clatter of their departure on the cobbles sounding like heavy rain, fading into the distance. Even the man who had attached himself to her side had gone, leaving her to her fate.

Linny stood and waited, watching him cautiously until he reached her. Her heart gave a hitch, as though she was having a minor heart attack, but she didn't want him to know that. She gave him her bored look. "What are you doing here, your lordship?" she asked him.

He rested on his cane, eyes sliding over her face, taking her in. There was a moment when she might have put her arms about him and kissed his cheek, like an old friend, but it passed. Because they weren't old friends and could never be.

"I'm not a lord," he said, but she thought he said it to give himself time to find an answer that wouldn't send her after the others. "My title was taken from me."

Linny shrugged. He was being scrupulously honest—he was dead and he'd been stripped of his title. Was he also going to tell her what he was doing here?

"I'm not alone. Maggie and Lorne are here, too," he told her. "And Sutcliffe and Loki. We're all staying in Blythswood Square."

Of course they were. Lorne had money, and friends with influence. She thought of the Sorceress and fought a shudder.

"Well that's all very nice," she said, "and I will see them when I can, but some of us have to work for a living."

Darlington shook his head at her, his eyes showing regret and perhaps disapproval, but she told herself it didn't matter what he thought of her. If he only knew it, she was doing him and the others a big favor. And yet she found herself checking out his face, trying to see if he was still the man she dreamt of at night.

She couldn't let herself become involved with him. He was two hundred years old and she could barely cope with life in the present century.

"We know he's back," he said the words she'd been dreading. "Stewart. He's here in Glasgow, pretending to be Simon. There have been sightings."

"Simon who's dead," Linny breathed. She couldn't, she really couldn't do this again. Last time she had gone south to Lincolnshire, worried about her sister, sensing something was wrong. But now Maggie had Lorne.

"We think he's doing it to draw us into his net again."

"So why are you here?" Linny repeated impatiently. "Shouldn't you be running as far and fast as you can in the other direction?"

"We're here because we have no option," Darlington replied in a heavy voice. "We have to find him and capture him, and this may be our only chance."

"So you thought you'd just drop in on my ghost walk and say hello, did you?"

She turned away at last but, as she'd known he would, Darlington accompanied her, his cane tapping along with their steps. "Linny, I wish you would join us," he spoke, slightly breathless, making her feel guilty for forcing him to keep up. "There's safety in numbers."

But she shook her head. "Oh no you don't," she said. "There's safety in staying well away from you lot. Nicholas, you don't know what it was like when-when …" She stopped, swallowed, and forced a smile. "Goodbye, my lord. Give my best wishes to Maggie. She knows where to find me."

And she was gone, quickening her pace, knowing he couldn't catch her up.

She didn't turn around but she had a feeling he was standing in the road like something from *Les Misérables*, watching her. It couldn't be helped, she told herself. The thing was, the others didn't understand. They had seen what happened to her when the Destroyer took over her body, and they had saved her life and brought her back. She was grateful, she truly was, but they didn't understand.

When the demon had been in residence, she had been … elsewhere. And when she'd come back from that other place something had come with her.

And it was still here.

About the Author

SARA MACKENZIE IS THE AUTHOR of The Immortal Warriors series. She also writes Historical Romance as Sara Bennett and Evie North.

You can visit her on her Facebook page: www.facebook.com/saramackenzieparanormalromance/

While you're there sign up to her Newsletter for the latest news: www.facebook.com/saramackenzieparanormalromance/app/152926008054123/

Look for these

Immortal Warriors

titles by

Sara Mackenzie

NOW AVAILABLE:
Return of the Highlander
Secrets of the Highwayman
Passions of the Ghost

Hellfire Club: Lorne

COMING SOON:
Hellfire Club: Darlington